MEET
THE CAST AND CREW
OF SATELLITE NEWS . . .

RIKKA COLLINS—ace reporter. She's got brains, beauty . . . and a built-in microphone.

HARRY SNYDER—anchorperson. As an intergalactic newsman, he's tops . . . when he's not tipsy.

JHONNY—cameraman. He's a robot, he's illegally employed . . . but nobody's perfect.

MICHELANGELO—technician. He may look like a grizzly bear, but this alien troubleshooter knows his nuts and bolts and microchips.

"ACE" DEITRICH—the brains, literally. His body died almost three decades ago, but his scientific mind is still ticking.

"BOX" AMBOCKSKY—program director. He gets the team into the heat of the action, brings them back to the studio . . . and sometimes bails them out of jail.

Together, they are the Satellite News Team: champions of truth and broadcasting. And the news will never be the same!

SATELLITE NIGHT NEWS

JACK HOPKINS

ACE BOOKS, NEW YORK

This book is an Ace original edition,
and has never been previously published.

SATELLITE NIGHT NEWS

An Ace Book/published by arrangement with
the author

PRINTING HISTORY
Ace edition/February 1993

ISBN: 0-441-75046-X

Ace Books are published by The Berkley Publishing Group,
200 Madison Avenue, New York, New York 10016.
The name "ACE" and the "A" logo
are trademarks belonging to Charter Communications, Inc.

PRINTED IN THE UNITED STATES OF AMERICA

10 9 8 7 6 5 4 3 2 1

To my good buddy, Nick Pollotta,
without whom this novel could not have been written

ACKNOWLEDGMENTS

And a special thanks to the Channel Six TV news team in Columbus, Ohio, for their kind assistance, technical advice, and, of course, for all that free coffee and Danish.

CHAPTER ONE

"WE DID IT!" cried Rikka, throwing her spacesuit helmet into the air. The clear Armorlite sphere banged off the low ceiling of the space shuttle and rebounded into the helmet rack with amazing precision.

Buried deep within the central computer, a disembodied human brain mentally chuckled inside his glass jar. NOT QUITE YET, scrolled Deitrich on the cockpit monitor.

"Oh, shuddup and fly," growled Harry, manually triggering the ignition controls.

Lifting on an array of silent flame from its belly jets, the sleek white shuttle rose from the gray dustpit it had been hiding in and rocketed into the starry black of space. Narrowly missing a jagged outcrop of rock, the shuttle leveled off at five klicks and the four-pound MainBrain pilot activated the primary engines. With a brutal kick, the ship quadrupled its velocity. On the control board, fuel levels visibly dropped and the speedometer pegged the red line with a resounding thud like a small lead salami going home for the holidays.

Below the hurtling ship, the barren landscape of the dark side of the moon moved in an accelerating blur: the dome and tubes of the British aluminum dust mines passed over in a flash, the sprawling complex of UN Naval Base Gagarin, the stick-in-an-apple structure of the French observatory, and the elegant crystalline cones and expensive glass-topped gardens of the American consortium-built Club Med Imbrium.

Rikka grunted at the fleeting sight. A vacation resort on the moon. Luna had certainly undergone some major changes since Neil Armstrong first walked on its surface. From uninhabited rock

1

to a thriving worldlet in less than three hundred years. Not bad. The United States of North America had gone from a wood-burning British colony to an interplanetary power in less.

Removing his gloves, Harry used a thumbnail to peel the plastic "Sears" name tag off his spacesuit to reveal the embroidered name of SNYDER underneath. Rikka did the same to "Roebuck" exposing the word COLLINS. And with the merest flick of an encoded thought, Deitrich changed the designation on the outer hull of the craft from QUILLER GEO-MEDICAL PLUMBING back to the original QSNT: ALL NEWS, ALL THE TIME.

Now directly ahead of the racing spaceship was a tiny white dot, rapidly growing in size and shape.

Tossing the crumpled fake ID into the garbage slot, Harry glanced out the portside Armorlite window toward the twinkling lights they were streaking over. "Hey, waddaya know! It looks like Madam Adam has added that new wing to the Pleasure Palace."

Rikka Collins crossed her arms and raised an inquisitive eyebrow at her anchor.

"And how the prack do you know where to look for that secret brothel?" she inquired suspiciously.

Harry flashed his worlds-famous megawatt grin. "I read it in a newspaper."

"A newspaper!" sneered Rikka. "And since when do you collect antiques?"

The two exchanged glances and then broke into laughter. Even Deitrich had the monitor on the control board scroll a short collection of HAHAHAHAHAHAHAHAHAHA—OOPS. TROUBLE COMING.

"Alert," said a calm mechanical voice over the ceiling speaker in the control room of the shuddering vessel. "This is the Lunar Police. Slow your ship. You are in violation of Speed Safety Law 164954673936."

"Fax me!" growled Collins, flipping switches to scramble the police radar. The expensive, highly illegal device was supposed to generate a ghost radar blip making it seem as if the shuttle was actually a full klick to the west of where it really was. QSNT had certainly paid enough for this military scrambler and now was the perfect chance to see if it worked.

"A bad attitude will not help matters," continued the speaker.

With a curled lip, Harry spat out one of the fourteen phrases the news anchor was not allowed to use over the public airwaves.

"Now that will go on your permanent record, Mr. Sears!"

"LP, or 45?" quipped the anchor.

"Eh? What?"

"Look it up, moron!"

The speaker growled at them, but the words were rapidly diminishing in clarity and then abruptly cut off as the police scooter went over the horizon in the wrong direction.

AMAZING, scrolled Deitrich on the monitor. THE DAMN THING WORKED.

Rikka brushed sweat-damp hair from her face. Whew.

On the main view screen, the white globe ahead of the ship was now softball size and steadily enlarging. Biting a lip, Collins glanced at the watch on her pinkie. Prack! Only five minutes till the start of the Martian General Assembly! Angrily, she thumped the throttle with the palm of her gloved hand. The lever indented the rubber stop at the end of its side but the engines did not noticeably increase their output.

Damn, prack, and hell! she raged internally. If only they could use their FTL drive. But Media was too close. Far below the minimum distance of a quarter million klicks. Even a microsecond pulse of those engines would put the news vessel *through* the orbiting station. Which would destroy the paint job on the shuttle and just ruin everybody's day.

Deitrich would have to do this the old-fashioned way: with chemical jets, raw skill, and a total disrespect for the law. The job was tailor-made for their daredevil MainBrain. A free-lance rocket jockey for over sixty years, Deitrich had made only one bad landing in his whole distinguished career. Of course, Rikka admitted, that last one had been a doozy. But the wonders of science were, well, wondrous, and so the old bold pilot flew on! That Brain really had guts.

In cold lunar majesty, the translucent glass peaks of the Royal Black Mountains shot by the cockpit windows. As the hurtling shuttle crested the volcanic ridge, the ten thousand lights of Starlet City filled the horizon with glorious illumination; the glittering towers and sprawling docks of the international settlement reaching to the far walls of the massive lunar crater.

Rikka glanced at the chart. They were almost home.

Then she looked at her watch. And almost out of time.

"Deitrich, can't you get any more speed out of this thing?" demanded Harry, trying to adjust the navigation submonitor. The computer-generated vector graphic of the homes and factories on the ground below was only a smeary moray pattern.

NEGATIVE, replied the MainBrain. NOT WITHOUT LIGHTENING THE LOAD BY JETTISONING SOMETHING USELESS LIKE THE CREW.

Rikka and Harry paused, then shook their heads no. The story they had wasn't quite that important. Not quite.

"Never mind."

I DIDN'T THINK YOU'D GO FOR THE NOTION.

"No kidding."

OH, WELL. MAYBE NEXT TIME.

Suddenly, the aft door of the cockpit slammed open and there stood a grinning youth.

"I broke the Martian security code!" cried Jhonny, brandishing a computer bubble card in his fist.

"Took long enough," growled Snyder, watching the slim being plop himself down into the third seat just aft of Collins.

Concentrating on mentally urging the shuttle to go faster, Rikka merely muttered a brusque hello.

The fourth seat in the cockpit was unpowered, a bit dusty, and bare of any personal effects.

"Hey. I'm just a camera-op, not a tech," replied Jhonny, strapping himself down. "And if you hadn't been so drunk that you stepped on the first computer cube we stole—"

"Media Station, this is the Satellite News Team," interrupted Harry, speaking quickly into this collar microphone. "We have a Priority One cargo! Clear the inbound zone. Repeat, clear our in zone."

"Wait your turn, SNT," came a nonplussed reply. "I've got six other Priority One shuttles ahead of you."

"Traffic Control, we're running against a deadline!"

"Who cares? Go prack yourself, Jack."

Synder's face went grim. "Oh, yeah? Traffic Control, clear our zone, or we'll blast anything in our path!"

Leaning forward, Jhonny killed the microphone. "Chief, we don't have any weapons."

From behind the wheel, Rikka evilly grinned. "Yeah. But do they know that?"

The camera-op blinked surprise. "Lying to our own traffic controllers? That's a new low even for us."

"It's a bluff," retorted the speaker. "You don't have any weapons. No news shuttle does."

"Oh, really?" purred Harry sweetly, fingering the metallic ring of his spacesuit collar.

"Arm the Bedlow laser cannon," said Snyder in a gruff, elderly voice.

"Gulp! Aye-aye, sir!" he continued in a young, frightened voice.

Yanking a miniature camcorder from his spacesuit pocket, Jhonny held the device next to the microphone and clicked the on switch. The tiny motors engaged with a soft revving sound and an ominous electrostatic crackle.

There was an audible gasp on the speaker, and one second later a hundred flames sprouted in the black space before them as tugs, freighters, and shuttles hastily scrambled for safety, as the shuttle soared away from the moon's surface.

Now looming ahead was Media Station. Resembling a white beach ball stuffed inside a colossal mirrored doughnut, the free space structure was roughly one billion metric tons of zero-G steelloy set in geosynchronous orbit above Starlet City.

As the corporate headquarters for the Wilkes Organization, Media had thirty-seven levels, five thousand employees, four hundred dish antennas, ten thousand windows, nine hundred external airlocks, fifty landing ports, and one very precious saloon.

Thirstily, Rikka licked the imaginary foam of a victory beer off her lips. "Hey, Traffic Control, open door twenty-three or we'll—" She released the switch on the mike. "Deitrich, can we crash through the doors?"

SURE. NO PROBLEM.

". . . crash through those doors!" she finished smoothly.

NOT AND SURVIVE, OF COURSE, finished the MainBrain.

Oh, swell.

Stifling a yawn, Snyder snuggled inside his spacesuit and closed his eyes. "Wake me if we crash."

"If we crash," replied Jhonny, "you'll be dead."

"Perfect," he murmured. " 'Cause I'm dead tired."

But as Media began to completely fill the forward monitor, a pair of burnished steel doors broke apart exposing a landing port, its pristine floor garishly decorated with the giant neon red number 23.

Cutting the engines, Deitrich applied full braking retros. The stout hull of the craft groaned loudly from the conflicting forces unleashed. A control panel erupted in sparks, then another. Jhonny tried to grab an extinguisher and failed, banging himself on the head. Unflappable, Harry snored. At subsonic speed, the ship went skimming low across the station's outer wheel, clipping numerous radio antennas in passing.

Throwing off dangerous-looking flames, the shuttle hurtled toward the landing bay. Struggling to maintain target, Rikka corrected their trajectory, then Deitrich corrected her correction. Gladly, the reporter accepted the MainBrain's assistance. The doors loomed about them and she only got a fleeting glimpse of other shuttles parked in neat rows before they hit.

Too hard and too fast.

Hull scraping against the space station walls, thousands of white ceramic tiles were ripped from the shuttle in a spray of shredded lithium. Twisting from the impact, the battered craft skipped along the deck, once, twice, and then *slammed* to a halt as its nose brutally rammed into an inner bulkhead, the thick dura-steel bowing dangerously.

WE'RE HERE, scrolled Deitrich on the sideways monitor of the smoking control panel. AND I THINK WE'RE STILL ALIVE.

Harry woke up and yanked on his helmet. "Let's go, gang."

Hastily gathering in the quarterdeck, the team didn't waste precious time attempting to cycle open the battered airlock. Hardwiring a control box to the push-button panel set in the door lintel, Jhonny breached emergency procedure and ignited the explosive retaining bolts, blowing the outer door off. It hit the deck outside with a strident clang.

"Deitrich, stay here and guard the ship," ordered Rikka, climbing out of the tilted airlock.

Locked permanently inside the core of the shuttle's computer, the Brain mentally shuddered. OH, GET A NEW JOKE, scrolled the pilot on the tiny computer screen of her wrist secretary.

"Sorry."

YOU SHOULD BE.

With Harry in the lead, the trio raced past cheering technicians who didn't have to pay for any of the damage.

Stepping past the veined metal slabs of the open blast doors, the team stepped through a sonic curtain and bounded up an escalator to the next level.

Skidding comically on the highly polished floor, the reporters kicked aside a set of ornamental swinging doors and braced themselves for the expected assault.

The air shimmered and there appeared a hologram image of a disgustingly cheerful and politically correct mixture of reporters.

"Welcome to QSNT!" the images announced in perfect unison.

"All news, all the time!" sang an invisible choir.

Resisting the urge to barf, the team hurried onward.

Dashing past the buxom android at the reception desk, Jhonny slowed only for a moment to smile and wave hello. Both gestures were returned. In a decorative wall niche behind her, safe under a thick sheet of Armorlite, was an ancient oil lantern, a chalk slate, and a hand bell of a town crier lying reverently on a cushion of museum velvet. A sobering memento of their inauspicious past.

But then a monster filled the corridor before them.

"Freeze!" bellowed the huge guard. "You are all under house arrest for violation of Space Speed Safety Law 164954673936."

Reluctantly, the trio came to a ragged halt. Rock-steady in the guard's big callused hands was a 40mm Peacemaker and Rikka could see that the barrel was set on the red setting: Maximum Stun. Prack, there was no way her team could dodge the ultrasonic stun field, the spray of Narcolipic gas, and the barrage of anesthesia darts. Set on Max, a Peacemaker could bring a speeding express train to a dead stop.

Swallowing her fear, Collins stepped in close. "Bob, I'm calling in that favor you owe me," she said softly.

The guard's eyes went wide, but the stunner never wavered. A precious minute passed. Then another as he chewed the unpalatable idea to tiny bits and bitterly swallowed.

"Get moving," he growled, holstering the mammoth pistol.

The team sprinted forward.

"But the score is even now and the next time you pull a stunt like this . . ." the guard shouted at the closing doors.

"Never," said the guard, angrily reminding himself, "*ever*, draw to an inside straight!" And returning to his duty post, the man got out his portacomp to type the axiom a thousand times.

At the end of the corridor, Rikka, Harry, and Jhonny made a scampering left and pushed their way through another sonic field with the usual sucking sound of *scaw*. At top speed, they entered the main newsroom of QSNT. It was a cavernous bay that completely filled the entire middle section of the space station. Countless desks stretched to the distant walls that were lined with computers, physical files, and coffee makers. The team didn't pause to speak with any of the milling horde of newsfolk. Again, they pierced a sonic field; this one was only there to divide the office into departmental pockets, reduce headaches, and hold down unnecessary chitchat.

The overhead lighting here was tinted a soft xenon pink to ease eyestrain and along one wall was a display composed entirely of video monitors showing every other televised channel in the solar system. Off to one side was a small stack of submonitors that showed the real-time broadcasts of the other four major news services. There was a badly stained spittoon on the floor beneath the stack.

It really should have surprised nobody that every major broadcast network was now situated in a high planetary or moon orbit. Out in interplanetary space, broadcasting companies were not bound by archaic state laws or foolish federal guidelines; they were free from the onerous shackles of mob-controlled unions, paid no taxes, and yet were fully protected by the United Planets Space Force.

Plus, out among the planets, news was considered much more important than entertainment broadcasts. Who needed simplistic adventure holos with 4.2 car crashes, unrealistic explosions, and pneumatic blondes whose IQ perfectly matched their bra size? Life was quite exciting enough with the strange secret societies of Venus, the endless antics of the mad aristocracy of Mars, industrial espionage from money-hungry Mercury, the general lunacy of Earth, and vicious attacks by the bloody Free Police. Who were neither.

Basically, deep space was as close to heaven as a broadcast company could get, and not have to do moronic game shows or socially embarrassing pledge drives to pay the rent.

Leaving the Viewing Room, the team was starting to slow from exhaustion, when a loud click from the mechanical clock on the wall renewed their speed. Move!

Scaw, and the trio pierced another field rigidly maintained to contain the lofty atmosphere of the Society Section. A small crowd of people in posh clothing were clustered around a young woman and a flickering monitor displaying a pedigree dog beauty contest.

"It's my first story credit," wept the girl. "I'm so happy!"

An elderly man patted her on the shoulder. "Nice going, kid. Good job."

"It's crap," growled a fat, bald man in a painfully neat jumpsuit of the very newest styling.

Savagely, the youngster turned. "Prack you, granddad."

"Anytime, anyplace, kid," he sneered, stressing the last word.

"Hack!"

"Slut!"

Scaw.

In the Sports Section, a crowd of cheering people wearing sports jackets over their business jumpsuits were gleefully pouring champagne on top of each other's heads, while a smaller group was ripping their team shirts to pieces and sourly eating what resembled betting forms.

Oh, well, even the mighty Chicago Cubbies can't win 'em all.

Scaw! and the team sprinted through Classified Ads.

"Hey, you!" called out a burly woman in a silver jumpsuit, almost bringing the reporters to a halt. "What is your goddamn extension number?"

A dozen people pointed a questioning finger to their chests.

"No, not you, spacebrain! You!" corrected the lady giant readjusting the aim of her digit.

Scaw! Politics and Crime.

"B-but he's our best gangland informant!" stormed the tall, thin woman, nervously adjusting the clip in her laser pistol. "Wave his extradition from Earth!"

"We can always claim political asylum," added an elderly woman, stropping the edge of a switchblade.

"Idiot, they'll never let him anywhere near an embassy."

"Do it at Luna," suggested a huge slab of muscle, adjusting the straps on his shoulder holster.

"And how the prack do we get him to the moon, Einstein?"

"Use the lunar refueling station in downtown Toronto."

"Brilliant!"

"Is it legal?"

"More importantly, will it work?"

"It has before," he smiled. "Abduhl Benny Hassan versus Superior Court of the United States of America, August, 2254, September, 2255, March-April-June, 2256—"

A gun wave interrupted. "Go with it!"

Scaw. The Electronic News Department.

"Yes, it's the Download News!" shouted a modem the size of a refrigerator and the device gave a resounding computer beep. "Condensed reports from across the solar system available every minute on the minute." Pause. "Yes, it's the Download News!"

Scaw! Administration and Executive Offices.

Nimbly, the team rushed through a carpeted maze of chairs and plush vibro-couches to charge into a glass cubicle that bore the simple legend PRODUCER, NEWS DEPARTMENT. Underneath that, some wag had used hydrofluoric acid to etch into the Armorlite plastic the indelible words "The Box stops here."

"Paul! We got it!" Rikka cried, slamming the card down on his desktop. "The story of the decade!"

Unperturbed, the tired-looking young man behind the cluttered desk lowered the sandwich he had been eating. A colorful cloth napkin hid the majority of his conservative brown worsted jumpsuit. His only concession to fashion was a demure paisley bow tie.

"What is it?" asked Ambocksky curiously, removing the napkin and wiping his mouth. "Proof that Vice President Nehoff of the Martian General Assembly has been taking youth drug bribes from the Air Commission to hinder the creation of the polar feed plants?"

Jaws dropped.

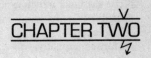

CHAPTER TWO

IN THE OFFICE, a very long minute passed in total silence.

"How did you know, Box?" asked Collins. Weakly, she dropped into a nearby chair that sported a large target bull's-eye on the seat cushion for just this sort of situation.

Jhonny hung his head in shame and Harry stumbled for the bar.

Ambocksky jerked a thumb toward a video monitor playing silently in the corner. "Interplanetary News Service just broke the story two minutes ago."

"Two . . ."

". . . minutes . . ."

". . . ago?"

Knuckles white around the neck of the container of blended Martian whiskey, Snyder spat out an oath that brought the ceiling fire alarm to alert status. Jhonny smacked himself on the forehead with a metallic clang.

Glancing at the pristine white computer card, Rikka gave it a farewell kiss and dropped it into the wastebasket. The top section magnetically deleted all recordings, the second ground the cassette into plastic strips, the bottom minced those into sprinkles and vaporized them into hot gases, which a vacuum pipe sucked into the main reactor where the material would get properly destroyed.

Snapping the cap off an ornate carafe on his desk, Box poured several white tablets into his hand and pushed the decanter across the polished wood. Rikka caught the precious container at the edge and dispensed mint antacids to everybody. Snyder dumped his into the whiskey and sipped in appreciation. The others tried to ignore him. It was an acquired taste for anchors.

"So goes the news biz," munched Jhonny philosophically.

11

"Now," began Ambocksky in a dangerous tone, "about that crash landing."

Quickly, the reporters started to marshal their arsenal of lies when there was a flash of light and a translucent figure formed in the middle of the room. Overlapping the laser hologram, Rikka stepped aside to see who it was. Oh, no.

Standing some two full meters alone without counting the additional hundred millimeters of her coiffured platinum-blond hair, the statuesque woman towered over even the android and held herself with the sure knowledge of a former beauty queen. Her sleeveless jumpsuit was of raw Japanese silk and molded to her ample form with the attention to detail of a lonely, myopic dermatologist. A gold Rolex secretary adorned her left wrist and her nails glittered with every color in the rainbow.

"Hi, Maria," sighed Ambocksky.

"So," the big blonde hissed in pleasure. "Missed the deadline by five minutes, eh?"

"Hello, Ms. Valdez," crooned Jhonny. "Always a pleasure to meet you, madam. My, what a lovely hairstyle."

Yeah, thought Collins dourly. Wonder if she did it herself or was simply hit by lightning?

Harry waved his half-full glass. "Hi, left. Hello, right."

Puzzled, then furious, Maria looked down at the ample cleavage displayed in her partially unzipped jumpsuit. The impudent toad!

"Sir," she said frostily, "I would greatly appreciate it if you would please address me and not parts of my anatomy."

A heroic slug. "Ah! Sorry. But I prefer to bypass subordinates and talk directly to the people in charge."

Valdez nodded. "Exactly." Then her face turned the color of murder. *"What was that again?"*

Harry started to repeat the statement as Ambocksky surged forward to stuff the remains of his sandwich into the anchor's big mouth.

"Eat, Snyder," the Program Director ordered. "Or else you may become delirious again."

Dutifully, the gray-haired man began to munch. Jhonny took the man's pulse and Rikka placed a hand on his brow.

"Temperature's down," Collins announced.

"Pulse is normal," added the android. "His spell of brain fever seems to have passed."

Tapping the end of her boot on the carpeted floor, after a moment Valdez accepted the charade as the only apology she was going to get out of these pracking lunatics. Brain fever, indeed. Ha! But there was still another bolt in her arsenal.

"Look at them!" Maria stated, her voice artfully dripping with scorn. "Our star news team and they haven't even removed their spacesuits before entering the office. A direct violation of station dress code!"

"Media has a dress code?" asked Rikka sotto voce.

Jhonny whispered, "So I'll get a dress."

"I have an address book. Does that count?"

Harry swallowed and started to speak, so more food was orally administered via knuckle sandwich.

"Now, Ms. Valdez," began Ambocksky.

"A team this sloppy doesn't deserve any replacement personnel," stormed the blonde, sitting in a chair off camera. "And if they weren't so damn popular, I'd fire the lot of them for that crash landing stunt!"

"What?"

"Eh?"

"Replacement personnel?" repeated Rikka eagerly. "Paul, you mean you finally got us another technician?"

Clearing his throat, Box stood, resting both hands on the desktop. "And that's where you are totally wrong, Ms. Valdez," he began lugubriously. "Because if these people had been properly equipped with a field tech, then they would not have had that trouble in the rings of Saturn and would have gotten here with the story on time."

The hologram of Maria glared hostilely.

Mentally, Jhonny upped the danger meter to Nuclear.

Snyder chewed heroically to get a word in before their fate was sealed without his participation. Damn, that artificial baloney!

Meticulously preparing for the worst, Ambocksky armed a switch set underneath his desk to set off the overhead water sprinklers. As a diversion, it was one of the best. Right up there with proposing marriage and making your head explode. He saved that last trick for true emergencies. Like the weekly budget meetings.

"Our ratings would have topped sixty plus," contributed Rikka, rallying to the defense. "And think what that directly translates into revenue from increased advertising fees!"

A glazed expression crossed the Station Manager's face and she wiped a bit of drool away with an embroidered handkerchief.

"Is this true?" asked Valdez, directing her question to the frantically swallowing anchor. The elderly man was a drunk and a letch, but he loved the truth more than life and had never been known to lie to a direct question.

One last mighty gulp. "What the man said," replied Harry, working a thumbnail on a incisor. "You want a list of the mechanical breakdowns and technical problems we encountered?"

With a sigh of resignation, Maria waved him silent. "No, I do not," she relented. Besides, Mr. Wilkes, the owner, wanted them to have another technician. This was merely a harassment visit.

The translucent woman stood and faced Ambocksky. "All right, Box. Our pet madmen get the tech you insisted upon. But if they're five minutes late on the next story . . ." Dramatically she drew a finger across her throat and made a noise like a rusty deli slicer.

"Understood." Ambocksky smiled and offered a hand. It was ignored. "You won't regret this, Ms. Valdez."

"Maybe. But I'll be watching!" And with a flash, the hologram faded from view.

Everybody exhaled in relief.

Then, taking a pile of computer flimsies, Ambocksky rolled them into a tube and soundly swatted Harry over the head.

"Ouch!"

"Next time this'll have a steel bar in it! Harry, when will you learn to behave?"

Appearing embarrassed, Snyder rolled his eyes. "Sorry, sir. But it's love."

Poised to strike again, the roll of papers lowered. "Come again?"

"It's love," repeated Harry, smiling. "I just love to piss her off."
Swack!

Thoughtfully, Jhonny tugged on a chin. "Hopefully our new technician can install a seven-second delay on his mouth."

"And maybe even get Deitrich's vocal circuits repaired," noted Rikka, chuckling. "If the tech is any good."

"He is," said Ambocksky smugly. "I saw to that."

Good enough. Turning, Collins added, "And by the way, Mr. Snyder, what engineering problems did we encounter on our journey?"

"None," he replied, reclining and lighting a cigar. "And I didn't say that we had any. I only asked if she would like a list of them."

"A classic number two evasion," smiled Jhonny. "Not bad for an ambulatory sack of mostly water."

"Why, thank you, Tobor."

"My pleasure, Monkey-Boy."

Shaking his head, Paul reclaimed his chair and pressed a button on the intercom. "Mrs. Seigling, please send in Mike."

"Okay, chiefy!" sang out the desk plate.

Smoking cigar in hand, Harry snorted into his whiskey, and Jhonny's face did the most incredible gymnastics.

"Chiefy?" sniggered Rikka, trying to cover her mouth.

Ambocksky held up a hand to cut her off. "Carol Seigling can read my handwriting, brings me homemade doughnuts, and has no aspirations of becoming a reporter. She can call me poopsy-whoopsy if she damn well pleases, and I wouldn't get rid of her if she set the place on fire. End. Of. Discussion."

Struggling against the internal laugh pressure, the news team managed to keep mum, but filed the delicious information away for possible future use. Maybe a nice discreet inter-office memo?

Just then, a huge dark shape loomed outside the office and as the doors cycled apart in walked a furry mountain.

Standing some three meters tall, the being was completely covered with a thick coat of short, chocolate-brown fur. The face was similar to a badger, solid black eyes, half-moon nose, but with the daintiest pair of spectacles precariously perched on the end of its elongated snout. The palms of its hands were smooth black skin, the fingers stout columns of taloned flesh.

The alien was wearing regulation space boots of a size Rikka and her team had never known existed, short hiking pants, and an unbuttoned equipment vest with ten thousand pockets. A Lavalear mike was clipped to his left ear and a full-size pocket IBM portable was strapped to his right wrist in lieu of a secretary.

Smiling, Paul motioned the colossus closer. "Hello, Mike. Come on in."

"Sir," rumbled the leviathan being.

"Wow!" cried Jhonny eagerly. "A Gremlin! Neat!"

Embarrassed, Harry hushed the android. It was a little known fact that Snyder himself had coined the nickname for the giant aliens when their sleeper ship was first discovered floating lost through our solar system. Only a youngster at the time, Snyder had done it as a joke on their huge size. But when it became apparent that the alien beings loved technology more than a Mercurian liked to argue, the silly name stuck. Permanently.

As the alien shambled closer, Collins braced herself for the worst and was surprised to discover that the fur wasn't musty, but smelled like springtime flowers. Hey, they must use the same shampoo, Industrial Spring 9! Immediately she began to warm to the new team member. Maybe he even had an answer for split ends. Certainly possessed enough of them.

"Mike, this is your new assignment. The top squad of QSNT, the Satellite News Team!"

"An honor," the alien replied in a stentorian bass.

"Rikka Collins, Harry Snyder, Jhonny Smith, may I introduce Michelangelo—" Box then snorted, burped, growled, and gave an eerie rendition of a door falling over.

"Just call me Mike," he rumbled, offering a paw large enough to hold a typewriter. And Rikka knew. She had seen one in a museum. Hesitantly, she shook the proffered limb.

"You are the writer?" asked the hirsute Goliath.

"And chief investigator," said Collins, retrieving her hand. Interesting. His grip was surprisingly soft and delicate. More like a surgeon's than a technician's. She had half expected to get her bones crushed to a pulp.

"I'm the anchor, chain, chief cook and bottle emptier," contributed Harry, rising to shake hands.

The scene somehow reminded Collins of a boy and his pet. Only she wasn't sure who was who.

"An honor, sir. But wasn't it you who covered the preliminary meetings between my people and the United Planets when our ship first wandered into your solar system?"

"Yep, that was me. I did a lot of free-lance work in those days. Of course, that was before . . ." The older man faltered in the greeting. "Well, it was just before."

Releasing his grip, Snyder turned and went to the bar for another Scotch. Nobody tried to stop him.

"Hi, there," grinned Jhonny, advancing to cover the social lapse of his friend. "I'm Jhonny Smith, the camera-op, jackdaffer, and burglary expert."

"Ja-hon-knee," said the alien, pronouncing the name carefully. "Not Jonny?"

"Correctamundo, big guy."

Feral eyes squinted in concentration. "You . . . are a J series android?"

Suddenly, the office went very still.

"Oh, good heavens, no!" declaimed the machine. "Hiring androids for anything but menial work is totally illegal. Why should somebody go to all the trouble of disguising an illegal android as a simple cameraman, even if it was to be considered a private act of rebellion against a stupid unjust law they hated, and the android in question was the best vidiot in the whole solar system and would work for peanuts because of his nebulous status?"

The towering alien gave a momentary pause and then nodded. "I quite understand. My apologies."

Nice recovery, noted Rikka appreciatively. The big guy might just work out okay.

Swirling amber liquid around crystalline cubes in his drink, Harry caught her eye and nodded in approval. Having a genuine alien on the team could be very helpful. He would give them different insights into old situations. New perspectives. Plus, the Herculean rug looked capable of punching his way through a dura-steel wall. A nice tactic to have tucked away for emergency exits. Good way to avoid bar tabs also.

Michelangelo glanced about. "And where is Deitrich?"

PRESENT AS ALWAYS, MIKE, scrolled the IBM portable on the alien's wrist after a small beep to attract his attention. I AM JUST EXTREMELY BUSY ARRANGING REPAIRS ON OUR SHUTTLE.

"Very costly repairs," the Program Director added for clarity, staring directly at the SNT members.

Three of the five people in the office assumed the most amazingly innocent expressions.

"Ah, yes," nodded Michelangelo. "I heard their arrival. Was the story of the correct temperature?"

The humans and android exchanged glances.

"Hot?" asked Rikka hesitantly.

"Yes. Hot. Did it have sufficient thermal residue to function properly on your children's entertainment show?"

ON OUR *WHAT*?

"Now wait a minute, Mack—"

"Hey!"

The alien seemed confused. "News is not educational?"

Suddenly, a red light on top of the monitor in the corner of the office began to rotate and flash. Then abruptly the picture on the screen changed from the 5:30 graph of the Dow Jones Industrials to a stock shot of the United Planets flag.

Rikka glanced out the transparent walls of the office to the newsroom surrounding them. Every monitor, television, and computer screen was displaying the exact same scene. And although the walls were supposed to be totally soundproof, she could still tell that everybody had stopped making noise. Even the coffee machines.

Paul glared at the picture. "Computer! Sound up! Level nine!"

"—peat," said the woman in a surprisingly pleasant voice. "This is the activation of the emergency broadcast system. This is not a test. Repeat, this is not a test. Until further notice, please do not use any Z-class transmissions, except in the case of a life-or-death emergency. Leave the communications band clear for the police and military. In five minutes there will be a vitally important announcement. Please summon everybody you can to a working radio, video monitor, and modem.

"Repeat," said the voice again. "This is—"

"Sound off," barked Box. "Half scroll."

Obediently, the monitor rolled and then stopped when the picture of the UN flag was half above the screen and half rising from below. A thin black line bisected the monitor below which glowed an encoded number sequence.

Rikka and her team said nothing. They knew that Box had memorized every government agency EBS code. He could identify what department the message came from before they officially announced it, a neat trick that often gave the SNT a full five-minute head start on the competition. Sometimes more.

"It's real," announced Paul after a moment. "No chance of a fake transmission with that code."

Harry placed his drink aside. "So who is it from? Venus Immigration? Martian DEA? Lunar DMV?"

Rikka was already typing notes into her secretary.

"This is a direct communiqué from the UP Security Council at the Hawaiian headquarters of the Earth Defense Force," stated the Program Director.

"And?" prompted Jhonny and Deitrich in unison.

"Ladies and newspeople," Box took a breath and let it out slowly. "Earth is at war."

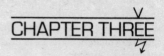

CHAPTER THREE

"A WAR?" SQUEAKED Jhonny. "A real-live shooting war?"

YIKES! scrolled Deitrich in a thirty-six-point font of terror.

Harry almost dropped his glass. "Bloody hell."

"Rhal-ca-shang," rumbled Michelangelo.

"On toast," the big alien added in English.

Collins also added that to her notes. A war? Wow. That was the one civil event her team had never covered. Had never wanted to cover, either. People got killed in wars. Even supposedly neutral news reporters.

Swiveling his chair about, Ambocksky opened a drawer and grabbed an executive microphone. The mike hummed for a second as it compared the fingerprints of the person holding it to those on file and when finally satisfied, it loudly clicked on, the noise echoing in the office over the PA system.

"Attention everybody," said Paul into the microphone, his words relaying throughout the entire station. "This is Paul Ambocksky. I want a full meeting in Conference Room A in nine minutes. All department heads and senior reporters will be there. No excuse for missing this is acceptable. Out."

Tapping commands into the desktop, Ambocksky cycled up a flat video monitor. Immediately, the screen swirled into a picture of a crew-cut woman in a tan Security uniform.

"Hertzoff," announced the guard.

"Hillary, Ambocksky here. Put Media on an Alert One status. Monitor all outgoing calls and nobody comes in or leaves unless I, Maria Valdez, or Mr. Wilkes okays them."

"Wilkes?" asked the woman, frowning.

Box relented. "Okay-okay, even if he does authorize somebody, check with me or Valdez also."

"Understood."

"See you at the meeting."

"No."

"Why the heck not?"

"Busy."

"Well, then send Harrison."

"Done."

"Later."

"Out." The screen went blank and cycled back into the desk.

"Someday I will discover why that Captain Hertzoff only speaks in single words," said Harry as he poured the remainder of his drink back into the liquor bottle. This was a time for sharp wits and black coffee.

"You folks got eight more minutes until the military makes their official announcement," commented Ambocksky wryly, locking his desk with a slap and a twist. "Now's a good time to clean yourselves up and become presentable."

Rikka nodded. "Done. See you in A!"

Leaving the office, everybody went off in a different direction. Not having been assigned an apartment yet, Michelangelo strode directly toward the conference room. People scurried out of his way until the alien reached the reception area where he was momentarily waylaid by Mrs. Seigling and a fresh plate of doughnuts.

Reaching the turbo-lifts, Collins hit nine, then three and two. Smoothly descending, the lift started to also circumnavigate the station to reach Level 9, Section 3, Corridor 2.

With a musical ding, the lift doors parted and Rikka hurried to her apartment. Her fingerprint unlocked the door. A shoe heel closed it behind her.

Inside, a wicker basket next to the mail slot was overflowing with physical letters. She ignored them. If anybody had sent an important message, it would be in her E-Mail on the computer. And there was no colorful wrapping paper to indicate a gift. Nor any yellow warning tags of a letter bomb—found and disposed of by station Security, thank goodness. As the public face of the SNT, it was poor Harry who got the majority of those. Some of his fans just wanted to love the man to pieces.

Over in the kitchen there was the skeleton of a dead cat lying before an empty water bowl. Rikka snorted at the sight. She had purchased the feline bones at a veterinary supply store in an effort to brutally remind herself that no matter how much she liked pets, for somebody on the road as much as she was, it was an extremely bad idea. But maybe a turtle? Nyah. How would she know if it ever did die on her?

Dashing into the bedroom, Rikka activated her Closet-Queen and impatiently waited for the green light to come on. Occupying its own entire room, the automated beautician was a civilian modification of the military Closet-Doc that could repair any injury from a stubbed toe to minor brain surgery. Having her own private home stylist was a shameful indulgence, and Collins had insisted upon the perk in her last contract only because she knew Valdez had one.

Green! Her thumbprint activated the menu and Rikka quickly flipped through the selection. Hmm, 821 would do. It had also been her ex-husband's favorite setting. Pity. Armand had been such a handsome, sensitive man. Collins would have happily put the welfare of their family ahead of her career. Unfortunately, Army wanted her to put everything ahead of her career. And that was a big no go.

While Harry was a drunk and Jhonny was some kind of a mutant android, if there could be such a thing, they were still better family than Armand and his snooty relatives.

And infinitely superior friends.

As the door cycled open Collins put those unconstructive thoughts out of her mind and stepped inside the Queen. The door closed on her and wiggling warmth filled the darkness.

A minute passed. Two. Three. Then the door opened with a hiss and Rikka emerged in a billow of scented smoke. Pausing for a moment before the mirror on her bureau, she checked the effect. Hair shampooed and combed, teeth polished, she was now washed, shaved, massaged, and dressed in a fresh new green jumpsuit with matching boots and headband.

Slapping a hand on the corner of her desk, the IBM secretary obediently wrapped itself around her waist. Retrieving her watch and wallet from a bin in the Queen, Rikka strode out the door.

Time for business.
A war, eh? Hmm.

Conference Room A was already filled by the time Rikka arrived. Pushing her way through a crowd of doughnut eaters, Collins forced a path to the main table and claimed her seat. Harry was in a neat, blue pin-striped jumpsuit. A black coffee Marlboro flavor stick dangled jauntily from his mouth. Jhonny had donned his work outfit of a gray leather jumpsuit covered with metal rings for equipment to hang on. His semisentient Toshiba camcorder was perched on his right shoulder like a pirate's pet parrot. As the android turned his head, so did the camcorder's lens array.

Dominating the whole table, Mike was occupying two chairs at the same time and still appeared to be cramped. Box was directly across from Rikka. The Program Director was talking on two Hush phones simultaneously while jotting notes and shredding a folder marked "Secret." Briefly, Collins wondered if juggling had been a basic requirement for his job.

At the arbitrary head of the circular table sat Maria Valdez in the flesh. Busy in executive contemplation, she was studiously filing her rainbow-colored fingernails.

The reserved chair next to her was conspicuously empty.

"Think the boss got lost again?" a movie critic asked Rikka, taking a seat alongside her.

She smiled. "He probably just forgot. Or had something really important to do."

A five-credit bill was pulled into view. "I say he's lost."

Crossing her arms, Rikka viewed the money impartially.

"At what odds?" she asked politely.

DON'T TAKE LESS THAN FIVE TO TWO, advised Deitrich prudently.

"Time," called Ambocksky, hanging up both phones.

All conversation stopped and recorders were activated.

A wafer monitor descended from the ceiling and the liquid crystal screen flickered into life. With perfect timing, the shot of the UP flag dissolved into a picture of a stout woman in a stiffly formal military uniform. On the wall behind her was the draped flag of the United Planets. Tactfully underneath were three smaller versions of the flags of Earth, Mars, and the Independent Asteroids.

"Excuse me, please," asked Michelangelo. "But why do those

three specific worlds also have their own flags posted? Why not Luna, Venus, or Titan?"

"Because those are the superpowers," explained Harry, tapping the clear tip of his flavor stick into a convenient tray. The drained end crumbled off at the touch. "They're the leaders in society, politics, economics, et cetera."

Pursing his snout, the big alien thoughtfully adjusted his tiny glasses.

"Actually, it's because they're the folks with the really big bombs," explained Jhonny succinctly.

"Ah! Top billing or else. This I understand." A toothy grin. "Your world is not so different from mine, my friend."

REALLY? HOW SAD.

"Greetings," said the Colonel in flawless Esperanto. "I am Lt. Colonel Victoria Wills, Public Information officer for the UP Security Council."

"We know who you are, Vicky," chided a reporter at the screen as he poured a cup of coffee. "Get on with it!"

The officer cleared her throat. "As of 1400 hours Greenwich Standard Time, the United Planets colony on Titan has declared itself an independent political entity and placed an official state of war between Titan and the rest of the solar system. Armed battleships from the rogue moon have already raided and destroyed several UP Navy bases in the ice rings of Saturn and attacked numerous outposts on the moons Mimas, Enceladus, Rhea, Hyperion, Phoebe, Tethys, Dione, and Japetus, wounding and killing hundreds of civilian personnel."

Shocked faces filled the conference room.

RIKKA, scrolled Deitrich on the IBM sec on her wrist. ARE YOU ALSO RECEIVING THIS, OR AM I HAVING A BOUT OF HARRY'S BRAIN FEVER?

Sadly, Collins informed the disembodied pilot that they were both seeing the same thing. It wasn't some local battle between regional neighbors, but interplanetary warfare.

Turning a page, the Colonel went on. "The Royal Martian Navy immediately sent the dreadnought HMS *Burroughs* on tour in the rings of Saturn to effect rescue and assist the Earth Defense Forces." There was a pause. "The *Burroughs* is reported destroyed with all hands lost."

"Ye gods," croaked a man, crossing himself.

"If this is what they're admitting," asked a pale woman, "then how bad is the real situation?"

Box quieted them both with a stern glance.

"Numerous appeals were made by the Secretary-General of the United Planets for a peaceful political solution to the situation, but to no avail. So, under the authorization of Amendment 23-A of the Earth-Mars Treaty, as of 1700 hours today, August 26, 2258, the entire solar system has been placed under martial law. All off-planet civilian travel is hereby restricted. All use of Z-band communications is strictly forbidden. Punishment by military tribunal will be swift and severe."

"So how the prack are we supposed to get more information?" loudly demanded a Crime reporter. "Stick our heads out the airlock and shout at the Earth?"

Stretching a leg, Harry gave the woman a kick under the table. "We'll use an X- or Y-band transmission."

"But those only travel at light speed! It'll take forever to contact Pluto and confirm the facts."

"Roughly thirty-two hours for a round-trip communication," corrected Michelangelo. "Due to the relative positions of the source and target goal."

"Thanks. Who the hell are you anyway?"

On the monitor, another page was turned. "Currently, the Earth Defense Force, the Royal Martian Navy, the Lunar Police, and the Enforcers of the Independent Asteroids are combining their forces.

"As per the United Planets information charter, we will broadcast details of all battles, including live footage, the regulation four hours afterward." A smile. "This announcement will be broadcast every five minutes for the next ten hours. Please consult your local news services for additional details."

As the message began to repeat, the screen faded to white and rose into the ceiling.

"Damn Titan bastards," growled a Sports editor. "They're always causing trouble. Even their pracking planet orbits backward."

"That's Tritan that orbits counterclockwise," admonished a Science editor.

"Yeah, them, too!" rallied the athletic curmudgeon.

Paul turned to Valdez and she gestured him on with a full spectrum wave.

"Okay, the basics first," stated Ambocksky. "Wu Chung, contact our Earthside affiliates and have 'em dispatch some cub reporters to go interview random naval personnel. Send a lot. That should make the enemy think we're on a hot lead and hopefully waste some top reporters on a wild-goose chase."

The big redheaded sales rep gave a wink. "Faith and begorra, consider it done, Box. Bullshit is my speciality."

"I know it is. Hey, Schwartz!"

A head jerked to attention. "Yeah, boss?"

"I want a composite report on the political factions of all the major combatants, plus their military firepower. Raid the file room for stock footage of prior battles, and add clips of some space battles with lots of big explosions from that *Iron Earth* movie series."

"Already working on it," stated the woman, busy typing on her wrist secretary.

Rikka approved. If you have nothing to say, then make your report visually stimulating. And full frontal nudity was always helpful in a pinch.

Ambocksky checked the list in his hand. "Sam, work up one of your tearjerker specials on the deceased soldiers and scientists."

"Done!" answered the Society editor.

The Religious editor sniffed for attention. "I can contact all of the major religious leaders to conduct public services for the dead and pray for a quick and lasting peace."

"Amen, to that," decried Harry seriously.

Peterson, the Union expert, raised a hand. "I'll do a piece on what the Gremlins think of all this and why the prack aren't androids allowed to fight."

Ambocksky jotted the suggestion on his old-fashioned notepaper. "Good idea."

"Why? 'Cause we're too damn smart for that shit," whispered Jhonny to nobody in particular.

Elbows on the table, Peterson leaned close. "Sir, exactly what do you think of this situation?"

Michelangelo removed his glasses before speaking. "I do believe," he stated ponderously, "that our probe ship chose a bad time to crash in your solar system."

"And amen to that," decried Harry again.

"Okay, so much for the basics," stated Paul, feeding the sheet of paper into a slot in the table. There immediately followed a grinding noise and a brief flash of light. "Now I want some unusual opinions, observations, and ideas. We're racing against the enemy and time is short."

"We fight in the war?" asked Michelangelo, concerned.

"Nyah," scoffed Snyder. "The enemy he was referring to is CNN, the BBC, and the Interplanetary News Service. Okay, how can we scoop the other networks?"

"Especially INS," added Jhonny hatefully.

The room growled in response.

"Smuggle a mole behind military lines for some shots of the battles before they're officially released?" suggested the chief Entertainment editor, an eager, dreamy expression on his face.

"And have us all arrested for receiving stolen data and then shot as spies?"

The avaricious look quickly faded. "Ah, perhaps not," recanted the dapper man.

"We could quote—mistakenly—end quote hijack a UP message drone," murmured a thin, wild-haired woman as she earnestly rubbed a crystal ball in her bony hands. "Get the inside poop on this hard copy."

"And break a Sig-Zine code? Even if successful, we're shot as spies again," frowned Ambocksky.

The Financial editor merely shrugged in reply.

Impatiently, Box glanced around the table. "Next?"

During this discussion, Rikka chewed rhythmically on a lip and was strangely quiet, a fact noted by most of the people present. They could almost hear the wheels grinding in her brain.

"We could assign a strategy room," offered a Sports editor.

"A what?" demanded Valdez, joining the conversation for the first time.

"It's a gag we use for sports events we can't, legally, broadcast. We have the Special Effects gang in the lab establish a conference room as a battle board and place the positions of everybody's ships. As information comes in, we duplicate the actual events with miniature holograms. Do the whole simulation in miniature laser holograms and we could even shoot for broadcast."

Paul squinted an eye. "You can guarantee quality?"

"Sure. You know that shutout game in last year's Worlds Series?"

"Yeah . . ."

"That was us," stated the man proudly. "However, it is expensive."

Ms. Valdez finished another nail. "Prack the cost. Do it."

"Wow," gushed a Business editor. "Couldn't get a better view unless we were on the bridge of a dreadnought."

"No thanks," said an elderly meteorologist. Sadly, his department wasn't going to have much of anything to do in this conflagration. Nobody had learned how to make the weather a weapon. Yet.

"Wasn't a suggestion," corrected the woman pleasantly. "Merely an observation."

The elderly man sneered in contempt. "Oh, a coward, eh?"

"Hack!"

"Slut!"

But the witty repartee was cut short as a laser hologram appeared in the middle of the conference table. The rotund man was in his mid-fifties, partly bald, and what hair he had was snowy white. His ample face seemed to have a cheery smile permanently tattooed between his apple-rosy cheeks. His luxurious blue jumpsuit was of an expensive Italian design, and the tiny initials GWB shined silver bright on each lapel and cuff.

"Sorry I'm late," smiled Gardner Wilkes, beaming his pleasure at the roomful of dour reporters as the hologram floated into position at his chair. "But I got los . . . ah, I was momentarily detained with station business."

Raggedly, the room said hello.

"Gardner Wilkes?" asked Michelangelo softly.

Jhonny nodded yes.

"What does the 'B' stand for?"

"Boss," replied Harry with a straight face.

BOZO, corrected Deitrich.

Puzzled, the alien accessed the Encyclopedia program of his IBM portable. Ah! Oh, dear.

"Where are we in the conference?" asked Wilkes amiably.

"Dictating assignments," purred Maria, moving her chair a little bit closer to the man. "I had finished outlining the basic thrust of our designs and had turned the meeting over to Mr. Ambocksky."

"What?!" gasped Ambocksky.

Wilkes gestured grandly. "Well then, please take over, Paul, I'm sure you'll do fine."

Grinding teeth, the Program Director resumed the discussion. "Val-Singa, who do you think will be placed in charge of the armadas?"

Lowering his monitor sunglasses, the UP liaison checked his private files. "Well, if it was a defensive fleet, Port Admiral Sullivan from Mars. But since it is an offensive fleet, then I would say Fleet Admiral Davis from Earth."

"Terrance 'Mad Dog' Davis?"

A shrug. "That's the man."

"Merciful heavens," gushed a Society editor, flushing with excitement. "There will be nukes tonight!"

"And what about Titan?" asked Wilkes curiously.

Paul consulted his voluminous notes. "They only have one person with the ability to successfully lead a war fleet, Admiral Kathryn Hamilton."

" 'Hellcat' Hamilton?"

"Whoopee! A Kat and Dog show," gleefully chortled a political cartoonist. "This is going to be great!" And he started wildly penciling starships on his board.

"What have the Asteroids to say about this whole thing?" asked Gardner Wilkes, filling a glass with hot coffee from a steaming urn embossed with his initials.

"Nothing. No official statement as of yet."

Maintaining a facade of total cool, the water glass was emptied into a coffee mug. "Now that is suspicious," sipped Wilkes. "Normally the Independent rocks have an opinion on bloody near everything and will tell it to you, ad nauseam. Reticence is not part of their culture."

"Air is precious, breath isn't," quoted Harry, amused.

A smarmy fellow dressed in solid white tentatively lifted a single finger. "Hey, Box. I have a secondary override flip-flop who'll cookie on a platter if I can shoot him a solid 86."

Covering his face with a hand, Ambocksky sighed a groan.

"Bob, I've talked to you before about this. We have a lot of newbies here so let's keep the slang to a minimum. Okay?"

"I understood what he said," commented Valdez loftily.

Nobody important paid her remark any attention.

Visibly, the reporter shifted mental gear. "There . . . is a person whose-name-I-do-not-wish-to-reveal-for-reasons-too-numerous-to-mention who will divulge secret information to me, and me alone, if I promise him total anonymity and sufficient monetary renumeration." Tenderly, he worked his jaw. Ow. That had hurt.

Ambockisky nodded. "Sounds good. Draw what you need from our Bribery clerk but try and get a receipt this time. Okay?"

"Do my best, chief."

"Okay."

"No, this is not okay. Not even slightly," stormed Rikka, standing and knocking over her chair. "This is total bullshit of the highest magnitude! Things like this simply do not happen out of the blue or black. The Titan colony was safe, warm, and well fed. They had minimal taxes and full cable. Why the whistling hell would they go to war with anybody?"

"Are you postulating that this is a fake broadcast by some prankster?" asked Maria, the tone of her voice highly suggestive that she would just love it if Collins would answer yes to the idiotic possibility.

"Of course not," snapped Harry. "Only a boobs would say that."

Valdez went dead white and started to sputter incoherently.

Placing aside the gold-rimmed mug, Wilkes laced hands across his ample belly. "Exactly what are you suggesting, Ms. Collins?"

"Oh, the war is real enough," she started to clarify. "Or, at least, there will be some fighting. The government couldn't hide that. But the reasons are totally false. I think the UP, Earth, Mars, Titan, or maybe even the Asteroids are hiding something. Something so big and potentially dangerous that they need a systems-wide war to help distract everybody from what is really going on."

"And what is really going on?"

"I don't know. But we can find out soon enough."

"No," stated Maria coldly. "We need our top team here at Media to delve into the subtle political machinations of the situation."

"Any damn cub can handle that," snapped Harry. "Just give 'em a list of phonetically spelled questions to read and tell them not to crap in public."

A smattering of laughter circled the room at the blatant truism. Although the two scowling cub reporters did not join in the merriment.

"Hesitantly, I agree with Mr. Snyder," said Gardner. "Ah, minus the profanity, of course. I think the SNT would do best to check into this interesting possibility."

Facial color slowly returning, Ms. Valdez chose her words carefully. "And how will they do that, sir? Go to Titan?"

"Sure," answered Rikka. "No problem."

Ambocksky spoke, "Ah, sorry. Problem. The UP has informed us that any ship traveling toward the general vicinity of Titan, or on a hyperbolic course that could theoretically take them to Titan, will be blasted without warning."

"News ships?" gawked Snyder. "They actually stated that the military would shoot at news ships?"

"Officially? No, of course not. But accidents happen."

"Hmm, would they shoot at a hospital ship?" asked Harry with a sly smile on his lips.

"Or a derelict Mercurian lifeboat?" asked Jhonny.

"Or a malfunctioning Gremlin probe?" added Michelangelo, getting into the spirit of things.

"A UP dreadnought has already vapped two meteors and one of their own supply ships," said Ambocksky.

There was a stunned moment of silence.

"Any further questions?" asked Paul, tapping a stylus.

Wilkes exhaled, making a raspberry sound. "When will the big hostilities officially begin?"

Box shrugged. "Unknown, sir. But the battle lines are here." A translucent map of the solar system appeared above the table. A series of different colored glowing lines formed complex patterns about the planets.

"What the pra . . . heck is this?" demanded Valdez incredulously. "Are both sides going to form neat lines of million-dollar ships and calmly sit there banging away at each other?"

Brows furrowed.

"It is a highly unusual way to fight a war," stated Wilkes. "In fact it violates every known martial philosophy."

"I am a black belt in kung fu," the station owner admitted humbly.

JELL-O BEWARE, scrolled Deitrich.

"Then we have a go on the fake war idea?" asked Jhonny hopefully. The android could feel his internal relays start to accelerate their rhythms as a prelude to fieldwork.

The plump millionaire tugged on an ear. "Well, I don't know about that . . ."

Sensing executive weakness, Paul jumped into the fray. "Give 'em forty-eight hours. To prove, or disprove."

"The war could be over in forty-eight hours!" snapped Maria. "And they're still exhausted from their Martian debacle."

Rikka did a double take. Since when did Maria give a damn whether or not they burst into flames.

"Forty-eight is awfully dang long," drawled Gardner Wilkes. "I'm willing to stretch things only so far even for my favorite news show."

Ah, another mystery explained. Collins vowed to remember this.

"Well, I can give them until the six hundred report tomorrow morning," recapitulated Ms. Valdez magnanimously. "That should be more than enough for any competent reporter."

"Twelve hours?" snorted Ambocksky, snapping the stylus in half. Tiny computer chips sprinkled onto the table. "Outrageous! They need at least thirty-six."

"They can have until noon," shot back the big blonde. "Eighteen hours. And that's it. Finito. End of discussion. Period."

"Thirty," retorted Box, gesturing with the jagged stylus stub. "Or I'll personally assign them to interview the cooks of the fleet to see how many beans the troops are eating this year!"

Grimly, Valdez pointed her nail file at the man. "Twenty! Or I'll have them analyzing yak droppings on the North Pole of Neptune!"

He leaned in close. "Twenty-eight!"

She leaned in closer. "Twenty-two!"

"Twenty-four seems a nice round number," stated Wilkes calmly.

Interrupted in mid-bicker, the flushed Program Director and Station Manager whistled breath through clenched teeth and tried to regain their composure. Privately, each had an unusually strong desire for a cigarette at this moment.

GEE, I LOVE THIS KIND OF STUFF, scrolled Deitrich.

Trying to act casual, Rikka hid the screen with her palm. Damn bigmouthed Brain.

Gardner Wilkes swiveled about, his chair remaining stationary. "Rikka, can you have something in the can for us by 1800 tomorrow?"

The stern expression on Maria's face added the dire codicil "or else."

"Consider it done," stated Collins, standing. "Come on, gang, we have an interplanetary conspiracy to bust open."

Or die trying, added Maria privately. Preferably the latter.

CHAPTER FOUR

"NOW ABOUT THAT simulation . . ." said Ambocksky's voice as the conference-room doors swung closed.

"Strategy is our first order of business," declared Rikka, streams of busy reporters and techs filling the corridor. "And someplace quiet where we can think in peace."

"The Horny Toad?" asked Harry.

"The Horny Toad," agreed Jhonny.

"The . . . what?" asked Michelangelo as they push/pulled him toward the nearest turbo-lift.

AUXILIARY LIFE SUPPORT, explained Dietrich as the doors closed.

As the lift doors musically parted, the team walked into a lobby reminiscent of pre-space times. The walls were lined with real wood and decorated with ancient flat photographs of men and women. Brass railings edged the floor that was covered with a fine woven plastic carpet of tremendous durability. Great leafy bushes in wicker tubs stood sentry in every corner and a velvet-covered chain blocked the set of wood and brass doors. On the lintel was a discreet sign of puce neon that audibly hummed with electrical power: THE HORNY TOAD. And underneath blinked: ALL BOOZE, ALL THE TIME!

"Quila!" cried Harry, gesturing grandly. "The best saloon within a hundred fifty kilometers!"

"The only saloon within one hundred fifty kilometers," corrected Jhonny.

Rikka threw the bar door open and the team entered. "Well, that makes it the best by reason of default."

Grudgingly, the logic of the argument was accepted. Of course, that also made it the largest, the smallest, the most expensive, and the bar with the greatest number of albino Lithuanian midgets who refused to vote the straight Republican ticket.

Inside, there was a noticeable change in the atmosphere. The saloon was darker than the rest of the station and several degrees cooler. The air was crisp, fresh, and thick with extra oxygen.

The walls were massive horizontal beams for the first meter, then red brick to the ceiling, which was painted a nonreflective black. Optical charts of the solar system and Scotland adorned the walls in no discernible order. Cushioned leather booths lined the room and huge hexagonal tables dotted the middle. Only a score of people were here today, munching on sandwiches or quaffing frothy drinks in tumblers the size of small countries.

A vintage CD player stood solitary and proud near the rest rooms. Floating above the music machine were two old men with very long beards and electric guitars singing about the amazing virtues of a young lady's lower limbs.

At the far end of the spacious room was the bar, its counter a single slab of dark granite. The top was polished mirror smooth, the sides were irregular and pitted deeply in several spots. A few indentations in the igneous rock looked suspiciously like bullet holes and laser craters to Michelangelo.

Spanning the wall aft of the bar was an aquarium tank filled with water and plants and plastic mermaids who displayed their mammalian attributes with brazen glee. And swimming about in the aquatic wonderland was a battle-scarred fish of Herculean proportions. Even its jagged teeth and bloodshot beady eyes seemed muscular. A small sign on the outside of the tank bore the warning: HIS NAME IS BRUNO AND HE HAS A SERIOUS ATTITUDE PROBLEM. BEWARE.

Alongside the big tank was a smaller glass cube filled with deadly South American piranha. The sign on their tank read: FOOD FOR BRUNO. KETCHUP AND YOUR FINGERS ARE OPTIONAL.

Situated behind the vast expanse of aged mahogany was Alonzo MacKenzie. A shaved bear was the usual first impression that came to people's minds. Barrel-chested, the man was dressed in an incongruous Highland tartan jumpsuit. His long strawberry-blond hair was tied off in a ponytail that hung to his waist and his hands appeared to be more scar tissue than healthy flesh. But the bartender's blue eyes twinkled as he stared with unabashed pleasure at the hairy skyscraper ambling toward him.

"Rikka, Harry, Jhonny," he called as a greeting. "Who is the *fal ishd-tbwk aaraa*?"

Mike stopped in his tracks. "You speak my language?"

"Only a few words, laddie," admitted MacKenzie, polishing a beer glass to a sanitary sheen. "Never want to lose a sale because I can't understand the customer."

The alien bowed. "A highly commendable attitude."

"So what do you think of my place?"

"Your place? The Wilkes Corporation does not own this establishment?"

"No."

"Interesting. Why not?"

MacKenzie turned to a small blackboard on the wall near Bruno and made a check mark. "That's one!" he announced.

Tugging on his equipment vest, Collins pulled the alien aside.

"Nobody knows why Wilkes doesn't own the Toad," she whispered to him. "And apparently, whatever the reason is, it's a sore point of contention. A customer gets to ask why three times, then they're barred from the club."

"Permanently," added Jhonny.

WHICH IS THE EQUIVALENT OF A DEATH SENTENCE TO A NEWS RE-PORTER, scrolled Deitrich.

"And what will you folk be having?" asked MacKenzie, filling a bowl full of pretzels and giving it a pat. Mechanical spider legs extended from the bottom and the bowl scuttled along the countertop until it reached the first person who said, "Ah, there they are!"

"A table in a quiet corner," said Harry, glancing about the dim room. "You got the sound dampers fixed yet?"

A bowl of potato chips was sent off in search of customers needing a quick intake of toasted grease and salt. "Ach, now. Business is it? Well then, take number one under the picture of Edward R. Murrow. And may his luck be yours."

"Thanks," smiled Rikka and the group ambled away.

In the background, the CD player had automatically switched to another recording. Now a swarthy man in a tuxedo was directing a fifty-piece orchestra composed entirely of assorted drums. The music was stirring, primordial, made for dancing. But as the report-

ers took their seats blessed silence engulfed the table as the dampeners activated.

"I thought we'd get a good night's sleep and then to go work in
the morning," stated Michelangelo, drawing a chair from another
table. Placing the two chairs side by side, he daintily lowered his
bulk. The stout wood creaked ominously, but held their structural
integrity. For the moment.

Behind the bar, MacKenzie pulled a pocket-doc from his apron
and adjusted its setting to Gremlin, buttock, splinter removal. Just
in case.

"Sleep!" gasped Snyder.

"Sleep?" asked Jhonny, shocked.

HA! scrolled Deitrich. FAT CHANCE.

Removing her headband, Rikka leaned forward on the table.
"Mike, you're not suggesting that we sleep when we have a time
limit on our actions?"

"Well, actually . . ."

SAY NO, BIG GUY, privately scrolled his IBM portable.

"No," the technician stated, sitting upright and proud. "I was
joking. Ha."

Harry smiled. "Better," he said, digging into the bowl of popcorn. "Then let's get some drinks here and get to work. Jhonny,
you're closer."

"Sure," said the android and he palmed a softly glowing sensor
plate in the middle of the table.

"Drinks? Will alcohol assist human concentration?"

"No, but it makes staying awake a lot more fun."

A tiny version of MacKenzie wearing a kilt and tam-o'-shanter
shimmered into existence on the tabletop.

"And what will be your orders," drawled the hologram, its High-
lander accent infinitely more pronounced than the original.

"A whiskey on the rocks," said Rikka. "Mineral water chaser."

The minuscule bartender scowled. "Scotch, you mean, lassie."

"Scotch," agreed Harry. "And leave the bottle."

A translucent nod. "Aye, bucko. That I know."

"Martini X," said Jhonny. "But reverse the ratios. Forty percent
Kahlúa to fifty percent grenadine."

"Natch."

"With a pickle. Gerkin, if you got."

"No problem, laddie."

Rikka tried not to openly shudder. The taste buds of an android were beyond human comprehension. It was well documented that they actually enjoyed the taste of high school cafeteria food, an item that had recently been officially banned from POW camps.

"I'll just have a small iced tea," rumbled Michelangelo in his stentorian bass. "No lemon, extra sugar."

Angling its head, the bartender eyed the alien suspiciously. "You over a hundred and six, boyo?"

Panic touched the black, pupilless eyes. "Ah . . . yes. Of course I am. Ask my friends."

The hologram waved that aside. "Let's see some ID."

Reaching into a tiny pocket of his bulky vest, Mike did as requested and held the card low for the computer-generated waiter to visually scan.

"Hey, this doesn't look anything like you!" snorted the small MacKenzie.

"It was before I grew the beard," explained the technician. Then he covered the bottom half of his hairy face with a huge furry paw. "See?"

The tiny head blurred as it attempted to compare the ID card and Michelangelo at the same time. After a moment, the bartender shrugged. "Okay. It's you. Sorry. House rules."

"Hoot, naw, no problem there, matey me bucko," said the alien, rolling his R's as much as inhumanly possible.

"Ha!" chortled the image. "Nice try, you big *aaraa*! Your first drink is free. Welcome to Media." And he vanished.

Harry reached across the table and tapped Mike on the forearm. The leviathan limb felt like a fur coat draped over a steel beam.

"Umm?" replied the alien, surreptitiously slipping the morsel of popcorn he had sampled under the table. Bleh!

"Mike, if you're going to become a member of a professional news team, then you have got to learn how to drink," warned the anchor, totally serious. " 'Tis a mark of distinction."

"He is drinking," said Jhonny, sprinkling powdered cheese on the popcorn. "Alcohol does nothing to his species. Caffeine gets them inebriated."

"We call it getting stiff," amended the technician, taking another pinch of the snack. Ah, much better! The alien and the android nodded at each other in culinary agreement.

Harry stole a fresh bowl from a nearby table. Bloody heathens.

Mike munched happily. "The dilatory effect of caffeine also tightens our epidermal layers and makes our fur stick straight out."

"Interesting," said Rikka, making notes on her secretary. This could come in useful if she ever had to pry information out of an uncooperative Gremlin. And some of them were going into politics. "Tell me more."

A massive shrug. "Your noses get red, we resemble a cactus. Eventually, our vascular muscles become so contracted that we're unable to move." A bestial grin. "Tricking a friend into getting stiff in a socially embarrassing position is an old bar game."

HEY, THIS GUY IS OKAY.

With a hum, the center of the table dilated and their assorted orders rose into view on a recessed pedestal.

"Okay, to work," said Harry, distributing the drinks. "First, we have to ascertain—"

With a yelp, Rikka scrunched down in her chair and tried to cover as much of her body as possible with the small wine list.

"Trouble?" asked Michelangelo, scanning the room quickly. He saw nobody new but a rather handsome human dressed in very expensive clothes.

"My ex-husband," growled Collins's voice from behind the vintage barricade. "Lord Armand d'Soyez of Mars."

"And you do not wish to speak to him?"

"Ha! Yeah. Right after I start doing ski reports in hell."

The alien gave that a moment's consideration.

"Never?" he queried.

Harry moved his chair between Rikka and the newcomer. "Correct the first time."

Moving casually, Jhonny placed his camcorder on the woman's shoulder to help hide her face. With a vibrato thrill, it happily settled into place.

"Does Lord d'Soyez work here at the station?"

Snyder made a rude noise. "Work? Hardly. But he recently purchased a huge block of Wilkes Corporation stock so that Security could no longer throw him off the station for bothering Rikka."

"Why?"

"Stupidity, I guess," Jhonny postulated, blowing out the flame of his drink and plunging their table into darkness. "He has more of that than money."

"And he has a lot of money," added Collins. Pity he couldn't buy some common sense with the family fortune.

"Oh, there you are, Rikki-tikki-tavi!" called out the man coming their way. "Darling."

Slowly, the menu lowered, exposing a classic face of extreme displeasure. "Hello, Armand," she said listlessly. "I have the Venusian Swamp Flu. Don't touch me. Go away."

Laughing, he tried to give her a kiss on the cheek and she managed to dodge out of the way.

"Oh, what nonsense," the Martian lord chided in amusement.

"Who is this human?" growled Michelangelo, standing to what seemed ten times his normal height.

Startled, Armand blinked in surprise. "Ek! It talks! Thought it was another of those dead stuffed things like the cow in the bathroom."

"It's a moose, ya putz!" called out Alonzo from across the room.

Jhonny tsk-tsk'd. "Bad move, studly," he said, pushing his chair away from the table. "Shouldn't have called him a cow."

Still growling, Mike advanced a step and blocked out the overhead light.

Dismissing the notion with a gay laugh, Armand rested a hand on Rikka's unoccupied shoulder. She stared at it as if something dead had fallen from the ceiling to land there and rot. "Ah, Rikka, sweetheart . . ."

"Remove your hand from my crumbcake!" roared Michelangelo at the top of his lungs. In a spray of electrical sparks, the sound damper shorted out and died.

Not sure if he should be amused or annoyed, the Martian lord offered the hairy mountain an aristocratic smile. "Do you mean cupcake?" he offered as a correction.

A hand the size of Jupiter rammed across the table to grab the dapper man by the lapels and bodily hauled him into the air.

"And who the hell are you to call my crumbcake a cupcake?" hissed the leviathan alien.

The smile melted and threatened to stain the lower half of his jumpsuit. "Rikka, poopsy, you . . . you're surely not dating this . . . thing! Are you?"

Michelangelo pulled the human male close so they were snout to face, the tips of his rose-scented shoes dangling limply above the table.

"Poopsy?" he breathed hot and wet upon the trembling man. "You're not an ex-lover are you? I don't like them. Any of them." A wide display of razor-sharp molars. "Maybe I should just *spartoone* you here and now to save time."

"Well, the floor is waterproof," chipped in Harry. "I say go for it."

Stifling a yawn, Rikka pulled out a file and started doing her nails. "Oh, darling, don't do another one. Security will ban you from the station."

Armand blessed her with his eyes.

"Well, maybe just one more," she relented. "I know how much you like it."

Space-black orbs narrowed to tiny slits and the alien's breathing took on an urgent quality.

"Anybody got a pencil?" asked Michelangelo in a throaty whisper. "A nice *sharp* pencil?"

Struggling against the titan's grip, Lord d'Soyez managed to wiggle free and drop to the floor.

"I see that I've caught you at a bad time," he said, backing away and tripping over a chair. Scrambling to his feet, the lord dashed pell-mell for the exit. "Perhaps later on in the week? Call my secretary!" And the double doors of the bar barely had time to separate before he was through them and gone.

Cheers and applause sounded from the attending patrons. The CD player materialized a vaudevillian band who immediately broke into a rousing rendition of "Happy Days Are Here Again!"

"What the hell is *spartooning,* anyway?" asked Jhonny, wiping fresh water tears of laughter from his face.

Aligning a fresh pair of chairs, Mike gave a massive shrug. "I have no idea. Just made it up on the spur of the moment."

WHY YOU CRAFTY BASTARD, complimented Deitrich.

Caught in mid-drink, Rikka started to have a choking fit and Harry roared with glee. "Mike, you're all right. Welcome to the team!"

"What about the mandatory probation period?" queried the alien. He was delighted, but surprised.

"Buddy, you just passed it with flying colors."

Rikka offered a hand. It was accepted. "Tones and bars, kid. You did great. Only next time . . ."

"Yes?"

She glanced at the door. "Don't waste so much time talking. Just go ahead and *spartoone* him."

AGREED.

Maintaining a dignified stance, the Gremlin technician promised that he would take the suggestion under serious advisement.

"Anyway," drawled Harry, refilling his glass from the bottle on the pedestal. "As I was saying before we were so rudely interrupted, since we are trying to expose a conspiracy, I think we should avoid our standard avenues of gathering information."

"Definitely," said Jhonny. "Since the announcement of war, everybody and their cousin is scampering for inside info. Trying every trick in the book to ferret out some juicy bit of hidden data."

Snyder turned. "Okay, kid. Unorthodox is your department. What do you got?"

Reaching into her shoulder holster, Rikka whipped out a phone. "I don't know yet," she admitted. "But let's see what a little bush beating can unearth."

Placing the flat box on the table, she booted the transmitter and flipped up the video monitor. With a low hum the screen segmented into four pieces and unfolded again nearly doubling its size.

Across the room a couple of reporters from Sports and Entertainment gasped at the casual display.

"Wow," sighed Entertainment. "An extending monitor!"

Sports agreed. "I've never seen anything like that!"

"And you still haven't," growled MacKenzie from behind the bar. And he dropped a glass from his hand. It loudly shattered on the steel floor. "Get me?"

After a moment the two men faced each other.

"Hey, what about those Yankees?"

"I understand they'll be making a new movie."

Back at the table, her face illuminated by the soft glow of the hinged screen, Rikka finished keying in the long coded telephone number. There came a series of clicks and hums as the signal was sent through a dozen relay points to reach its destination some quarter million kilometers away.

"Hello, UP Records and Archive Department," happily sang out a voice. "How may I help you?"

"Fernando, it's Rikka," stated the woman. "How is everything on the ol' L5?"

There was a one-second pause. "Ah . . ."

She dimpled and lifted a thick sheaf of fifty-credit notes into view. "By the way, I need a small favor."

A one-second pause. "What was that?" blinked the man, sweat dampening his brow. "Rikka? I'm sorry, but I do not know who you are. Are you sure you dialed correctly? I'm not allowed to accept personal calls. Time for my lunch. Crackle, crackle. There seems to be trouble on the line. Oh, dear, the computer crashed. Good-bye."

The picture went black.

Smiles blossomed.

"Okay, there's a conspiracy," beamed Collins in pleasure. "So let's see how big it is."

She dialed again and this time took even longer to get through to the other end, even though the goal was only to Gagarin Naval Base on the moon below them, a scant few hundred klicks distant. But finally, the monitor cleared to a sharp picture of a mustached man in the painfully well-pressed uniform of a major in the United Planets Navy.

"Hello, Major Harrison, here," announced a crisp voice.

Rikka dimpled again, but this time the woman put everything she had into it. "Bob," she breathed lustfully, trying her best to put the stress test on the front of her jumpsuit. "It's Rikka."

There was no response.

"Bob? Hello? Can you hear me?"

There was an audible swallow. "There is nothing I can say to you, Ms. Collins."

Okay. So much for diplomacy. "Hey, Bob, cut the crap. You owe me big and it's time to pay."

"No."

"Listen, Major . . ."

"No!"

A sly tone creeped into Collins's voice. "Then perhaps you

would not mind if I called your wife? I have some information she might be interested in. And some swell video disks."

Recoiling, the soldier paled. Then set his jaw and began typing off screen. There was a hum, a click, and the monitor split in half. Standing beside the major was a woman in curlers and a bathrobe.

"Bob? Sweetheart, what is it?"

He swallowed with some difficulty. "Susan, I have been unfaithful to you. One year ago I cheated with a news reporter named Collins."

Thunderstruck, Rikka's jaw unhinged and hit the table with a dull thud.

Unabashed, the major continued. "You and I had just had a bad fight and I was very drunk, but that is no excuse. I humbly ask your forgiveness and will not return home until you deem to forgive me."

The woman slumped a bit. "Come home at the usual time tonight, dearest. I thank you for telling me. But a minor indiscretion twelve months ago doesn't really matter now that—"

Harrison hit a button and the woman blinked out.

"Good-bye, Ms. Collins. Never call me again."

The phone went black.

wow, scrolled Deitrich.

"This is big," gushed Rikka, reclining in her chair.

"Really, really big," agreed Jhonny with a whistle. At the sound, the camcorder on Rikka disengaged its hold and crawled down her arm to climb up the chest of the android and return to its usual post.

Harry didn't want to, but he simply had to know. "Excuse me, kid. I know you'd do almost anything for a story, but you didn't actually—"

"No. Of course not," she snapped irritably. "I only let the drunk yutz think we did, so that he would be forced into being friendly with me and I could occasionally exert gentle pressure on him to squeeze out information."

"And he just threatened his marriage to call your bluff," mused Jhonny. "This is weird. Very, very weird."

yowsa, added the MainBrain.

Studiously watching and listening, Michelangelo kept his peace. He was not a reporter. When they had a technical problem, then he'd speak.

"Why should an Intelligence clerk be willing to ruin his happy marriage for an interplanetary conspiracy? What the hell is the UP covering up?" asked Jhonny, stroking his mecho-pet. The camera lenses rotated in pleasure at the caress.

Rikka set her jaw. "Let's find out."

Another call. The usual noises of transmission. But as the monitor cleared of hash, the screen was overfilled with an endless processing scroll of TV sitcom ratings from the 1960s.

"Office," said a garbled voice.

"Mr. Nobody? Newshawk, here."

A chuckle came from the phone. "Lady, I am impressed. How ever did you find out about it so quick?"

Exchanging meaningful looks with the rest of her team, Rikka wet her lips. "I have my sources," she truthfully lied. "But tell me everything in case some of the data got garbled."

"The usual rate?" asked the disguised voice.

"Done."

The Beverly Hillbillies . . . Mod Squad . . . a chortle. "Get ready for a download. I was expecting you to call sooner or later."

"Ah, Mr. Nobody, you never disappoint me."

"That's cause you always pay on time."

The telephone gave a hum and click as the protocol was established between the two communication units, then a monotone beep sounded as the information was flashed to Rikka in a single byte.

"Got it?" asked the voice over a bad year for *Laugh-In.*

"Got it," she answered. "Anything else for me?"

Get Smart was climbing to the top of the chart fast. "Well, as of today I can offer you the bargain price of a two-hour delay on the data being sold to anybody else for a measly thousand. Or a total one day exclusive for five thousand. Interested?"

Five thousand. What had she just purchased? The true name of God? "Let me look at what I've got first. Call you in five."

Mannix . . . Land of the Giants . . . "I'll be waiting!" And the screen went mercifully blank in the middle of *Here Come the Brides.*

Trained fingers danced across the controls as Collins linked her secretary to the phone. The compressed information was expanded and then converted to the prominent language in her SpellCheck program. The others watched impatiently as words appeared on the screen. The report was only a paragraph long, but Rikka read the message twice, and then once again before being able to believe what she saw.

"Ohmigod," she gasped, staring at the telephone monitor. "They've launched the Ark!"

Harry spit out his mouthful of Scotch.

The camcorder fell off Jhonny's shoulder.

"The Ark?" asked Michelangelo curiously.

Slowly regaining her composure, Rikka explained. The Ark was a deep-space sleeper ship designed to take a group of one thousand colonists to another star system. But not by using a StarDrive. No ship could be built big enough to hold sufficient control elements for an interstellar journey. The Ark was a sublight ship. The crew would journey in Cold Sleep, a state of suspended animation. That way they would not age on the millennium-long voyage, and thus save valuable air, fuel, video cassettes, condoms, all the basic necessities of life.

The big alien nodded sagely. "This is very similar to how our own probe came to your world."

Unashamed, Harry admitted that the UP had blatantly stolen the notion. If it worked for the Gremlins, it should for humanity. Only . . .

"They have launched the ship two years early," stated Jhonny, reading over her shoulder. "And the target star has been switched, from Alpha Centauri only a few light-years away—"

"To R47D in the Orion Coal Sack," continued Rikka. "Which is just about as far away from Earth as a star can be and still be considered part of this galaxy."

There was a moment of silence as this unsavory news was digested along with the liquor and popcorn.

"It's an escape pod," stated Michelangelo.

Harry raised his head from his glass. "Eh? By gawd, you're right! The UP doesn't think that anybody will survive this war."

"Why?" demanded Collins, her instincts surging at the concept of a new mystery. "The Earth Defense Force, the Royal Martian Navy, the Independent Asteroids, and even the Free Police don't have any kind of a doomsday weapon that would wipe out pracking everybody!"

"That we know of," said Jhonny, retrieving his camcorder. It was dented, but still chipper.

"Okay, we can forget about normal channels," stated Harry, refilling his glass. Then he paused and pushed the booze away. "We need a back door. A line of investigation that nobody else has thought of."

Lost in contemplation, Rikka placed both elbows on the tabletop. A back door. Hmm. As her eyes glazed over, Michelangelo started to reach out a furry hand to roust the reporter, but Harry stayed him and Jhonny shook his head vehemently no. They both knew better than to bother the chief when she was cooking.

Minutes passed in silence.

Then Rikka's eyes opened with a snap. "Back door," she stated. "Literally. We'll do it backward. To hell with what is going on now. Let's find out what the UP Security Council was doing immediately prior to the official outbreak of war."

" 'Nothing like this happens without some prior warning,' " repeated Jhonny in a good mimic of her voice. "Gotcha, chief. If they were studying Mercury, then Merc is the real source of the war. If drug running, ditto."

THIS WILL BE MOST DIFFICULT TO DO WITHOUT A Z-CLASS TRANSMISSION, scrolled Deitrich across everyone's personal screens. AND YET IF WE USE ANYTHING LESS SECURE, THEN THE INTERPLANETARY NEWS SERVICE MIGHT INTERCEPT OUR TRANSMISSION AND SCOOP US.

"Again!" stormed Harry, slamming a fist on the table.

Rikka shuddered. An event that would probably put them all on the Saturday morning garden show. A fate worse than death. At least there was some dignity in death.

Acting casual, Michelangelo reached into his vest and withdrew a flat unmarked box. Adjusting a dial set on top of the burnished metal surface, he swung the concave end around them as if it were a light meter and he was a photographer searching for the perfect illumination level.

"The bar is clear of insects," he stated, tucking the scanner away.

"Bugs," corrected Jhonny. "And yeah, we know. Anybody tries to do EM surveillance in The Horny Toad gets fed to Bruno."

The alien felt his stomachs lurch. Perhaps it was another bizarre human joke. He certainly hoped so.

"What should be our first step?" asked the technician, glad to change the subject.

"Getting access to the UP information network," murmured Rikka, chewing the inside of her cheek. "But if we land at the news dock, we'll be under constant surveillance."

"Don't trust us, eh?" said Harry.

Collins batted her eyelids. "And gosh o' willickers, I don't know why."

"We could go to the bathroom and flush ourselves down a toilet," offered Jhonny, leaning forward on the table. "Mike might be a problem, but at least I could do it. Scuba along until I reach a major coupling and tap into their terminals."

"I always knew that reporting was dirty work," said Harry with a straight face.

Mike shook his wooly head. "That would not work, my friend. I spent many months on Geneva in educational assimilation and know much about the inner workings of the L5. There are grinders, shredders, and sickening narts spaced every meter along the sewage lines against just this sort of invasion."

"Sickening narts?"

The big alien adjusted his glasses. "Umm . . . ill narts? Diseased? Woozy? Nauseous narts?"

"Queasy?" supplied Rikka hesitantly.

A big smile. "Yes! That is the model type."

Glancing across the counter, MacKenzie saw the pained expressions on the reporters' faces and went to the storage room to obtain an industrial strength bottle of aspirin.

"But there has to be a way to tap their network!" admonished Jhonny. "We aren't after top secret files, but their buffer zones, default bins, and garbage dumps. Don't need to know what's in a file. Only where it came from!"

"Agreed," snapped Collins.

Snyder raised his hands to heaven for assistance. When none was forthcoming, he undertook to bestow the revelation by himself. "Listen, folks, the best minds of three planets have worked for decades to safeguard the UP computer files against just this sort of an invasion. It's impossible."

"Unless we tap into the external lines," muttered Rikka.

"Possible," admitted Mike hesitantly.

"How?" asked Harry bluntly.

"Or," said Rikka.

Patiently, everybody waited for the woman to finish.

"No, that's it. That's the whole idea. Or," she repeated.

Understanding brightened Michelangelo's furry countenance. "You mean or, as in o, r, e?"

"Yes!"

"The new L5 Russia is building!" exclaimed Jhonny, standing in his excitement. "Yes! It can be done!"

With a karate chop, Harry hit the android at the back of a knee making the camera-op drop into his chair.

"That's pracking brilliant," whispered the droid softly. Yes, it might just work. There was a lunar-based gravity slingshot that hurtled tons of moon dust past Geneva in a hyperbolic curve to reach the construction site of the new L5 colony.

"We hide our shuttle inside a load of aluminum dust," the android said, still whispering. "And at the right moment, just rocket out of the dust ball and land on a blind spot of the colony."

I HAVE A SMALL PROBLEM WITH THAT, stated Deitrich in urgent red type. UNDER NORMAL CIRCUMSTANCES THE LUNAR DUST SHOOTS BY UNDER 400 GRAVITIES OF THRUST. WHICH WOULD CRUSH EVEN ME INTO PRIMORDIAL OOZE.

Rikka dismissed that with a wave of her hand. "Precision isn't important in a slingshot operation. I'm sure we can bribe the operator to give us a slower gravitational boost. Deitrich, what's the highest thrust factor our compensators can take, and we survive."

Mathematical figures scrolled wildly in four directions across the screen on her wrist.

TWO HUNDRED AND FIFTY.

Harry chewed a cheek. "That's pretty damn slow."

YES, IT IS.

"And there's another minor problem," stated Jhonny. "Once on the station, the only way to gain access to the infonet is through the solar array. We would have to wiggle past the six-story-tall mirrors, squeeze under the twelve-ton prisms, and dodge the focus of the main collector. But then, shazam! We're in!"

"A blast furnace," scowled Rikka. "Those solar arrays have an operating temperature of two thousand Celsius."

"Military powerarmor can take that," offer Michelangelo, consulting his IBM portable. "For a little while, at least."

"Yeah, great. And where the prack are we going to get some Mark IV Samson powerarmor?"

"On the one place on the moon where soldiers of both sexes take off everything they wear," stated Rikka with a smirk.

"The Pleasure Palace?"

"A forthcoming battle builds a lot of tension. Sexual tension," Jhonny agreed. "It's a well-known medical fact that admirals can't think straight without their privates happy."

A smile was shared at the age-old joke.

"Are not there any . . . ah, establishments such as this in Geneva?"

The humans and android stared at him agog. "With all of those damn nosey reporters everywhere? Not bloody likely, friend."

With a sigh, the big alien accepted the inevitable and started composing his death poem. There once was an alien from Nantucket . . .

A finger snap from Rikka shattered his artistic muse.

"So, in essence," said the woman slowly, "the plan is for us to burglarize the Pleasure Palace in order to steal a few million dollars' worth of military powerarmor, an act punishable by death, then bribe a slingshot operator to lance us near the L5 at a slow enough speed for us to survive the journey and make an undetected jump to the colony and boldly walk straight into the main solar array and hardwire a link to the master computer through the power system before we vaporize."

And for a single moment, the true dire implications of what they planned to do permeated the hearts and souls of the stalwart news reporters.

"Nyah!" chorused the team in unison. Prack it. No story was worth that much trouble.

Taking her whiskey and water, Rikka spread her arms wide. "Okay, any other bright ideas?"

"Just one," said Harry, cocking his head. "If we can't call Geneva without INS tapping our transmission." A sly smile. "Then let's give them a transmission to remember!"

"Or two," added Jhonny meaningfully.

CHAPTER FIVE

THE TURBO-LIFT OUTSIDE the Toad took the reporters to the topmost level of Media with amazing speed, with only a slight delay being caused by a mild altercation with another turbo-lift filled with Armand and all of his luggage heading for the main space dock at emergency exit speed.

Nobody waved good-bye.

As they reached Level 37, Snyder rummaged about in his pockets to find a mint flavor stick and quickly sucked it into life. Hiding smiles, Rikka and Jhonny pretended not to notice.

Not quite cognizant of human customs, Michelangelo offered the anchor a light from his tool vest, but it was politely refused.

In well-oiled silence, the doors parted.

That is to say, it was a general belief on Media that the doors to 37 opened that way. Nobody had ever heard them over the incredible thunderous noise.

Machinery. That was the overpowering impression of what filled the room. No people. No walls. Just machinery.

And noise. A chorus of laser scanners hummed along as they faxed news reports into physical existence. Scanners clicked as the documents were recorded and grinders annihilated the paper and flushed it off to Recycling. A thousand relays for ten thousand telephones click-clacked as circuits opened and closed. Bells rang incessantly signifying nothing. It was the technological heart of Media.

As the team proceeded past the battered couch and water cooler in the waiting area, a complex robotic printing press *ker-chunked* out paperback operating manuals, while another did phony IDs and a third embossed office stationery and business cards.

Powering the X- and Y-band transmitters, giant vacuum tubes hummed and glowed like glass toaster ovens. A multisectioned wall of white Master bubble memory cards constantly flipped and changed position as reporters at their desks accessed files and deleted others. Immense Sterling motors revved complex gears to slowly rotated support shafts that keep the fifty-meter communications dish on the outside of the station in perfect alignment with the assigned target. Superconductor cables in a rainbow of colors hung like vines from busbars overhead and snaked away on the floor to feed the all-important Z-band broadcast units.

Jhonny started to twitch as they neared, so Mike switched places with the android. Something would have happened to a human with a pacemaker back in 1880. Or was that the 1980s?

"Sasha!" called Rikka through cupped hands.

A sheet of perforated metal lowered from a catwalk far ahead of them and an orange figure waved hello.

"Hey, guys," said a speaker hanging from the mesh cage around a circulation fan next to them. The voice was female. "Wait a sec. I'll be right with you."

The battered neutrino shield lowered into place, and a moment later a woman in an orange jumpsuit stepped out of the shadows between a roaring decollater and a strident gum machine.

"Wow," shouted Jhonny, impressed. "Howdidyadodat?"

"Ladder," yelled the woman matter-of-factly.

Rikka offered a hand. They shook while Harry got a strong hold on his tongue and valiantly stuffed it back into his mouth, trying not to drool in the process.

In a skintight jumpsuit necessary for unencumbered travel between so many sharp bits of machinery, Sasha Parson displayed a trim figure. The flame-retardant fabric was a brilliant neon-orange, making her only slightly difficult to find in the mobile mechanized jungle rather than totally impossible. Her flexible boots were military combat footwear for needed protection from electrical shocks and mild explosions. A silver button on Sasha's collarbone indicated a surgically implanted command mike, similar to Rikka's, a similar metallic dot on her left ear denoted a BonePhone, and Parson was wearing a N.Y. Yankee baseball cap of no known technical application.

Small, petite, deliciously shaped, with a sweet angelic face and a right hook that once put a drunk Space Marine down for the count, the ComTech was Harry's idea of the perfect woman. Her ebony hair and blue diamond eyes often filled his dreams at night, and occasionally made him stop drinking for days at a stretch.

Although amiably inclined, Jhonny thought she was too short to be pretty. Mike liked her hat. Rikka called her friend.

"Sasha," smiled Harry, feeling slightly giddy.

"Hi, Harry," the ComTech bellowed, her tone strangely friendly.

"Greetings," said Michelangelo, his voice oddly clear in the thundering environment.

In ritual greeting, Parson touched a finger to each temple and displayed empty hands to the towering male. *"Gritt-kal firtz, Mike-ting!"*

"Qarl čo hugft, Sasha-ting?"

"Company newsletter," she explained.

The alien chuckled. Of course, how obvious.

Lifting a leg, Parson parked her fanny on the edge of a vibrating trough filled with endlessly processing shredder gears. Snyder fought the urge to pull the woman to safety. Here, he has a neophyte and she the old pro.

"Okay, folks," her amplified voice asked over a nearby speaker. "What's the down and dirty?"

Rikka enjoyed the directness after the psycho warfare of the conference with Maria. "We need to send a double message."

"A very special message," cried Jhonny for enlightenment.

Harry shouted, "Secret and illegal."

A casual shrug. "Why else would you be here? A social call?"

Snyder started to speak, then retreated a step. No, don't be a fool, old man. You're twice her age. Why embarrass yourself in front of friends and coworkers?

Exasperated, Rikka and Sasha exchanged glances. Men! Couldn't take a hint if they were hit in the groin with a fifty-gigawatt laser. Well, maybe then.

Rising, the ComTech waved them on. "Let's get going. Work Station 8 is free at the moment. I'll let you have a new Runamuck I cooked up last week."

"Is it good?" asked Michelangelo, stooping under a red-hot pipe. "The success of this broadcast is paramount."

Snyder started to rally to her defense, but Parson was tolerant of the newbie. "Son, it's so flaming insane, even the program doesn't know where it's going."

Grandly, Rikka gestured. "Sounds like exactly what we need," she shouted. "Lay on, Parson!"

Leading them over, under, around, and through the metallic jungle of communications equipment, Sasha brought the news team to a small alcove whose controls extended from the main console to the walls and ceiling.

With a mental command sent through her cybernetic link, Sasha snapped on the sonic dampers and blessed silence exploded around them. Everybody sighed in appreciation. This place was worse than an indoor concert by the pyrotechnic rock group Bombs an' Roses.

Purring with delight, Michelangelo took the human-sized seat and began throwing switches with gay abandonment. Meters flickered into life. Power gauges glowed into racing numbers and a series of submonitors showed a booting fandango of programs.

Sasha watched him for a minute. "You know your stuff," she complimented. "Train under WizOp Wilma on Geneva?"

The nonvocal reply was in the affirmative.

"It shows." Parson turned. "Rikka, do you need a Z-class transmission? With the war going on, that's restricted. I'll need to Macross in an extra Fool Ya 5.1 to hide the source."

"No, thanks," said Collins, cycling an extra chair up from the floor. "X will be fine."

"Heck, we want the INS to know it's us!" explained Snyder, depositing the stub of his flavor stick into a waste receptacle.

Unobtrusively, Parson slid a hand inside her boot and retrieved a tiny rainbow disk. "Wanna give them a virus from hell?" she demurely offered. "Made it myself. Guaranteed to do twelve things illegal in the state of Omaha to their main DPU."

"Let's save it for Christmas," suggested Jhonny.

With a nod, the ComTech stuffed the disk back into her footwear.

Michelangelo looked up from the console, his furry face scrunched into a vague approximation of a human scowl.

"Oh, dear," he said in a worried voice. "Is this . . . immoral?"

"Nyah," gestured Parson. "Just illegal."

Unconcerned, the alien went back to work. Part of the job.

Walking over to a wall-mounted sheet of clean white plastic, Harry palmed the control and accessed a diagram of the solar system. "Okay, how are we going to bank it?"

Taking a wax marker, Sasha did a zigzag pattern. Jhonny added a curlicue, Harry a backswitch, and Rikka an inverse sine wave. Expectantly, they looked at the ComTech and she nodded in approval. Then added a diedo as a fillip.

Both paws wildly programming, Mike glanced at the travel route and bared a grin. From what little he knew about human society, this little message should cause more excitement than an honest election!

Mars. The purple planet.

Its historic reddish hue was long gone with the terraforming of the planet's atmosphere to include oxygen. But still orbiting high above the violet world were the two tiny moons, Phobos and Deimos. Both moons were now private property owned by unscrupulous individuals due to an erroneous legal loophole in the colonial treaty of two centuries ago; a contractual flaw that had eventually been repaired in the royal courts of Martian law and at the hot end of a democratic gun barrel.

Nestled deep inside a millennium-old impact crater, at the very North Pole of Phobos, was a single titanic dome emblazoned with the kilometer-high, holographic letters: INTERPLANETARY NEWS SERVICE; and underneath in slightly less noticeable letters: SUBSCRIPTION RATES AVAILABLE UPON REQUEST.

Inside the dome was a faceted hive of divisions and sections, endlessly complex. Indeed, it was rumored that the original architect was still here, lost and wandering about in the lower levels. Still others whispered that he was not lost, but safely entombed in the concrete foundation.

Waste not, want not, the boss always said.

In the center core of the dome was the circular tower of offices for QINS executives, their staff, protégés, and bootlickers. And at the pinnacle of the core was a spacious penthouse with deep pile rugs, extra-large real wood desks, a Jacuzzi built for twelve, and a control console designed to do anything the operator wished, short of assigning themselves a pay raise.

Thunk! And another feathered sliver impacted on a large photograph of Rikka, Harry, Jhonny, and the retired Apache technician, Kneeling Strongarm, that was pinned to a dart board.

Removing the projectile, a large calloused hand savagely ripped off the photo and tossed it near a trash receptacle. A tall and muscular human male, the owner of the hand was dressed in a black leather jumpsuit and jeweled earrings. Stepping to his desk, the svelte Hercules opened a drawer and turned to replace the old photo with a fresh new one of the SNT that now included the massive alien Michelangelo.

Then retreating a few meters, he turned and threw a dart directly into Mike's furred face. *Thunk!*

"Good shot," approved the ample blonde at the desk across the room. All apples and curves, and wearing a summer print taffeta jumpsuit, the woman seemed as fresh and wholesome as Sunday morning milk.

A grudging smile exposed perfectly pearly teeth. "Thanks."

Then her pocket telephone rang.

In the background, at the ready board, their technician played a computer game of Strip Solitaire and a nameless camera-op slept with feet up on his equipment case. Paid by the hour, the workers had no interest in the sage machinations of the reporters. Only what was broken, should they fix it, and when was lunch. Forty-five minutes and counting.

"Interplanetary News Service," answered the phone in a terribly cheerful voice.

"News, *News, NEWS*!" sang a genderless chorus.

"Whom do you wish to speak to?" finished the phone.

There was a guttural reply.

Fast, the woman snatched up the receiver in mid-chorus.

"Sunshine and Hardcopy, ace reporters!" she announced with the dull rhythm of familiarity. "Susie Sunshine here."

Patiently, Susie listened for a moment and then slammed the telephone shut, cracking the plastic case.

"Prack!" she screamed furiously and then broke the phone in half. "Prack, hell, shit, fuck, and whistle!

"And double prack!" she added as a vitriolic afterthought.

"What now?" asked Jason Hardcopy, pausing in his game.

"That's the second Mafia assassin who flatly refused to kill the Satellite News Team!" stormed Susie, brushing the sparking circuitry off her lap. "I even claimed it was my birthday. But, no . . ." A muscle in her forehead flicked tautly. "By God, you just couldn't hire good help anymore!"

"What was the reason this time?" queried Jason, throwing again. *Thunk! Thunk! Thunk!* Expertly, the darts neatly feathered Rikka in the stomach, heart, and eyes. Ha! What a fun game this was.

Ice-blue eyes met those of space-black. "Same as before. He likes them! Once even canceled a hit so he wouldn't miss one of their special reports!"

"Well, we beat them with the Martian VP story," boasted Hardcopy, retrieving his darts.

A rueful smile. "That's true, and we did it legitimately. No bribes, no stolen photographs."

Lost in rumination, Sunshine went back to dialing assassins and Hardcopy returned to his primitive voodoo ceremony.

Thunk! A Gremlin. Now how the prack had they pulled off that miracle? They had an alien technician, the award-winning Jhon Smith as their camera-op, and a MainBrain as the pilot for their shuttle. He was almost tempted to do a story on them. Boy, if they ever crossed the line and got caught doing something illegal, like . . . oh, hiring an android, the normally thrifty bosses here at INS would happily spend millions to manufacture evidence to put the SNT away in the dread Neptunian prison, SnowBall Hell, till the sun went cold. Longer, if possible. The dire establishment had justifiably earned its infamous title because it accurately described a prisoner's chance of escaping.

Someday. Ah, someday. *Thunk!*

On Level 37 of Media, at Work Station 8, banks of lights turned green and power meters pegged the red line.

"Ready?" asked Rikka nervously, cracking her knuckles.

A hairy nod.

Jhonny crossed his fingers.

Harry gave a thumbs-up.

"Then do it, big guy," smiled Parson.

And the button was pushed.

From the primary dish atop Media Station a boiling beam of total gibberish hurtled down toward the innocently slumbering Starlet City. The garbled transmission hit the main city receiver and was broken into five separate calls. One went to Madam Adam him/herself at the Pleasure Palace. Another to Sergeant Buckley at Mare Imbrium Station of the Lunar Police. The third to directory assistance. The fourth went to a holding modem in a vacant apartment in a downtown housing complex wholly owned by a secret subsidiary of the Wilkes Corporation. There it was cleared of all unnecessary hash, fine-tuned, strengthened, and released in the next microsecond. Upon hitting the city central circuits, the fifth call fragmented into a dozen smaller impulses, each ordering an uncooked spleen pizza to be delivered PDQ to the nearest QCNN news reporter.

COD, of course.

Whether each call was answered, or disconnected, the core signal pulses stayed whole in the electron flow and followed the complex programming. Tapping into the first available relay unit, the messages scattered and forced themselves across the globe to reconverge at Tycho City on the other side of the moon.

Now with Earth filling the sky, again the transmissions stormed the closest X-, Y-, or Z-band transmitter and hurled themselves off into space.

One hundred fourteen priority signals bombarded Geneva switchboard with everything from heavy breathing to a religious message on the virtues of foot polishing.

Unnoticed amid the noise and thunder, a small weak signal trickled out of the magnetic melee, casually strolled over to the garbage dump, and politely asked for a report on the last week's activities.

In the office of the head computer hacker for the United Planets colony, the desk monitor of WizOp Wilma Meijer stopped its scrolling of a demographic chart and suddenly flashed the words "Hi, teach!" for the briefest possible second, and then returned to its previous program. Amused and flattered, the woman chuckled and went back to work.

Under the gibbering and howling invasion, the automatic defenses of the UP colony repulsed the magnetic nonsense and forcibly shoved it out into space—where a strategically situated Wilkes Corporation weather satellite caught them and rebroadcast the EM assault toward Earth, Luna, Mars, Mercury, and the sun—where no radio transceiver was known to be owned or operated by the local fiery inhabitants. If any.

At each point, sans the sun, the process was repeated, with infinite variations, until the beams all converged on their final, ultimate point of the ThunderBay Danger Club, 13-13 Ambush Avenue, Annihilation City, South Venus.

In the INS team office, a flashing light on the communications console suddenly disrupted the obscene card game of the dawdling technician. Eh . . . what?

"Mr. Hardcopy! Ms. Sunshine!" called a young man, adjusting dials and levers among the vast array of lights, meters, and dials showing the status of the X, Y, Z communications bands. "QSNT is sending a message!"

"So what," growled Hardcopy. Tired of darts, he had opened a refrigerated cardboard box on his desk and was snacking on a sugar-filled ToothCrumbler. It was palatable, but what the man wouldn't give for a real doughnut.

"It's Priority One, encoded and scrambled!"

Sunshine dropped the phone and pastry sprayed the air. A secret broadcast? "Why the hell didn't you say so, idiot!" berated Susie, hurrying across the office.

On the balls of his feet, Hardcopy pivoted about, already next to the technician. "Get ready to intercept!"

"But I need authorization to do that," started the man.

"Do it or you're dead meat!" bellowed the blonde, hot blood in her eyes.

Seeing that none of this concerned him, the camera-op went back to sleep.

Bracketed by the two grim-faced reporters, the technician swallowed a beating organ that had risen unexpectedly into his throat.

"That's good enough for me," he agreed with a sickening grin. "Activating the sensor feedback loop . . . locking in the main CDPU . . . and cutting in primary circuits . . . now!"

Twirling a dial, Michelangelo tried to elevate a secondary fluctuation in the carrier wave of the transmission. Tried and failed. "There's a disturbance in the flow!"

"The INS is trying for an intercept?" asked Rikka eagerly.

"Yes!"

Jhonny leaped into the air in celebration, but Sasha Parson crowded in closer to the console.

"At what link?" demanded Harry, empty hands reaching for the controls in a reflex action. Damn, he felt so helpless! "Where did they connect?"

"I don't know yet," growled Mike, his big hands moving with amazing grace and fluidity across the console. "Gimme a minute."

"We don't have a minute!"

"Got it!" cried the INS tech in triumph. Whew.

"What? Who? Where?" demanded Sunshine, avarice distorting her voice into a high-pitched slur.

"Can't tell details yet. The damn thing is in some kind of bizarre binary code. Maybe a book cipher. Very complex. But it was sent to the ThunderBay Danger Club on Venus."

Unable to halt the flow of words, the technician added, "It's a brilliantly crafted Runamuck. A real work of art!"

"Parson," growled Jason Hardcopy, shaking a fist at his distant enemy. The hated ComTech used to work for INS before she got offered inane things like paid overtime and sick leave.

Sunshine crossed her arms. "So, they called in Parson, eh?" she contemplated aloud, drumming sharp nails on her biceps. "Now why would they bother? Unless this is incredibly important."

"Gotta be about the war, then."

"Some kind of insider information?"

"Perhaps a stolen file. They specialize in that."

"Or a set of the battle plans!"

"Maybe even a traitor!"

Face-to-face, noses almost touching, the teammates shared a brief moment of satisfaction as their glands pumped raw adrenaline fuel into cold hearts and minds.

"Let's go," declared Hardcopy, and the two reporters dashed for the door, dragging their camera-op along behind them.

"Move it, putz!" roughly urged the bouncy blonde.

"Thanks for waking me," yawned the man, stumbling after his bosses with a bulky equipment bag in hand. "Was having a terrible dream 'bout the ThunderBay Club."

"That's where we're going!"

He dropped the bag and halted. "I quit. Those prackheads greet the doorbell with a grenade toss! Sometimes it's live, and sometimes it ain't. No way. I can find work elsewhere."

With a nimble leg sweep, Sunshine tripped the man using a judo throw and Hardcopy slung him over a beefy shoulder.

Sunshine grabbed the equipment bag and threw it at the dangling tech. "You're under contract, Mack! End of discussion. We're going to Venus!"

"No . . . !"

"It worked!" cried Parson, correcting the balance on a submonitor. "They intercepted between Earth and Mars!"

"Then they aren't aware of our subtransmission?"

"Impossible!"

And the group cheered until the sonic dampeners threatened to blow a circuit from overload.

"But what about our request?" asked Collins anxiously, releasing Jhonny from the impromtu hug.

"It's coming in now," stated Michelangelo, watching the paper roll off the teleprinter. Nobody had hugged him, which was just as well. To his race, it was a challenge for lethal combat. Or sex. Which were pretty much the same thing when you got down to details.

Eagerly, the people crowded close as the alien ripped the sheet free from the machine.

"*Zarl-nif!* It is in code," he stated in disgust.

"Of course," said Harry, radiating confidence. "But one we can break. Jhonny!"

"Here," said the android, lugging an armful of books over to the workbench. "Alphabetical, numerical, sequential, and religious."

It only took them a few minutes to match the prefix, crossmatch the suffix, and fill in the middle. It was sort of like doing a crossword puzzle—without the questions. No big deal.

"Koop!" cried Rikka, slamming the massive tome shut.

"God bless," said Michelangelo, offering her a hankie.

A smile. "No. I mean Koop Hospital."

The alien tech had to dig into memory for that. Ah, yes. Koop Memorial Space Hospital. It had been designed by the great Mozart Da Vinci and paid for by the legendary Onassis Rockefeller under the direction by the worlds-renowned Sir Alexander d'Caesar.

Pierpont Koop was merely a clerk who had accidentally tripped and fallen down a flight of stairs to die delivering coffee to their first meeting.

Overcome with guilt, it seemed the least they could do.

Mostly the hospital handled degenerative cases and the odd wrecked spaceship, with an occasional foray into zero-G recession and the space heebie-jeebies; i.e. incurable cases of contra-agoraphobia, the fear of enclosed spaces inside the ultimate out-doors. Part claustrophobia and part acrophobia, it was an unknown illness in the annuals of humanity until the advent of space explora-tion. Now it ranked up there on the disability chart along with such classics as the Asteroid's Revenge and the Jupiter Drip.

Nowadays, the facilities had been expanded by the UP. And that meant some of the money went for learning how to extend the ser-vice period of suspended animation and designing advanced tech-niques for the robo-docs. Medicine was the one profession where the experts did their best to put themselves out of business.

"Koop," Snyder prompted the android. "You sure about that?"

"Definite," agreed Jhonny, perusing the material. "And if we have this correct, every damn superpower in the solar system, and most of the minor nations and Independent Asteroids, were all given a top secret report from Koop Memorial Hospital."

"Including Titan?" asked Parson, aghast.

A nod. "Damn straight including Titan."

"What kind of report?" asked Mike, standing and stretching his back to the sound of snapping castanets. Ah . . .

Rikka fought the urge to dance to the musical interlude. "The specifics aren't clear. But Koop only does medical research."

"That we know of," averred Snyder.

"Paranoid," joked Jhonny.

With a terrified expression, Harry spun around fast. "Who said that?" he demanded, drawing an imaginary gun.

Michelangelo took the anchor by the head and gently rotated him back to the conversation. Humans. Sheesh.

"A medical report," mused Collins. "Or study, or investigation, that is so important and/or shocking that it forces the worlds to stage a fake war to hide . . ." Her voice trailed off.

"A plague?"

Sasha thought for a while. "Uh-uh," she decided. "Merely quarantine the location until the disease ran its natural course. And if necessary, burn the place clean with a bombardment of neutrinos. Zap! Not a microbe or DNA strand would survive. End of plague."

"And the people."

"Could the sun be going nova?" asked Parson, sucking on her lower lip.

"That would explain the sudden departure of the Ark," noted Jhonny, tickling his camcorder under the lens. It revved in delight. "But not the phony war angle. And besides, there are a thousand scientists studying the sun. If there was any irregularity, it would be public knowledge long before anybody could stomp a lid on the fact."

"Plus, why would they hide the data in a medical report?" insisted Collins, pacing about the work area. One step too far and she broached the dampener field, the noise of Level 37 hit her like a sledgehammer and she quickly retreated.

"No. It's a medical issue we're dealing with," she continued, wiggling a finger in her ear. "Nothing else makes sense. Something that wasn't important before, but now suddenly is."

"This doesn't make any sense!" stormed Snyder furiously. "How can any possible medical issue threaten the whole solar system?"

"Maybe the plague is on Earth and the war is a cover-up for purging the homeworld," offered Michelangelo.

All conversations stopped.

"Prack and hell," swore Rikka. "Maybe some archaeologist found a live vial of a war germ in the ruins of an old pre-space military laboratory."

Dutifully, the pet camcorder recorded everything said and done.

Then Collins shook her head. "But again we hit the problem of the Ark. Why send it off? Where's the connection?"

Harry lowered the paper. "Christ, what have we uncovered? This isn't between Earth and Titan. Every government in the solar system is involved. Including archenemies."

"Can we raid the Koop files the way we just did the UP trash bin?" Rikka asked Sasha.

Removing her baseball cap, the ComTech shook her head. "No way. A blue code, see?" She indicated a thin border on the report.

"Ah, yes. Not kept on computer, only on physical hard copy. Must have been transferred to bubble card at Geneva."

"Very top secret," agreed Harry, thoughtfully fondling the blue line. "We're going to have to go there in person to burglar . . . ah, pursue their files."

WHICH IS GUARDED BY A MAINBRAIN LIKE MYSELF, scrolled Deitrich.

Nobody was surprised by the sudden intrusion of the shuttle pilot. He often went silent for long periods of time. Nobody knew why.

"Okay," said Jhonny cordially. "So we'll need a two-sided approach then. Maybe even three."

"With a diversion and a secondary," added Rikka. "Just in case."

Michelangelo covered his face with both paws. "Gods above and below, we're not going to have to ride another meteor, are we?"

Eyebrow raised, Sasha stared at the trembling alien.

Rikka chuckled and patted the tech on the arm. It was as high as she could reach. "No prob, Mike. Koop is not a military installation. We'll simply stroll in. No problem."

"Of course, all of this still depends upon flight clearance from the military," noted Parson pragmatically. "For that you'll need official authorization from the station."

Jhonny smiled. "We can get it while en route and save time."

"Good idea. Let's go."

Mike started shutting down the work station. "But what if we are refused clearance?" he asked quizzically.

"Then the military blows us to atoms with their nuclear lasers."

The big alien slowed in his work. Had he braved the infinite dangers of deep-space travel only to become marooned in an alien solar system as a field technician for the most lunatic bunch of news peepers in the history of mass media?

With a toothy grin, he finished with a flourish and turned to join his new comrades.

Amazing. Sometimes, you just get lucky.

CHAPTER SIX

A COLOSSUS STRODE through the infinite blackness of space.

Stars cascaded from his fingers and suns dimmed in honor at his mighty approach. Casually, he toyed with whole planets, watching them spin on the palm of a hand. Blazing comets detoured about him forming a halo. Meteors impacted with pyrotechnic results on his shirt. Indeed, the entire galaxy itself appeared to revolve about this huge man-shaped being as if he were some primordial deity of old and the source of all power. The supreme master of Nature itself, he was plainly more than man. More than even a god!

It was the Executive Producer. And owner.

"This simulation is wonderful!" complimented Gardner Wilkes, passing his hand through the laser hologram of the Earth. Australia blurred, tendrils of land extending into space briefly clinging to the disrupting biomagnetic field of living tissue.

Standing behind the sun, the Media SFX crew took a bow, momentarily setting their hair on fire.

"Thanks, sir, we did our best," said the Chief Technician. A lot of this was old hat. But the big boss had never paid much attention to their work before and the whole gang was grateful for the chance to show off. There was nothing her pack of lunatic geniuses loved more than ego-boo. Except getting paid regularly.

Leaning close to the moon, Gardner watched as a tiny Media orbited close and then phased straight through his nose. It tickled! "How will the linkage with the military go?"

With the endless avalanche of the asteroid belt cascading about her sweat-stained jumpsuit, the Chief Tech bit a lip and crossed her arms. "Well, we have a small problem there since Z-band scanners are forbidden . . ." began the woman slowly.

"Yes, they are," said Wilkes sternly. The Law was the Law. Especially since he would be the one going to jail for breaking the military sanction.

The Special Effects expert shrugged. What the hey. It never hurt to ask. "Okay, then what we will do is a passive monitor of all military channels. Our resident analyst will weed out the wheat from the deliberate chaff and then move the model ships into the correct positions."

"As for the actual details of the battles," continued somebody masked by the steaming molten surface of Mercury. "Well, those we make up as we go along. Concentrating primarily on accuracy, believability, and timing."

Wilkes appeared bewildered. "Timing?"

"Sure. Can't have a commercial occur at the end of a dramatic missile salvo. It's too satisfying. The audience might lose their impetus and go make a sandwich."

The millionaire shuddered at the horrible concept. Losing viewers. Brr! Obviously, these folks really knew their stuff! Of course, the scale and dimensions of everything were totally wrong, but that was only so the whole solar system could fit on a standard TriD view screen. With just enough room remaining for the famous, transparent, annoying QSNT logo to fit in a corner.

"We also have a team of wargamers from Entertainment preparing a wide assortment of attack scenarios," added the Chief Tech, as the multicolored Jupiter moved silently behind her. "So in case the station receives partial info, I can go with one of their premades, modified to comply with existing knowledge."

"Watch this!" cried out a voice from Venus.

Suddenly, an armada of silvery warships appeared about Wilkes, the scintillating beams of their lasers and blossoming fireballs of nuclear missile explosions illuminating the space about him like miniature fireworks.

"Wonderful! Terrific!" the grinning man complimented from amid the violent bombardment. One impetuous dreadnought rained death and destruction on the top of his partially bald head to no apparent effect. "This is sure to boast our ratings!" Then his gold wrist secretary began to beep vying for his attention. Eh? Ah! Oh. Rats, and he had been having fun.

"Well, I've got to go do a final revue on the noon broadcast," said Gardner Wilkes, temporarily masked by a tremendous thermo-nuclear blast. "Keep up the good work!"

Stepping out of the war, he glanced about the solar system in mild confusion. "Ah, by the way, just where is the door again?"

Silently, the technical staff pointed toward Uranus.

With a sniff, the boss strode off in that direction.

How drool.

With screeching tires, a station wagon roared out of an alleyway on Earth and crashed into a luxury limo stately rolling along the street. Glass exploded at the impact and hubcaps went sailing. Air bags ballooned into view from steering wheels to instantly cushion the drivers. As always, the passengers were on their own.

Then the doors to the station wagon slammed open and out scurried a man with a professional camcorder and a woman with a glass cutter. As the camera-op balanced light and focus, the woman sliced a neat hole in the driver's side window of the limo and popped the section free with a small suction cup. The hard inflated crash balloon inside the limo expanded a bit to fill the sudden opening.

"Hello!" called the woman. "Senator Hardwick!"

". . . help . . ." weakly called a voice from within.

"Rolling," said the man and the camera lights winked on.

Tossing aside the glass cutter, the woman fluffed her hair and checked her makeup with a palm mirror. Perfect!

"Hello, this is Sandar Kinney of QSNT in Buenos Aires, Argentina, Earth South. I'm here with Senator Raphael Hardwick, the pro tem Secretary-General of the United Planets Security Council. Although usually reticent in these matters, today he was kind enough to grant us an interview. Senator, what can you tell us about the coming military action? Is it truly punitive?"

". . . murmprh . . ." replied the politician, making the taut crash balloon wiggle and jiggle.

The cub reporter glanced at her amateur camera-op.

"Sounded like a yes to me," he theorized.

"Ah! Well, then, Senator, what about the rumor of—"

A fine misty spray kissed the teakwood deck of the sleek Bentley yacht as it sliced through the crisp blue Pacific Ocean at over a hundred knots. On the aftdeck, a slim, tanned woman in a scandalous small bikini was strapped into a safety chair and straining to operate a fishing rod and reel over five meters long.

"Here it comes!" cried the woman in unabashed glee as she frantically operated the manual ratchet to take in the slack on the line.

. . . and a magnificent swordfish broke the surface of the sea spinning and flapping as it arched into the air.

. . . and kept on coming. Higher and higher, up and over the gunwale until it wetly crashed onto the deck at the feet of the almost nude woman.

"Hans. Olga! Give me a hand! It's a monster!" cried the beauty as she unstrapped herself and reached for the impaling hook to secure her catch.

But suddenly the mouth popped open and inside was a small man with a waterproof camcorder perched on his shoulder.

"Greetings, Madam President," he called. "I'm Braf Thompson, QSNT. May I have a few words with you about the upcoming war?"

The words the outraged American politician used were not fit for the public airwaves.

Nor were the words the reporter used as Hans and Olga tossed him back overboard. Along with the heavy-duty sea anchor and several meters of stout chain.

"You h'ain't got a friend on your left," chanted the Marine Sergeant alongside the column of marching troops.

"You're right!" chorused the combat troops in machine unison.

"You h'ain't all the time in the right!"

"What's left?"

"Sound off!"

"One, two!"

"Sound off!"

"Three, four!"

"Cadence count!"

"One. Two. Three. Four. One, two, three-four!"

An odd shadow on the ground made the Sergeant glance suspiciously upward in time to scamper aside and avoid being engulfed by the parachutist descending from the sky.

"Hi, troops!" called the woman, punctuating her statement with a grunt of pain as she hit the concrete.

Rolling to her feet, she snapped on the camera gun in her hands. "Hi, I'm Amanda Dillingoff, QSNT. Private MacDowell, as the secret bastard son of our beloved premier, can I have a few words with you about the upcoming . . ."

In Bangor, Maine, a retired admiral opened a garbage can to dispose of some trash, when he discovered the can recording his actions.

"Morning, sir! Leon Sardouichi, QSNT. Do you believe that Titan colonists are really—"

The lid dropped shut.

"Yeow! Nice punch there, Madam UnderSecretary . . ."

"Hi there, Your Majesty! QSNT here and—"
Crash!

"Excuse me, General . . ."
Slam!

"Hello there, Don Salvatore!"
Kaboom!

On Luna, near the Sea of Tranquillity where mankind first set foot on Earth's closet neighbor, was a bare patch of lunar soil and in the middle was a large lucite block containing the famous plaque and original space capsule that successfully made the perilous voyage. A noble permanent monument on the tenacity and undying courage of humanity.

Surrounding the landing site at a distance of fifty meters was the sprawling metropolis of Green Cheese City, the first and oldest settlement on the moon. Armorlite domes soared above the crater walls. Surface tunnels twinkled with a thousand lights. The ground vibrated constantly from ever-busy subterranean industries that produced the necessities and luxuries for the indigenous population of two million.

Indeed, there was even a small export trade with the other

worlds of the ultra-difficult to find and thus fabulously expensive, blue-white crystal Lunar Geodes; reputed to have magical healing powers and the ability to significantly increase one's sexual potency. However, the only scientifically proven attribute of the hollow crystal spheres was that of a common paperweight. And, to the esthetically dull, the more plebeian function of a poorly designed nutcracker.

However, there were many other sources of lunar revenue.

On the surface of the moon, just off to one side of the inner city encircling the Eagle Landing Park, was a prim geodesic dome that had a tall row of artificial trees erected outside in the bitter vacuum to block the sight of the American antique from the lofty sight of its aristocratic diners.

As the only proper French restaurant on the Earth side of Luna, Chateau la Manga was extremely selective in its clientele and, in fact, possessed a private access tunnel that wasn't listed on any map. The secret entrance being a disguised door hidden in the small, but dignified, Antiquarian Spoon section of the downtown Green Cheese Library. The basic idea was, if you couldn't bankroll a team of private detectives to find the place, then you couldn't afford to eat there.

So, of course, it immediately became the place of choice for every news reporter on the QBBC staff. Purporting themselves like true Englishmen, the staff considered that expense accounts were like promises, made to be broken.

With a hiss of properly trained hydraulics, the armored portal to the posh establishment silently swung aside and in walked a man and a woman.

She gasped. He grinned.

The place was dazzling. Multitiered chandeliers hung directly above every single table and each location was isolated by a set of velvet ropes suspended from highly polished brass stands. The tables themselves were made of real wood, fine Irish linen draped every place setting, and the centerpiece for the day was a slim Steuben crystal voz—not a vase, but a voz—adorned with a single fresh flower.

And even more impressive was the simple fact that it was possible to identify all of the people eating there. Millionaires, celebrities, politicians, gangsters, actors . . . it almost seemed as if everybody who was anybody was here at the same time. Sporting a dapper pin-striped mumu, with vest and bowler hat, Lord Alexander Hyde-White of QBBC viewed his colleague with pleasure.

"Impressed?" asked the anchor.

Tucking her hands into the pockets of her sheer taffeta jumpsuit, Hannabel O'Toole cocked a wry smile.

"Hmm? Nyah, I volunteered for this," quipped the CNN reporter.

Scandalized at their jovial banter, the maître d' standing at the podium in the foyer dutifully scanned the new arrivals with a pocket WatchDog and was enormously relieved to find that the two reporters were carrying no weapons or doggie bags.

"Good afternoon," mouthed the chief butler, his French accent demurely lowered to intelligible speech. "Do you have a reservation?"

Lord Hyde-White glared at the man. "Certainly not!"

An oily smile. "Ah! Then, right this way, please."

At his approach, the velvet rope snaked out of the way and he marched off down the main aisle.

Each section of the restaurant was divided by the type of flower in the voz; rose, carnation, lily orchard. The floor itself was a living carpet of thick green grass. Hesitantly, O'Toole approved. It was pretty, removed unwanted smells from the air, hid nasty food stains wonderfully, plus, you merely had to rake the floor once a week to recover lost silverware and hope that somebody's escargot didn't escape.

With a flair of his hand, the maître d' showed them a table as if expecting applause. As none was forthcoming, he turned on a heel and marched back to his post, en route accidentally crushing a lone bold snail that had spent the last two years racing for the door and precious freedom.

Taking a napkin, Hanna dropped it into her lap as instructed by her prep-school teacher in Etiquette 101. Which, unfortunately, she had failed.

"So, Al," she began without any preamble. "Why the big lunchtime spread? Trying to get me in the sack?"

Caught in mid-swallow, Lord Hyde-White choked on his imported Saturn mineral water and valiantly tried to cover the social breach with his own napkin and as much panache as he could muster under the circumstances.

A passing waiter paid the incident no attention at all.

"Great heavens, miss, what effrontery!" he finally managed to gasp, mopping his vest dry.

"Is that a no?" she asked sweetly.

"Really, now," said the anchor, clarifying nothing.

Becoming excited, the news reporter leaned closer to the veteran anchor. "Okay then! Got some inside info on the war you need a hand in ferreting out?"

Summoning his pluck, he viewed her with disdain. "Sorry. I asked you here merely as the new top investigative reporter for your network and I thought a genial lunch would help cement a friendly working association."

As a second waiter detoured around them, Hanna tried not to pout. Damn. He was either gay or married. Oh, well.

Another waiter went by.

"What the . . . hey! How do you get some service around here?" she asked, annoyed. "Fire off a flare gun?"

A sophisticated smile. "It's so much more complicated than that. Allow me?"

"Please," she gestured, returning to scan her menu. A total lack of printed prices had been expected, but no, the prices were blatantly there and each appeared to be the speed-of-light with a dollar sign in front. Geez!

"Garçon!" the British lord cried as if expelling a piece of rotten fruit from his mouth.

Busy in the kitchen a Parisian waiter, seeing that somebody was being exceptionally rude, hurried over immediately.

"Hello, I am Pierre, your outrageous French waiter. Welcome to the most horribly overpriced restaurant in town. How may I help you?"

Hanna croggled. And she wasn't even sure how to spell the word. Wow! Well, at least they were honest about it!

"As my guest, please go first," suggested the lord anchor.

The menu was briefly consulted to verify her choice. "I'll have crêpes suzettes with strawberries."

What pronunciation! "And would madame care to see the wine

list," sneered Pierre in a manner to suggest that anybody wishing to do so would certainly unclog their nose on the Mona Lisa.

Missing the sarcasm entirely, Hanna declined the offer. "Just more mineral water, thank you."

Pierre turned to his next victim. Perhaps this one would not be so cheap. "And for monsieur?" he asked through his nose.

Even though the British anchor had already made his decision, Hyde-White let the waiter cool his heels for a full minute before deeming to answer.

"I'll start with the vichyssoise soup," he said, tossing aside the menu. "Immediately followed by an endive salad with raspberry vinaigrette dressing. The entree will be a Japanese Coby beef chateaubriand steak, black and red, please. With Neapolitan carrots and brandied cheese as a side."

"But of course!" thrilled the waiter, utterly delighted to finally have a real customer to serve. His computer stylus fairly danced with joy across the monitor of his hand-held computer.

Judging the moment to be perfect, White went for the kill. "For dessert, I'll finish off with a café mousse and the wine shall be an '02 Chateau La . . . no, a '99 Dom Pérignon . . . no, aw, just gimme a beer."

The stylus broke in half, the shattered point spearing straight through the computer pad.

Beer! screamed the waiter's bulging eyes.

"And don't bother to bring a glass," said Hyde-White with a bored expression as if he did this every day. "I'll just use the can."

Pale lips fluttered for a minute before coherent words issued. "O-o-oui, monsieur," the poleaxed waiter somehow managed to croak and the man stumbled off to the kitchen where he could faint in private.

As the kitchen doors closed with the sound of crashing pots and pans, O'Toole turned to eye her colleague intently. "You did that deliberately," she accused.

"But of course," laughed White in his very best bad French accent.

"Why, you bloody bastard," chuckled O'Toole. Well, at least this initiation had been more amusing than the snipe hunt she had undergone on Earth.

"Now, as for the war," her companion picked up their former

conversation. "In my opinion, the military has released all of the pertinent information that the public should be allowed to know. Our jobs are merely to relay that information in a precise and coherent manner."

"There's no secret agenda?" she asked disappointedly.

"No. This is a straightforward revolt by Titan."

"Yeah, that's my opinion also," she admitted, disgruntled. "But as the new kid on the moon, I was really hoping for something hot from you."

A pause. "Business-wise, that is."

"Sorry."

"Damn."

Suddenly, there was a terrible commotion at the front portal of the dining establishment and in strode a young man in a garishly striped delivery uniform.

"QCNN!" the teenager cried, snapping his chewing gum with every juicy word. "I have your spleen pizza!"

As the crowd feigned to swoon in response, burly security guards moved in quickly to oust the boisterous invader. At their table, Hyde-White and O'Toole exchanged thoughtful glances.

"QINS?" she asked.

"Far too subtle," he denied. "Theirs would have exploded. No, it must be QSNT. But for Rikka and Harry to pull a practical joke in the middle of declared war is beneath even them!"

"Then it's a diversion," decided the reporter.

"Indubitably," agreed the anchor.

"And a diversion means . . ."

"They have a hot story lead!"

"After that pizza!" cried the reporters in unison as they wildly scrambled over their table.

And the chase began.

CHAPTER SEVEN

STEEL HANDS CLOSED around the soft flesh of the woman's throat and began to expertly knead the tense shoulder muscles.

"Mmm," purred Maria Valdez. "A little lower, Danny."

The J series android did as requested and resisted the temptation to slide his hands forward and cup those beautiful full breasts. Danny was terribly ashamed of the fact that he found human females incredibly desirous.

He ran his powerful hands down her back, palms paralleling the spinal column until he reached the lower lombar region. There his fingers spread to the swell of her hips, while his thumbs teasingly caressed the soft warm flesh of her partially exposed buttocks.

With her silk jumpsuit pulled down to around her waist rendering her half naked, Maria squirmed in her office chair and tried not to show her rising excitement. It was only her android butler simply doing his standard daily massage, she reminded herself. People would think her a pervert if she told anybody what she longed to do with the anatomically correct machine male. Sigh.

Unnoticed in the corner, a Hush monitor silently spat out duplicate reports of official government announcements, synopses of recorded interviews, random street polls, and a running tally of reporters arrested and/or hospitalized. Happily, the total was surprisingly low. Excellent! Maria had known that sensitivity awareness training sessions for the staff would pay off! Maybe she should have gone herself.

Nyah.

Just then her wrist secretary buzzed and a message scrolled on the tiny monitor.

"Ah! Time for the twelve. Let's see what Box and Rikka have

prepared for our kickoff report." She reached for the control panel set flush in her desktop.

Hesitantly, Danny J touched the limp jumpsuit top around her trim waist. "But, madam," he objected. "This is unseemly!"

Bemused, she glanced over a shoulder and gave the android a quick smile. "Oh, I'll use the censorship circuit. You just continue."

With pleasure. "As you say, Ms. Valdez."

Operating the control panel with practiced fingers, an illuminated rectangle was formed in the middle of the office. The center of the hologram window fogged white and then cleared to a view of Paul Ambocksky in the control room of Studio One, with technicians scurrying about and a bank of assistant directors doing frantic last-second corrections on the prerecorded scroll on the teleprompter. On the stage beyond was a distinguished woman in a somber business jumpsuit getting a quick application of theoretical makeup from a youngster in an artist smock.

"Box?"

Hearing his name, Paul Ambocksky turned and the smile faded. Floating in the air, he saw a view of Maria sitting at her desk framed by a glowing rectangle. The background and her clothes were slightly out of focus and he assumed she was using the censorship circuit. Probably got her pet robot on his knees under the desk.

"Hello, Ms. Valdez. How can I help you?" His tone beguiled the polite words.

"What's our lead?" Maria asked without any preamble.

"A recap of the main facts, followed by a brief history of the combatants, then a Wilkes Corporation Yummy Noodle Soup commercial and a shotgun of troops frolicking on leave, cross cut to the same preparing for battle."

That was the lead? Excellent stuff.

"And?" she prompted in her best unimpressed voice.

"Then we're doing an exclusive interview with Admiral Davis and Hamilton onboard their flagships."

"An exclusive? How the hell did we get that gem?"

"Rikka set it up as a PR stunt for the military during a turbo-lift ride."

Damn the woman's efficiency!

"Sounds okay," Valdez relinquished. Then something caught her attention. There was only one chair on the phony newsroom stage. There was six behind her, but those were for the professional actors who played the parts of SNT reporters. Hired entirely for the sincere looks and honest noninteresting faces, they added a nice touch of realism to the daily broadcasts. And unfortunately actors were needed—mostly because the majority of reporters in existence weren't housebroken, much less showpieces.

"Why is Lois Kent doing the anchor instead of Snyder," demanded the woman petulantly.

" 'Cause he ain't here," replied Box impatiently. "Number two, start with an establishing shot and then do a tight zoom during the intro. Angle up and mind those light shadows."

A hand wave. "You got it, chiefy!"

The crew chuckled. Paul covered his face and groaned. Oh, Lord, the whole station knew his nickname by now.

"What do you mean he isn't here!" shrilled Valdez.

A shrug. "Security says they're still somewhere in the station, so I assumed the team was hard at work. Probably on Level 37."

Even as her shoulders relaxed, Maria tightened her lips. The hated Level 37, where nobody could go, even Wilkes or Security, unless the demigod Parson deemed them admittance.

"You want I should go find him?" asked Ambocksky, gesturing toward the working crew and busy techs on soundstage below.

The wall clock audibly clicked to the one-minute slot.

"No, of course not," purred Valdez, heroically controlling her temper. "I'll find him myself. Please carry on with your usual fine work."

"Gee, thanks." Box put his back to the Station Manager, something he would never do if she were here in the flesh. "Bye. Nice to see you. Call again. Hey, number three! Hit your mark! Where's the auxiliary teleprompter? Cue the actors! Where's my coffee!"

Exercising willpower, Maria bid the man adieu, closed the window, and yanked on her jumpsuit. Smoothing the material into place, she marched out of the office with Danny in close tow, his hands partially extended as if to help her with something. She would personally find Rikka and her cowboy team. And if they didn't have their teeth in the throat of a genuine page one story, she would cancel their contract for *non compos mentis, or malfea-*

sance, or some other legal mumbo-jumbo, then fire the lot of them and damn Wilkes. Damn her career.

Damn everybody!

In downtown New York City, America, the Secretary-General of the United Nations and combined Earth Defense Force rapped his gavel on the dura-wood of his podium, his microphone picking up the sound and relaying it to the earphones of the multitude filling the General Assembly room. "Ladies and gentlemen, order, please!"

The murmuring in the cavernous room dropped to a more tolerable level. The upcoming war between Earth and Titan was the absolute top priority on everybody's agenda and yet this unscheduled meeting had been called for the ungodly hour of noon. Half of the delegates were still in their pajamas. What conceivable new disaster could be so important that it rated disturbing their last chance of sleep before the possible end of civilization?

"Oh, what now?" yawned Afghanistan rudely. "Has Russia also attacked somebody?"

The Russian ambassador turned red. "We never attack!" he disclaimed loudly. "We only act to defend ourselves from future aggressions!"

"Yes," said Poland and France in unison. "They only act to defend themselves."

"Amazing how he does that," said America to England. "You can't even see him pull their strings."

"Once, I actually saw him drink a glass of water while each of them delivered a speech."

"Really?"

England made an X on her chest. "Cross my heart."

"Besides," continued the Russian unabated. "My country has been far too busy on our Great Project to bother with such puerile actions."

"Stupidest thing I ever heard of," muttered Monaco to Korea. "Imagine, building a fifty-foot wall around your entire country. Just who does that crazy czar of theirs think he is? Pharaoh Rameses?"

"It's impossible!" agreed Finland. "Ridiculous! Think of the cost!"

"What I want to know," chirped in Brazil, "is, are they doing it to keep their enemies out, or population in?"

"Yes," said Iceland coldly.

Puerto Rico harrumphed. "It'll never work."

"Worked in old Berlin," reminded Belgium.

Spain agreed. "True, but only for a few decades."

"My people have never had much faith in walls," stated China for the record.

Egypt smiled. "Ah, but remember what the Koran says about faith and mountains, my friend."

"Russians have no faith," replied Poland hotly. "Or friends. Only strong backs."

"The Koran mentions those, too."

As the muttering was getting out of hand, the Secretary-General set the volume control of his microphone on maximum and spoke clearly. "In case any of you haven't been paying attention to the outside world as usual, QSNT will be broadcasting a special report of the upcoming war."

The assembly hall quieted with the speed of an assassin's bullet as every diplomat present reacted according to his personal opinion of the free press: fear, loathing, apprehension, dudgeon, indigestion, or confusion. Mostly it was fear.

During these facial gymnastics, the Secretary-General kept his own countenance neutral. "I thought it would be appropriate for us to watch together, in case prompt political action is needed to be taken. Agreed?"

More muttering. To the affirmative.

A gavel rap. "Fine. Then let's see what they think is really going on in the worlds."

As the room lights dimmed, the wall behind the podium flickered into a picture of a man and woman kissing passionately. Then the woman drew away and started to cleanse her mouth with a blowtorch, while the man looked very embarrassed.

Behind them a chorus began to sing, "Oh . . . if your girlfriend won't, 'cause your teeth aren't bright, then brush with Luck and you'll"—pause—"*hug* all night!

Then a deep, booming announcer's voice spoke. "When you're outta luck you're out of luck. Luck toothpaste! Another fine biodegradable product from the Gunderson Corporation! A wholly owned subsidiary of Wilkes Incorporated."

Irritably, the politicians scowled. Bloody commercials.

In the heart of Media, a studio tech stood just off camera at Stage One and displayed three raised fingers. "We have a go," he announced, "in three . . . two . . . one!" The last finger went level and pointed at Ms. Kent just as the lights brilliantly illuminated the stage.

An overvoice chattered away. "From the fiery sun to the nebulous Ort Cloud, from the depths of the sea to the farthest reaches of space, QSNT is there!"

"All news, all the time!" sang the chorus.

Kent flashed her famous toothy smile and a light operator aligned a colored gell to focus on them to cut down on the reflected glare. Whew. She must use Luck.

"Good afternoon, ladies and gentlemen and all the ships in space," announced the anchor, pretending to read from the blank sheet of paper in her hands. "This is the QSNT twelve hundred news report. I'm Lois Kent filling in for the ailing Harry Snyder."

Ailing sounded so much better than AWOL.

In the control booth, a communications monitor started to scroll with sympathy calls for poor sick Harry. An automatic CC logged the return address of each caller so they would receive a catalog of QSNT goods; including the brand-new "SNT: The War Days" T-shirt. Ambocksky nodded approval. Gardner Wilkes might be absentminded and slightly goofy, but the man would refuse to die unless he could somehow make a profit on the act.

Kent continued. "Soon we'll be going live to Admiral Davis of the Earth Defense Fleet and Admiral Hamilton of the Titan Navy for an *exclusive* QSNT double interview." She shifted blank papers. "But first, a quick recap of today's top story, the revolt of Titan . . ."

The Lunar Police watched the report hoping for news of peace. War was the ultimate crime.

Seated with their king and queen in the throne room of the palace, the commanders of the Royal Martian Navy twiddled their thumbs and waited for this nonsense to be over. It was impossible for anyone to have discovered the truth in this short a period of time.

Meanwhile, Rikka, Harry, Jhonny, and Mike took this as a golden opportunity to raid the supply lockers of the station and refuel their shuttle when everybody was too busy watching the double interview to notice their departure.

Busily engaged in another battle with a heavily armed contingent of the Free Police, who were neither, the Enforcers of the Independent Asteroids let their VDR machines back home record the interview for later.

The Earth and Titan crews listened over their spacesuit helmet radios, but did not even slow their frantic preparations.

Using a riding crop to brush the sweaty hair out of his/her face, Madam Adam called a hiatus to all mattress merriment for the duration of the broadcast.

Wilkes pounded on his desk, trying to unjam the controls.

". . . and now we take you to space rendezvous point Alpha for an SNT *exclusive,* where diplomatic ships from the United Planets and Titan have met for this important, and *exclusive,* QSNT interview. At this time they also intend to have a preliminary parlay to decide on nonstrategic targets and the exchange of prisoners."

A smile. "Which is highly unlikely given the destructive nature of the superscience weapons of today. Long gone are the days of limited nuclear warfare and the idea of surviving.

"Such as it was," she added jokingly.

On cue, the screen cut to a view of two tremendous vessels floating in starry space. Each had a bare unpainted hull of polished silvery metal, a holdover from the old days when lasers were the ultimate weapon and a reflective hull could give a ship precious minutes of extended life.

In an effort to seem strong, the UP had sent the Earth Defense vessel *King Arthur,* an Excalibur-class dreadnought. Roughly resembling a loaf of bread with a needle tip and a flat end, the hull was staggered and irregular, making the vessel appear as if it had fought and been damaged in a hundred battles.

That was a false impression. The *King Arthur* was brand-new off the assembly line. Actually, the ship had two hulls. The inner shell was a standard formation of reactive armor, sheet lead, lithium fiber tiles, and dura-steel. But the outer hull was composed of thousands of curved sections of armor plating with their own independent power supply and magnetic treads. If any portion of the hull was damaged, then these mechanized platelets would converge to cover the wound and protect the vulnerable ship underneath. The experts knew that, occasionally, a plate would blow a fuse and start blocking the doors or windows, but that was a rare event and easily corrected with the quick application of a crowbar and a good hard shove into space.

The mobile armor could also move to uncover gun turrets and missile hatches, so it was generally unknown how much armament the massive vessel carried.

However, the needle prow was an exception. Upon closer inspection, the tip was actually a hollow, ferruled pipe whose internal dimensions were large enough to accommodate an entire space shuttle. This was no escape hatch, but an Einstein-class Gatling gun, a machine cannon that fired streams of nuclear bombs like old-fashioned bullets. Io, the moon of Jupiter, no longer existed because of the hellish weapon, along with the main headquarters of the infamous Free Police (who were neither).

Attempting to appear dangerous, the ship from Titan was the *Schwarzenegger,* a Barbarian-class superdreadnought (patent pending, Wilkes SpaceMilitary Corporation). Roughly resembling a manta ray, the vessel had a wide curved hull that tapered to a stingerlike tail in the rear—a jamming antenna for enemy Watch-Dog scanners.

The top bristled with laser cannons, and the bottom was bubbly with hundreds of anchored drones, whose functions and capabilities could not be discerned from an external examination.

The round armored hatches of missile ports lined the gunwales and at its bow was a charred cone set inside a pitted ring. The muzzle of a hydrogen lance. Although a short-range weapon, even planetary shields could only last for a few minutes against the brutal onslaught of controlled fission.

There were no logos, symbols, ID numbers, or anything else to indicate the allegiance of either spaceship. The physical design of each vessel alone told of its national origin. For the viewers at home, Box had the techs superimpose a UP flag under the *King Arthur* and the new Titan flag under the *Schwarzenegger*. The flag was a blue and white diagram of Saturn with a red star on the outer ring.

"Nice flag," noted a tech at the balance board.

"Has the communications links to the two vessels been successfully established?" asked Kent for the viewing audience. Nobody moved or did anything.

"Excellent," she smiled after an appropriate pause to simulate off-stage conversation. "Then let's go to the bridges of the *King Arthur* and the *Schwarzenegger*."

The video signal from Media split into three sections: the middle one still displayed Lois, smiling and confident.

But now on the left side was a corpulent man with a face too small or a head too large for conventional beauty. Fleet Admiral Terrance Davis. Smoking contentedly on a steel pipe, his uniform was of spotless white linen, dripping with gold braid and trim. The emblem of the United Planets Space Navy was emblazoned on his right breast and underlined with his massed collection of colorful decorations. None of them were for good conduct. His mathematically straight Navy cap had its brim covered with fancy gold filigree, scrambled eggs it was called in the service. A mark of distinction. And Davis had enough to qualify for an omelet. His splendiferous belt of red, white, and blue leather stripes sported an inlaid gold scabbard whose ornate sword pommel was adrip with crimson tassels. On the other hip rested a standard-issue Bedlow laser pistol of extremely functional design.

On the right side was a large woman whose very presence seemed to fill a room before she actually physically entered. Admiral Kathryn Hamilton: black hair, green eyes, freckles, and a knife scar on her cheek that disappeared into her collar on its way to her hip. Her long hair hung in a braided club to the small of her back where it ended with a copper clip attached to her belt to keep the hair from lashing about freely in combat situations. Her soft cloth cap bore the single initial "A" for admiral, showing that the Titan Navy was not such a stickler for protocol as the EDF and that it had a much higher level of literacy. The short jacket and jumpsuit of her uniform were a strict utilitarian black, only the sleeves and ammo clips were edged with light blue. On her right shoulder was the brand-new emblem of the Titan Military Forces. On her left shoulder was a small green patch for marksmanship.

A brown leather body rig of a belt with shoulder straps supported around her waist a ring of molded batteries whose armored cable fed directly into the butt of a squat MBA Neutrino pistol nestled in a fast-draw shoulder holster. While the array of power packs and cable seemed immaculate, the pistol grip was faded and the muzzle of the dire weapon shiny from constant usage.

"Greetings, Admiral Davis, Admiral Hamilton," said Kent. "First of all I would like to thank you for this"—she faced the camera—"*exclusive* meeting with QSNT. And I am sure all of humanity hope and pray for a swift end to this possibly bloody situation."

Davis smoked.

Hamilton shrugged.

Feeling the tension like a noose about her throat, Kent nervously chewed the inside of her cheek. This was an inauspicious beginning. Time for a little levity to lighten the mood. These two soldiers can't really be that angry at each other.

"Actually, I'm not sure which of you I should start with," she chuckled good-naturedly.

Silent, the two admirals stared at each other.

"Perhaps, age before beauty," offered Kent jokingly to break the ice.

Silent, the two admirals stared at each other.

"Admiral Davis," said the anchor, crossing her legs and using her best interviewer voice. "What can you tell us of the incidents that preceded the outbreak of hostilities?"

"Before I comment on that," drawled the Admiral in a thick Alabama accent. "As a southern gentleman, I am, of course, dismayed at the prospect of waging brutal warfare on a delicate member of the fairer sex." Davis paused and drew contentedly on his stainless-steel pipe.

"However," he added, after blowing a smoke ring, "if that uppity Titan bitch doesn't surrender immediately, then I shall nuke her till she glows." A slow stately smile grew as he emptied the hot ashes of the smoking pipe into a bare palm.

"Then I'll shoot her in the dark," chuckled "Mad Dog," crushing the burning leaves in a scarred fist.

"Hellcat" Hamilton's reply was a juicy raspberry and a salvo of missiles from the belly of her ship.

"External view, now!" screamed Box, tearing at his hair.

Cut!

Shimmering lasers from the *King Arthur* stabbed at the streaking missiles, detonating half before they hit their target.

A glowing ball surrounded the vessel as a hard-driven force shield struggled to withhold the awful load of the incoming energy. Then a return salvo of missiles launched from the sides and top of the *King Arthur*, more than four times the number the Titan ship had launched.

Anti-missiles jetted into space to counter the attack, along with more missiles, anti-missiles, and even some anti-anti-missile-missiles. Pyrotechnics blossomed in a never-ending display of explosive technology. Now radiating spheres surrounded each vessel as lasers and neutrino cannons added their awful destructive bids to the general madness. Streamers of energy flared off the warships to impact on the other, so close were the two combatants.

Then the tip of the *Schwarzenegger* glowed red-hot, yellow, white, and a burning lance of atomic annihilation vomited from the prow of the Titan ship to violently impact on the immaterial boundary of the EDF forcefields.

The shields of the *King Arthur* struggled heroically to withstand the volcanic outpouring of tortured nuclei. Some of the shock wave leaked through charring sections of the hull and the armor plates performed their defensive dance.

Then the Einstein cannon began to stutter a stream of white pellets and as they crossed the shield to the other side the entire volume of space was filled with a blinding fireball of staggering proportions.

Back in the control booth in Media, Paul Ambocksky turned about and saw that the digital tote board of their viewers was solid 8888 as viewer after viewer called in friends to see the swell show.

Already they had hit fifty percent of the market and were just about ready to push the smash hit afternoon soap opera *Sex, Drugs, and Rock 'n' Roll* off the air.

Yep, there it went!

On the video monitor, as the dissipating gas in space thinned to invisibility, Kent audibly gulped to clear her throat.

"Wow," she offered as an opener.

Most of the viewing audience agreed, then gasped. Davis and Hamilton were still on screen. What the prack?

"Mine was a drone," stated Davis, refilling his pipe.

Thumbs hooked in her belt, Hamilton laughed. "Mine also. Did you honestly think that I would trust murdering scum like you?"

"You think, madam? Amazing."

"Next time, Admiral Davis," warned the furious Titan woman.

Applying a light to the pipe, the Earthman puffed agreement. "Indubitably. Next time, Admiral Hamilton. Ah, next time."

And the pictures clicked off.

Pandemonium raged across the ten worlds of civilization and the QSNT studio. With a throbbing headache, Box held a pocket-doc against his temple for whatever relief the machine could provide. It hummed, clicked, and hissed as a hypo-spray directly applied Wilkes Corporation aspirin to his beleaguered brain.

Returning the doc to his pocket, Paul tried to make sense of the events he had personally witnessed. God, he couldn't believe this! It was almost as if the two enemies wanted to generate public fervor! Hell and damnation, could Rikka have been correct about the conspiracy theory?

On stage, Kent moved her fingers in an unusual pattern. Thinking fast, Ambocksky gave her a sign from the control booth.

"We'll be rebroadcasting a repeat of this historic event in only a few minutes," stated the anchor confidently. "But first now we take you to Jim Smith, our statistically average person from Peoria, Illinois, USA, North America, for his usual in-depth analysis of this confrontation. Going to you, Mr. Smith!"

Cut to a man in blue jeans, smoking a corncob pipe and rocking in a chair on a front porch of a farmhouse. In the distant background androids wearing straw hats loaded tomatoes the size of Buicks into a hovering aircar.

"Howdy, folks!" called the farmer, removing his pipe and spitting a long stream of black fluid off camera. "Well, now t'ain't much to say really. Except this sure was a hoot! Now, Davis, he's a simple country boy gone corrupt, and Hamilton, she's a street fighter made mad with political power. To be blunt, they're each excellent commanders and more than slightly crazy."

A stained tooth grin. "So all in all, folks, this promises to be one hell of an entertaining war!"

* * *

Four hundred kilometers away, in the Mercurian Building of Important Talk, the television was turned off and the liquid crystal screen slid into the wall again.

"Well, that was certainly fun," grumped the representative of Tin.

It was an odd fact of life on Mercury, but the planet was so close to the sun that the heat had long ago leached the lighter metals from their soil and formed great oceans of nearly pure elements. Each had been claimed by an individual group, and in time those groups became political parties.

"I liked it!" chimed in the representative of Gold.

"How much is this stupid war going to be costing us?" demanded Lead, annoyed. "And isn't there some clever way we can weasel out of paying?"

The Speaker of the Congress stared at the man. "Haven't you read the report yet?"

"What? Eh? Nyah. Been to busy. Why?"

The single sheet of paper was passed to the man posthaste.

Idly, he glanced at it. Paused. And then started to read in earnest. Turning the paper over, he consumed the rest of the report and then turned it over again to read it once more from the start.

"Bloody-bleeding-pracking-jumping-jesus-in-hell-selling-ice-water-to-my-enemies!" he exploded in a single breath.

Almost ripping his jacket open, the Congressman got out his chit book and penned in his name.

"Here!" he said, giving the sheet to a page who promptly scurried away. "Carte blanche. However much you need, you got! My people will empty the treasury if necessary!"

"Thank you," said the Speaker. "It is appreciated."

"I just had a thought," announced Copper, standing, her thumbs under each suspender strap.

"Ah, novelty night," whispered Iron.

"Fined! Ten dollars!" roared the Speaker of the Congress with a rap of his gavel. "Any more witticisms?"

With two friends holding his mouth shut, the official merely nodded in the negative.

"Okay, then. Please continue, madam."

Shooting a dirty look to Iron, the lady from Copper went on.

"We actually have a choice as to which side we want to be on in this war," she announced. "We can choose."

Heads jerked up across the room.

"Bloody hell!"

"Solar storms, she's correct!"

Snapping her suspenders, the politician took a stance. "So, does anybody have an opinion as to which side we should—"

"We fight against the Earth!" chorused the entire assembly of fifty elements. At last!

"Ah, who is the other side anyway?" asked Aluminum.

Steel snorted in disdain. "Who cares?"

Primly, Titanium checked her notes. "Ah . . . the colonist at Titan." How nice!

"We fight for Titan!" chorused the room.

"My favorite people in the universe!" declared the man, placing a foot dramatically atop his desk. "Why, in the history of mankind, there has never been a more undertrod people as these valiant deep-space colonists. Plus—"

As the rhetoric wailed on, the Speaker of the Congress smiled benignly at his boisterous brood. Ye gods, the entire Congress had actually agreed on the same item. It was a first in Mercurian history. A unanimous decision. It was unique! Amazing! Prophetic!

Suddenly, the door was slammed open and in rushed a young representative of Silver.

"What's going on?" he asked, breathless.

"We've reached a decision," stated the Speaker proudly.

He gaped. "Without me? Well, then, whatever it is, I'm against it!"

Of course, a riot ensued.

Watching the combatants boil over desks and broken furniture fly through the air, the Speaker sighed in contentment and relaxed in his chair. Ah, normalcy. Much better. If only their problem in space would be this easy to handle.

He glanced at the clock.

Eight hours to go. And counting.

CHAPTER EIGHT

"THAT'S THE LAST of the supplies," said Rikka, shutting the hatch on the cargo bay and turning the handle to lock it closed. As she stepped away from the shuttle a sheet of lithium-fiber heat shielding slid over the hatch covering.

AND THE INTERVIEW IS OVER, scrolled Deitrich. WE'D BETTER GET GOING.

She nodded. "Check. I'll see the Flight Controller."

"Maria won't like us leaving during a prime-time emergency," noted Harry, standing halfway in the airlock of the shuttle. "Lloyd may say no."

"So I'll persuade him," retorted Collins, over her shoulder.

"And I bet she will," chuckled Jhonny in the middle of a grunt as he dragged a burlap sack of rocks up the inclined ramp to the airlock. "Come on, Mike."

With an identical sack under each arm, the leviathan alien did as requested, even though he had no idea what a space shuttle could possibly need with two megagrams of stone. Ballast?

Appearing carefree and chipper, Rikka strode along the cavernous area of Launch Bay 23, waving hello to friends and coworkers. Rectangular in shape, the mammoth space dock was a pristine expanse of white paint with an orderly array of shuttles neatly lined on the floor and another row of them parked overhead on the ceiling. Space not, want not, was the motto here.

Although over a hundred shuttles were parked here, all were nearly identical in design. Merely another example that function dictates shape. Strongly resembling flat-bottomed airplanes with clipped-delta stubby wings and a cluster of rocket vectors at the rear, the outer hull of the vessels were an intricate jigsaw puzzle of lithium-fiber tiles whose heat resistant abilities enabled the sturdy crafts to make fiery descents into atmospheres. Thus saving tremendous time by bypassing the BeanStalks of Earth and Mars. In essence, the BeanStalks were two-hundred-kilometer-long tubes whose fore end was moored in space while the aft hovered a few scant meters above the planetary surface, allowing passengers and cargo to be loaded into an elevator pod and casually descend to the world in relative comfort. Although safe and cheap, not many reporters wished to undertake the sedate voyage, as the trip took six full hours to complete and few indeed were the hearty souls who could endure that much Muzak. And the hors d'oeuvres were terrible.

Ambling past the pumping stations and tool room, Collins approached one section of the dock floor that seemed even a more pure white than the rest, by which the reporter concluded that was where she and her team had made their hasty entrance this morning.

Gawd, was it only this morning?

Hopping over a small wire fence and dodging around massive steel columns reported to be able to withstand a shuttle crash, she found the Flight Controllers Office, a plain prefab plastic cubicle with a counter and open front. It rather resembled a ticket booth at a fair. Seated at the cluttered desk was the bedraggled chief operator, Lloyd Peterson, a pale harried man who either badly needed a haircut or a week's sleep; the matter had never been settled to anybody's satisfaction. Especially for Mr. Peterson.

"Hey, Lloyd," called the news reporter smiling broadly.

"Hi, Rikka. No, Rikka," he said without even glancing up from his encoding. There was a staggering mound of bubble memory computer cards on his left and a much smaller pile at his right. Finished typing on an old battered keyboard, the man took a bubble card from a function slot, placed it atop the small pile, and took a new one from the big batch. As with most clerks in the universe, exactly what he was doing was not readily clear, but he managed to make the task radiate an aura of absolute importance. As if the universe would grind to a halt should he be interrupted.

Collins hid a knowing smirk. Oh, you don't get rid of me that easily, Mr. Peterson, she mentally chuckled.

"By the way," said Rikka, resting a friendly elbow on the

counter. "Out of curiosity, what did you send to your girlfriend for her birthday yesterday?"

Instantly, the encoding stopped and a frightened face rose into view. "Bloody hell!" cried Peterson in anguish. "I forgot! Again!"

"Oh, you workaholics," soothed the news reporter. "However, like a good friend I assumed the worst and sent her a nice card with your forged signature, some live flowers, a five-pound box of those Belgium chocolates she likes so much, and a copy of an appropriate Lord Tennyson love poem."

The man just sat there, relief and terror fighting for possession of his features.

"Now, if you want, I can always tell her you simply forgot," said Rikka, toying with a loose thread on her cuff, "and that a female friend of yours actually sent her those things, but on the other hand, if I was, oh, say, busy elsewhere in the solar system . . ."

With a sigh of resignation, Peterson handed her a pair of bubble cards. "Launch authorization and priority clearance for immediate evac." He offered a sickly smile. "Friends help friends."

Rikka took the cards and stuffed them into a waiting pocket. "Gee, thanks, Lloyd. Guess I owe you this time."

He mumbled something that sounded vaguely like "then don't come back," but the reporter was sure she was mistaken.

Returning calmly to the shuttle, Rikka climbed inside and dogged the hatch shut.

WE MONITORED THE CONVERSATION OVER THE PA SYSTEM, scrolled Deitrich on the main monitor in the dashboard. VERY NICE. MY COMPLIMENTS.

"Thanks," she snapped, climbing into her seat at the control console. "Now let's go. Fast."

In the copilot's chair, Harry glanced up from snapping on his safety harness. "Why the hurry?"

"It's not his girlfriend's birthday."

Filling the corner of the control room, Michelangelo sat in a Gremlin chair and looked down at the tiny humanoids. "Then why did you send her all those gifts," he asked, puzzled.

The humans slowly turned to stare up at the alien.

"I'll explain it to him later," said Jhonny, cutting off the air vents and putting the shuttle on internal life support. The meters hit green and stayed steady.

Trained hands throwing switches and pulling levers, Collins fed the bubble cards into the dashboard console. Deitrich did the rest. "What's our element status?"

Swiveling his chair around, Mike consulted a wall-mounted console. Most of the gauges and meters were in both Esperanto and formal Gremlin, which was strangely reminiscent of ancient Hebrew, to the utter puzzlement and total annoyance of the Arab community.

"The main control elements in the FTL engines have some two hours of service life remaining," rumbled the tech. "Our auxiliary is fresh with a full ten hours and our emergency reserve element has three."

For a moment, Michelangelo contemplated the wonderful FTL engines now under his command. Able to shunt the shuttle to twice the speed of light, the whole of the Sol system was no more than a day's journey away. But the stars were still denied humanity, for despite every possible technological tactic, the control elements of the field generators could not last for longer than thirty-six hours maximum. And with the nearest star system over two light-years away, no ship could carry enough replacement elements to get them anywhere worth going. What a pity. So close and yet so far. It was no wonder that humans drank so much. What surprised him was their low suicide rate.

"Hydrogen for the Sterling?" asked Rikka.

Roused from his musing, Mike turned to check a meter. "The mains are at ninety-eight percent, warmed to operating release temperature." He would have preferred to physically thumb the tank to be sure, but the vessel was not designed for Gremlin techs. Gauges can get stuck, but acoustics never lie. Swiveling, he consulted another readout. "Reserve tanks of liquid hydrogen are ninety percent full of ninety-nine percent pure. Insulation is good. Vapor values are stable."

The readings on the control panel matched perfectly those called out by the tech. "Roger that, Mike."

Holding a phone to his head, Mike minutely adjusted a dial and listened to the sound of the engines in the aft compartment with a trained ear. Functioning well within operational limits, although it did seem as if they could use a new muffler. Did Midas have a base on the moon yet?

"Chemical fuel?"

"H$_2$O$_2$ tanks are full, solid fuel rods are locked in place, and I just started the coffee maker."

FUEL FOR THE CREW, scrolled Deitrich.

"The man's good," noted Harry, running a preliminary check on the navigational computer.

Suddenly, a pale, harried face appeared on the main monitor.

"Hold it, you con artist!" raged Lloyd, flecks of foam on his lips. "My girlfriend's birthday isn't until next month!"

"All clear?" asked Snyder frantically, glancing out both the sideview windows.

ALL CLEAR, reported Deitrich, doing a fast sweep of the launch bay with maser and radar.

"Launch!" cried Rikka, hitting the ignition button.

And almost as fast as it had arrived earlier today, the QSNT shuttle shot out of the dock and into space. The sonic fold that held in the atmosphere of the station offered no more resistance than Lloyd.

Trailing flame, the white ship streaked past incoming vessels, marking buoys, and lumbering transports.

"Going Fatal in five," counted Harry calmly. "Four . . . three . . . two . . . one."

Calmly Snyder pressed a large red button. There was a momentary blurring of the control room around them, then all was normal. Except that Media and Luna were gone, replaced by the endless black of interplanetary space.

"Setting the collision deflectors for automatic," garbled Collins, stifling a yawn.

"Coffee?" offered Jhonny, unstrapping his harness.

"Sleep," countered Harry, rubbing his face. "We have hours till we reach Koop, and I strongly suggest that we put in some sack time. It's been a busy day and we have lots to do tomorrow."

"Agreed," yawned Rikka openly. "Forty winks sounds good."

"What can I do," asked Michelangelo, hunching down to speak to his comrades directly. "I recently slept and am not tired."

"Keep Deitrich company and learn the ship. If something breaks, we want you on it, ASAP. Harry runs Navigation, I handle the sensors and secondary piloting. Jhonny is quartermaster and you handle the engines."

"Ah, the engines," cooed the alien, lovingly running his paws against each other. "My people do not have hyper-speed engines."

"We call 'em Fatal," explained Jhonny. "As in F, T, L."

A shaggy nod. "An excellent name. One should always be aware that the fatality of organic life is similar to the time limit set on the control elements of the engines. All must die when the predestined time arrives. It is a happy thought."

Everybody stared at the big tech.

"Of course, it also sounds very pretty," he added hastily.

As the rest of the team wearily trundled off to bed, Michelangelo adjusted the engineering console to buzz a warning should anything unusual occur and proceeded to prowl about the control room and cargo bay familiarizing himself with the vessel.

As the Venusian ambulance drove off into the crowded city streets of Annihilation City, Hardcopy and Sunshine dusted off their tattered jumpsuits. Behind them burned the decimated ruins of the ThunderBay Danger Club; the crackling flames wildly licking at the distant Armorlite dome covering the city.

Nearby, a team of fire fighters stood idly by the pumpers and discussed the relevance of doing their job as compared to the noteworthy social service of letting this enclave of pyrotechnic nutcases burn to the ground. There was no general consensus, so the debate continued.

"You do realize that we have been tricked," cursed Hardcopy.

"Agreed," said Sunshine, fingering a laser hole in her jumpsuit that almost displayed too much torso. "Okay, where did they really go?"

Jason Hardcopy plucked a dagger from his sleeve and tossed it on the pile of broken weapons lying on the cracked sidewalk. Feh. Bad balance. "Elementary, my dear, Sunshine. If you wanted to trick a competitor into going into the wrong place, which direction would you send them off?"

"The total opposite." Her black and blue eyes went round. "Ah-HA!"

"But, boss, what's the opposite of Venus?" asked the camera-op, returning from behind the FreshAir machine where he had retreated during the very early stages of the donnybrook. Hey, the sign on the door had been in plain Esperanto: "No Knives, No

Guns, No Service." Although, he had to admit it, it was the most unique meaning of a club's weapons policy that he had ever encountered.

Activating their pocket-docs, Jason and Susan scowled at him.

"Venus is named after the goddess of love," explained Sunshine rudely, as the medicinal robot crawled over her head picking out shards of glass. "So that means they really went to the planet named after the god of war."

"Earth?" asked the man, scratching his head. Born a Unitarian he wasn't very cognizant of these obscure religious deities.

"Mars, you idiot!" roared Hardcopy, keeping motionless so the doc on his forearm could finish stitching a nasty gash shut.

"And if they sent us to the most violent place on Venus, then they went to the most peaceful on Mars!"

"The Vatican, or Koop Memorial?"

"Vatican! What could there possibly be at Koop?"

"Exactly!"

"Okay. Mars, and then Koop. Just to be sure."

"Good thinking!"

"Child's play, my good Hardcopy."

"The Pope of Mars," repeated the camera-op, aghast. "That gentle, quiet man who once said that rabid dogs, the Free Police, and news reporters are the only creatures exempt from the Fifth Commandment of 'Thou shall not kill'?!"

"Exactly."

"Taxi!" shouted the man, stepping into the busy street, heedless of the traffic that roared and zoomed all around him. "Taxi!"

As a vehicle screeched to a halt, the QINS reporters grabbed him under the arms and hauled the camera-op into the cab along with themselves.

"Space dock!" snapped Hardcopy, throwing the driver a fifty.

"And step on it!" added Sunshine as the vehicle zigzagged its way into the tumultuous stream of traffic. "We're off to see the Pope of Mars!"

"No . . . !"

CHAPTER NINE

FINISHED WITH HIS cursory prowling of the shuttle, Mike grinned in triumph as he solved the mystery of why they had a ton of rock onboard. Deuced clever, actually.

Returning to Engineering, the technician cycled a chair from the deck, then another and another until he finally found the one designated for him. The nameless vessel was amazing, it was so exactly like the one that had greeted his people as they disembarked upon arrival. The crafts were identical. He had only been here for about an hour and already he knew the intimate details of its operations backward. However, there was still a very important question on his mind.

"Deitrich?" the alien asked of the ship around him.

YES? scrolled a wall monitor.

"Where would I sleep?"

IN THE CREW QUARTERS UNDERNEATH THE CARGO BAY. I HAD A SLEEP-ING PALLET FOR A FAMILY OF FOUR INSTALLED DURING THE RENOVA-TIONS. SHOULD EVEN BE ROOMY ENOUGH FOR YOU AND A GUEST.

"I wish," snorted the alien. There had been only sixty females in the crew of four hundred on the Gremlin probe. It would be a long time before he enjoyed the pleasure of hot fur again.

PLUS, I REQUISITIONED AN ADDITIONAL SIX HUNDRED KILOGRAMS OF FOOD. A BODY THAT HUGE MUST SUPPORT A HOMERIC APPETITE.

The alien shrugged. "Homeric" was a word he had learned very early in his relationship with the tiny humans. Along with Hercules, Goliath, Samson, and Ek!

"Any apples?" he asked eagerly.

NATURALLY. BUT NO CHOCOLATE, ONLY HERBAL TEA AND DECAF COF-FEE.

Mike licked his chops. It wasn't sex, but apples ran a definite close second. Yum.

"No problem. I have no wish to get stiff and miss out on all the excitement."

YEAH, RIKKA AND THE GANG DO LEAD INTERESTING LIVES. I AM KEPT PRETTY BUSY PATCHING THIS OLD SHUTTLE BACK INTO WORKING ORDER EVERY FEW WEEKS. THANK GOD YOU'RE HERE TO HELP NOW.

A thought occurred to the technician. "Deitrich, if you control the entire vessel, then why do they need me along?"

MOSTLY FOR EVA ASSIGNMENTS, scrolled the monitor. ONBOARD I PRETTY MUCH RUN EVERYTHING. BUT THERE ARE A FEW TASKS THAT ARE AWKWARD, OR IMPOSSIBLE, FOR ME TO DO ALONE.

Interesting. "Such as?"

WELL . . . I HAVE GREAT DIFFICULTY IN DOING MAINTENANCE ON THE MACHINERY THAT SUSTAINS ME. NEGATIVE PSYCHIC FEEDBACK, THE SCIENTISTS CALL THE EFFECT. GIVES ME ONE HELL OF A BRAINACHE.

Instantly, the technician's instincts flared. "Anything in particular that needs immediate adjusting?"

YES! MY VOCAL BROADCAST UNIT. I'M MIGHTY TIRED OF SCROLLING EVERY DAMN MESSAGE.

Standing, Mike pulled a probe from his vest. "Okay, show me where the schematics are kept. I'll get busy."

BLESS YOU. BUT THE CIRCUITS ARE DIRECTLY CONNECTED TO THE MAINS. REPAIRS CAN'T BE DONE WHILE WE ARE TRAVELING AT FATAL SPEEDS.

And when they got to Ganymede there wouldn't be any free time to do the work. "Then we have no duties to perform at the present?"

NOT FOR THE NEXT 30 MINUTES. EXCEPT ONE.

"What is it?"

TELL ME ABOUT YOUR WORLD. IT'S AS CLOSE TO STAR TRAVEL AS I AM EVER GOING TO GET.

Michelangelo smiled. Ah! The technician got this from almost every human he encountered. The story of their arrival had been told endlessly in the media for the past thirty years. But the *aaraatings* of the Gremlin probe were still hounded with endless inquiries about the homeworld and what it was like. Hmm, there might be big bucks in an alien travelogue. And Mike had some photos from home he could use. But, not that awful shot of him as a child on the bearskin rug. And then there was always the conference route, talk shows, and possibly a movie deal . . .

PLEASE? asked Deitrich, mistaking the silence for reticence, and a large bowl full of apples scuttled into the room. On the side was the inscription "stolen from The Horny Toad, please return and be executed."

Chuckling, the big alien took a pawful and reclined in his chair. Business later. "Our world was named Earth, like your own," he began, munching, eyes unfocused in memory. "But then, I suppose, that all worlds are called that in the beginning. Later we chose an arbitrary name of Nestal. But to me it will always be *uhrta,* Earth."

SAME HERE, AMIGO. I THINK TERRA IS SILLY.

Terra? Oh, yes, the official name of the human homeworld. "We are nowhere near as populated as human earth. At the peak our population reached twenty-five million."

GEEZ, WE GOT CITIES WITH MORE THAN THAT.

"Yes, I know," shuddered the alien, brushing imaginary humans off his fur with the back of a paw. "Which is why I took a job in space. I need to earn a living, and at least out here I have room to breathe."

HA! OH, YOU MEANT THAT? SORRY.

Graciously, the tech accepted the apology. And more apples. The empty bowl scuttled away for a refill. "The most notable feature of my homeworld are the three staggered rings set on a diagonal to the equator, a fact that simply drives our mathematicians insane trying to explain." Mike chuckled to himself remembering the TV debates on the how and why of the off-center rings. Just prior to the departure of the probe, the scholarly talks had degenerated into weekly fistfights, where the only limitation was no hitting in the mouth. That way the battling scholars could keep arguing their pet theories straight into unconsciousness.

"Anyway, the first and third bands about our world are mostly water, but the second is primarily rock. Ore-bearing rock perfect for large-scale mining operations. So, that's where we built our probe, the *Reaching Hand,* up among the rings. Launching was easy."

I'LL BET. A RINGED WORLD. MUST BE PRETTY AT NIGHT.

Mike glanced out the porthole of the shuttle, watching the discolored stars streak by outside. "Very. Saturn strongly resembles our planet."

Tactfully, Deitrich decided to change the topic. HOW DID YOU CHOOSE EARTH AS A TARGET?

A bestial growl exposed sharp canines. "Our supposedly top scientists said the third world of your sun was perfect for us to colonize. Air we could breathe, water to drink, plants we could eat, and most importantly no sentient life."

HAHAHAHA! "OOPS" I THINK IS THE OPERATIVE WORD HERE.

Privately, the alien would have used a slightly stronger, more vitriolic phrase. "We traveled a hundred light-years only to find our new home already filled to the bursting point. Gone were our dreams of an interstellar empire. I sincerely hope that when the UP message drone arrives, citizens carve the slang word for total incompetent fool into their chest fur with permanent depilatories!"

Hmm, a new curse word. This could come in handy. WHAT IS THAT WORD?

"Putz," Mike sneered around a mouthful of apple.

REALLY? BUT THAT'S OUR WORD ALSO! WHAT A BIZARRE COINCIDENCE.

And for a moment, the two space travelers silently pondered the incredible cosmic mystery.

EVER DREAM OF GOING HOME? asked the MainBrain eventually.

"Often," chewed the alien, removing his tiny glasses and polishing them on a forearm. "Ah, to run barefoot through the forests of the Etal Plains! To sun on the mountainside beaches of South Foolgara!

"Near the big rock that looks like a fish," explained Mike needlessly, replacing his eyeware.

OF COURSE, scrolled Deitrich politely. WHERE ELSE?

Slumping, Mike hung his furry head. "But it is impossible. The *Hand* was fueled for sixty years and it took us forty to get here. Even with suspended animation, we cannot return."

Just then, the heavily ladened bowl returned.

"And before you suggest it," said the technician quickly, gesturing at the empty room with half an apple. "Human ships operate on entirely different principles. To convert our vessel to your power systems . . ." He shrugged. "We might as well build a whole new ship. It would be much easier and faster."

BUT SURELY YOUR PLANET IS WONDERING ABOUT THE RESULTS OF THE COLONIZATION ATTEMPT.

Mike swallowed the core. "Oh, the United Planets sent a message drone off to our homeworld. But once again, without Fatal drives, the journey is forty years there and forty back." The alien faced a blank section of the hull. "So I will be very, very dead before it returns."

Quickly, Deitrich changed the conversation. BY THE WAY, WHAT DID YOU DO ON THE SHIP?

"Janitor," came the amazing reply.

WHAT?!

Bemused, Mike raked a paw across his face. "Our word does not directly translate into Esperanto. To humans, a janitor is an unskilled worker who performs menial cleaning. To us, a janitor is directly responsible for maintaining every function of the spaceship. They must be able to tune, repair, and build a replacement unit if necessary for everything onboard.

"Perhaps the term 'maintenance engineer' is more appropriate."

HMM.

"Deitrich?"

YES?

"What were you . . . before?"

The MainBrain privately chuckled. That was delicately phrased. Ah well, turnabout was fair play. WAS, AM, AND WILL BE A PILOT. AS FOR DETAILS, I WAS A MAJOR IN THE NORTH AMERICAN AIR FORCE, AND A TOP ASTRONAUT FOR NASA, BACK IN 2180 WHEN NASA WAS STILL UNDER GOVERNMENT SUPERVISION. BEFORE PRESIDENT HARVIN, BLESSED BE HIS NAME, MADE THE AGENCY AN INDEPENDENT ENTITY.

"Explain, please?" asked Mike, puzzled, combing his snout.

Deitrich hunted for the correct words. NASA, THE SPACE AGENCY OF NORTH AMERICA, WAS A DIVISION OF THE GOVERNMENT AND THUS HAD TO OPERATE BY GOVERNMENT GUIDELINES. SUCH AS: IT COULDN'T MAKE A PROFIT, OR EVEN PATENT THE DEVICES IT INVENTED.

"I do not think I have that straight," said Michelangelo, leaning forward toward the hull speaker, elbows on knees. "The makers of inventions could not have a patent on their own creations, because then they would make a profit? But what did they do? Pay others for the rights to use their own developments?"

EXACTLY!

"But wouldn't the others have paid money that would have helped for the advance into space?"

SURE.

"Then I definitely do not understand."

JOIN THE CLUB.

Anger overwhelmed confusion, but then reason dispensed with both. It was only a familial expression of solidarity.

ANYWAY, I WAS AN ASTRONAUT WHEN NASA WENT ON THE FREE MARKET. IT WAS A REAL ZOO AT FIRST, BUT SLOWLY I STARTED BUILDING UP CONTACTS AND CLIENTELE. SOON I WAS ABLE TO RIG A LOAN FROM WILKES'S SAVINGS AND LOAN TO START MY OWN INTERPLANETARY FERRYING COMPANY, SPACE FOR HIRE.

An appropriate chuckle.

AH! WHAT A LIFE! FOR THE NEXT FEW DECADES, I HAULED LIQUID STEEL FROM MERCURY, ICE FROM SATURN, PASSENGERS FROM EARTH, AND DIRT FROM NEPTUNE. INTERESTINGLY ENOUGH, SOME OF THE MUTATED BIOLOGICALS THE SOIL CONTAINED LED TO THE DEVELOPMENT OF THE MARTIAN YOUTH DRUG.

"Yes, I have heard about that substance. But detailed information seems to be most scarce. What can you tell me about this drug?"

BUDDY, NOBODY CAN TELL ANYBODY ANYTHING ABOUT THE MARTIAN YOUTH COMPOUND. I DON'T EVEN THINK THAT GOD KNOWS HOW THE STUFF IS MADE. AND IF HE DID, ROYAL MARTIAN SECURITY WOULD KILL HIM TO PROTECT THE IMPERIAL INCOME.

Idly, Mike scratched at his hard belly with the sound of nails on concrete. The youth drug had little interest to him as the medicine would not work on his species. Besides, death was inevitable. Why fight it? Humans were just so . . . defiant.

"So what happened?" he prompted.

WELL, I WAS ON A TSD RUN, THAT'S TIME/SPEED/DISTANCE, WHERE THE SOONER YOU ARRIVE WITH THE CARGO THE MORE YOU ARE PAID.

"Understood. I have a semi-cousin who does such things for a local snood factory."

Quickly, Deitrich accessed the word. Ah, hairnets. Okay, that made sense. The Gremlins probably mass-produced the thing by the metric ton. And going to the barber . . . !

ANYWAY, scrolled Deitrich, returning to the subject. THERE WAS AN ACCIDENT.

Patiently, Mike waited.

BUT IT WASN'T MY FAULT, denied the Brain. I SWEAR, THAT ISLAND
JUST JUMPED OUT IN FRONT OF MY FREIGHTER! AND I WASN'T REALLY
SPEEDING. WELL, NOT MUCH ANYWAY. NOR WAS I DRUNK. JUST OVER-
WORKED. BESIDES, I NEVER WAS AN ATMOSPHERIC PILOT. SPACE IS THE
PLACE!

Not a fool himself, the alien knew lying when he read it, but decided to keep mum. Everybody had secrets. Even him.

BUT WHAT THE HELL, WHO CAN COMPLAIN? THERE'S LOTS OF WORK
OUT THERE FOR MAINBRAINS. WE'RE CHEAPER THAN COMPUTERS, UP-
GRADE FASTER, LAST LONGER, HAVE GREATER FLEXIBILITY, AND AREN'T
BOUND BY THE THREE LAWS OF ROBOTICS.

Whatever those were.

HOWEVER, YOU KNOW WHAT THE WORST PART WAS?

Losing his body wasn't the worst part? What did they do? Make
him watch? "Pray tell."

THE DAMN HAWAIIAN POLICE SITED ME WITH 392 TRAFFIC VIOLA-
TIONS . . . AT MY OWN FUNERAL! HOW HUMILIATING.

"Quotas," nodded the alien sagely. The bane of drivers everywhere. Along with speed bumps and cheery morning disc jockeys.
Bleh.

YEAH. I AM STILL PAYING OFF THE FINE IN MONTHLY INSTALLMENTS.
Pause. THIS IS ONE TIME WHEN A SPEEDING TICKET ACTUALLY COST
MORE THAN AN ARM AND A LEG!

As HAHAS scrolled across the monitor, Mike squirmed uncom-
fortably in his huge chair. Their talk had raised an interesting point.
And since the alien wasn't exactly sure about the proper procedure
for a request like this, he simply plowed directly in. "Deitrich, may
I see you?"

The laughter stopped abruptly.

A PICTURE OF ME, BEFORE? asked the pilot for clarification. OR ME,
AS IN—NOW?

"Yes. You now. If it does not violate some social or religious ta-
boo I am unaware of."

WELL, NO . . . IT'S ONLY THAT NOBODY HAS EVER ASKED BEFORE.
There was a crackle of static on the monitor. I'M NOT SURE THAT I
CAN ANYMORE . . . OH, THERE IT IS! SURE, MIKE. HOLD ON.

A section of the floor lifted an inch and then broke apart, the two
sections sliding into the deck. Exposed was a seamless cube of

metal completely filling the cavity. Slowly, the cube was elevated to chest height, then a red band of light encircled the upper section of the column and arched over the top. There was the briefest stink of ozone. As the glow faded, hair-thin lines were discernible. With a hydraulic hiss, the segmentations disengaged and swung backward. Inside was a steel framework over a fibrous dome of spongy material. Mechanically, the framework lifted up on telescoping support rods until it was well clear of the dome. Then the protective cushion separated into pie slices that retracted into the column of machinery underneath and suddenly clouds of lemon-scented steam obscured everything.

As the fog wafted away, there was exposed a transparent dome covered with moisture. In gradual stages the condensation evaporated and now visible inside a triple thick covering of military Armorlite was a pulsating human brain. Tubes and wires linked and ran everywhere.

On the side of the case was a pretty blue ribbon and an old faded newspaper clipping whose headline read: PRIZEWINNING CAULIFLOWER DISAPPEARS FROM THE TACOMA STATE FAIR. POLICE HUNT CONTINUES.

Michelangelo goggled at the notice, then roared in a wild guffaw. And he had been afraid of offending the pilot!

"Lord, I've waited a long time for somebody to see that gag," chuckled a speaker on the pedestal. "Hey, I may only be a brain, but I still have a sense of humor."

Michelangelo gasped. "You can speak!"

"Only on this one monitor," sighed the four-pound astronaut, conveying more emotional range than the technician would have thought possible.

A glitter of gold caught Mike's attention and on the side of the machinery he spied a tiny set of gold rocket-'n'-wings. Inscribed under the flaming spaceship was the name Lt. Major Uther Deitrich.

"Uther?" queried the alien.

"OH, pleeeze! I hate that name! Deitrich is fine. Thanks."

Going to his paws and knees, the technician got closer to the dome and inspected the miniature life support systems. "Is there any pain or discomfort?"

"Hell, no. I love it in here."

"Really?"

The speaker gave a snort. "Are you kidding? I have full virtual reality mode. By modifying my own sensory input I can create my own world. Complete with sound, smell, taste, the whole enchilada. At this very moment, I'm in my mansion at the beach, wearing silk pajamas, sitting in my favorite chair, drinking a cold can of beer that never empties, with Marilyn Monroe giving me a manicure and Dolly Parton cutting my hair, while I watch you eat apples on a video monitor."

Delicately, Mike ran a taloned finger along a set of coaxial superconductors leading from the rheostat to a transmodem. "And how do you fly the shuttle?"

"Easy. I step into the control room next door and climb into the pilot's seat. Mine is a perfect duplicate to the real one in the ship."

Standing erect, the alien tech exclaimed, "Well, I am sorry that the doctors could not save your body in the island disaster. On the other paw, I do think we may become good friends. I have a half brother also a pilot and—"

"Huh?" exploded the speaker. "I wasn't hurt in the crash. My copilot, Yolanda, and me jettisoned without a scratch! This was the story of how I joined QSNT. Wilkes covered my mound of tickets and I'm paying him off from my weekly salary."

"Such as it is," added Deitrich softly.

Now the alien was totally confused.

"B-b-but, then how did that happen?" stammered Michelangelo, pointing a talon at the bare lump of pulsating human tissue under glass.

"Actually, it's fascinating! First they removed the hair and skin from my head and then using a surgical chain saw formed a lateral incision along the frontal—"

"Why was this done?" corrected the tech hastily.

A long meaningful pause.

"Never," said the Brain. "*Ever,* draw to an inside straight."

CHAPTER TEN

WITH A BLURRING effect, the stars on the forward monitor shifted from a reddish hue to the original colors and the shuttle slowed to sublight speed, then stopped.

"Scanner horizon reads clean," announced Harry, manipulating the navigation controls.

"Opening cargo bay doors," said Jhonny, typing in the command on his keyboard. Surrounding them, the controls of the cockpit hummed and blinked in stately procession.

"Roger," muttered the voice of Collins.

Deep inside the bowels of the QSNT shuttle, Rikka was busy with her own work. For her part in today's charade, the reporter was dressed in a chrome yellow jumpsuit with lots of extra pockets and Velcro flaps in the oddest places.

Barely squeezed into the normally roomy cargo bay of their vessel was another smaller spaceship. About the dimensions of a planetary luxury car, the mining scooter was a brilliant neon green, rendering it easily detectable among the asteroids. The complex control panel wrapped around the one seat, with painfully honest sanitary facilities and a masseuse that could relax any but the most ardent space traveler. A one-person ship designed to allow a sole operator to work the debris fields of space for months at a time. Its entertainment library was larger than the computer space given to the navigational log. Of course, it was difficult to get lost when you could still see the sun.

At the nose was a set of six extendable robot arms to do the work of coring and sampling asteroids. Underneath the cramped living quarters was the cargo hold where rich mineral-bearing chunks would be stored until a planetary official could assay the ore, officially register the find, and assign taxes. Miners often dreamed of using the coring drills on other than asteroids.

Michelangelo had been surprised to discover that traditionally precious metals were not the target materials of the miners. Since the advent of industrial asteroid mining, gold, platinum, and silver had lost their vaunted status of rarity and became merely useful conductors and pretty jewelry. It was the transuranic elements that fetched the big money: vallidium, thullium, pallidium, etc. Even small amounts could make a months-long trip well worth the trouble and expense.

Since miners habitually worked alone, the vessel even had minimal shields and a modest arsenal. These were a needed protection from the Free Police. Who were neither. "Pirates" was the correct description, but that term invoked images of bearded men with peg legs and cutlasses, drinking rum and walking a plank on the Spanish Main, not deadly serious raiders in homemade powerarmor and converted ore transports whose weapons and forcefields gave the military a real fight. Worse, the brigands often took prisoners. And ransom was only one of the possibilities for a captive. There were many other uses.

Many others.

The reward for the death of a member of the Free Police was a year's income. Tax free. The capture of one alive: five years. The destruction of a mother ship had no bounty as the noteworthy event had never been accomplished by anybody outside of a major military expedition.

But after their great destruction at Io, the sightings of the Free Police had dropped drastically and they were now considered only a minor nuisance. Officially, however, it was still a misdemeanor punishable by a stiff fine to meet a Free Police and not even try to kill him.

Opening the weapons locker, Rikka inspected her collection of offensive ironmongery. The weapon rack held an assortment of knives, a Smith & Wesson 2mm needler, a Wilkes Corp. Peacemaker stun pistol, and a Bedlow Universal, not a weapon, per say, since the energy beam could be altered to do welds, heat food, sear wounds, flash messages, and, in an emergency, even give a fair to middling tan.

Choosing the Bedlow, she set the pistol to charge in its bracket and closed the sliding panel.

"Fuel levels are at fifty percent," reported Michelangelo, closing a bleed-off value. "Fatal elements are drained to forty-five minutes of flight and food stock supplies are depleted to register a journey of two weeks."

"Ready," she called, flipping switches and feeling the enginettes under her rump vibrate in response. Hee-hee. It tickled!

"We rendezvous at Koop in thirty-five minutes," said the voice of Harry from her ceiling speaker. "If you're not already there, we'll come arunning."

"And bring a casket," added Rikka to herself.

"Eh? What?"

"Oh, nothing."

On her waldo monitor, Collins saw the outer doors of the shuttle cycle open wide, and felt the holding clamps release the scooter.

"It's showtime," she announced, biting the top of her tongue.

"Tones and bars, kid."

"Luck, chief."

"Couldn't we ask them very, very politely for the information?" wheedled Mike plaintively.

As a response, Rikka hit the ignition. With a lurch, the scooter was blown free of the shuttle and darted off into space.

Lacking a MainBrain, the woman had to pilot the craft by herself, but the old skills came back easily enough. Guess what they said was true, flying a spaceship was like having sex on a bicycle: a difficult skill to learn and not easily forgotten.

On her aft screen, the QSNT shuttle shimmered and disappeared.

She wanted to be in the direct proximity of Koop for them to rescue her, but not so near that it seemed suspicious. This one time, she did not want to make any news. Just damage her ship and get rescued.

The distance was short, only fifteen Fatal minutes and Rikka was at the location chosen. Close enough to dictate a response from Koop, but not unreasonably so as to warrant questions as to what was a mining scooter doing in this quadrant of space?

Carefully sealing the wrist coupling on the gauntlets of her spacesuit, and making damn sure the helmet was close by, Rikka, readjusting the focus on the Bedlow, closed her eyes and shot at the floor.

Searing pain erupted in her foot and the reporter screamed as a sudden whistling filled the cabin of the tiny ship. Holy prack, she hit her own foot!!!!

Alarms sounded and a purple foam began bubbling from the edges of the hole to retard the escape of air. Tears of pain blinding her eyes, Rikka had to admit it was a nice touch of realism. Nobody could believe that she would vap a toe for a disguise. A person would have to be an *idiot* to do that!

Warm on one side and cold on the other, the foam hardened into a concrete blob and the whistling stopped as abruptly as it had begun. The indicator lights of life support were going disco as the machine raced to equalize pressure and temperature. The flexible cable arm of the pod's doc snaked out of a wall and attached itself to her arm. Then a second, third, and fourth wiggled out adhering to her foot.

Damn the machine! At this rate, she wouldn't need the assistance of Koop! Okay, time for another weapon malfunction. Then inspiration hit and the reporter started draining her laser into the wall-mounted doc.

"Help!" she called on Z channel 1. "This is the mining scooter *Sierra Madre*. My doc has malfunctioned and is attacking me!"

That should get everybody's attention.

Zap! Zap! Purple goo was everywhere in the ship, clogging the holes in the hull and tiny droplets floating free in the air like some weird hallucinogenic delusion of purple rain. Hmm, nice title for a song.

Just then, a fast series of blips appeared and disappeared on her Z scanner. More were spotted as a barrage of Hunter drones scattered about in space trying to locate her tiny ship. Damn, she had forgotten about that, the doc had an emergency signal generator inside. Destroying the doc also zapped her best chance at being located. A cold shiver took her spine. Oh, dear, this could get ugly real fast unless the folks at Koop were as good as reported.

Then a spherical drone jerked into a stationary position immediately outside her bow window.

"Here-here-here-here-here," screamed the drone in mindless radio delight.

Starting to feel woozy from blood loss and oxygen deprivation, the news reporter threw it a kiss and prepared to be rescued.

Sometime later, Rikka awoke on a gurney in the Emergency Room of Koop Memorial. It resembled the ER of any major hospital, with the sole exception that all four walls were adorned with equipment and patients.

Next to the reporter, a stately man in the classic white of his profession was probing her body with an advanced model of a Watch-Dog military scanner. "Mild decompression, exposure, a laser hole in the left foot," the doctor said to his collar mike. "Cauterized nicely. No danger of infection. Patient was wearing white socks. A smart move. Minor blood loss. No trauma. No shock. No deprivation of oxygen to the brain. Oh, hello, miss."

"Hi, ya, Doctor," mumbled Collins, making damn sure to use the full version of the word. For some reason, physicians were very touchy about being called Doc.

"What happened," he asked, cool fingers testing her pulse in an unnecessary, but pleasing ritual.

"Was on my way to Earth to sell my load, when the doc . . ." She waved her arms about wildly. "Oh, God, the doc!"

While the human physician did his best to comfort the distraught woman, the nurse walked into the examination room.

"What's in the hold?" asked the physician softly.

"Minerals and rocks," said the nurse. "Can't tell if they're actually ore-bearing, but there is certainly no drugs or contraband. She's a miner."

The doctor tried not to pout. Darn, not a member of the Free Police. Oh, well, there went the new sauna for the med lounge.

Slightly woozy, Rikka bit a lip at the hushed conversation. Geez, was she an amateur not to have something in the hold? A laugh escaped her and the doctor mistook it as a groan of pain.

"Easy, madam," consoled the physician, holding a hypo to her throat. There was a short hiss and everything went numb.

"Say, aren't you Rikka Collins, ace reporter of the SNT?"

Panic hit her belly with acid, as a meter on the WatchDog hit the red line.

"Huh? Me? Nyah. Just look like her. Get that all the time."

The physician offered a secret smile. "No, you're Collins. I watch the show constantly. Hey, what are you doing here? An undercover assignment for the station?"

"Doctor, you got it wrong," she tried again. "No! Really!"

Ah, the lady did protest too much. Proof positive. In a consoling manner, he patted her on the arm. "Well, don't worry. We'll keep your accident and identity a secret. Koop handles lots of celebrities and nobody ever knows they visited. Wouldn't want to disrupt the hospital, would we?"

Straw. Camel. Snap! Exhausted, doped, frozen, and shot, adrenaline flooded her body, drastically overloading her weakened state, and she fainted.

Puzzled, the physician bent closer to examine the woman. Now what could have caused that? It was almost as if he told her truly terrible news. Hmm.

With its pristine hull displaying only a civilian ID number, the QSNT shuttle landed nice and quiet at the Koop Memorial Space Dock and Souvenir Stand.

Ever moving to maintain its tenuous position between the speeding worlds, Koop was located at the apex of an equilateral triangle 'twixt Earth and Mars, set above the plane of the elliptic. Far out of the path of commercial traffic, yet within easy commute of all the major worlds, especially the island nation of Japan on Earth with its state-of-the-art medical facilities in cloning, bionics, cryogenis, and fourteen tournament quality golf courses.

The hospital was built in a series of cylindrical tubes set inside one another like concentric circles. The outermost rested relatively motionless for ease of patient access while the innermost ring moved at a velocity that gave the equivalent of a full Earth gravity. Four massive tokamacs powered the hospital even though at its heaviest draw only two were needed. Safety was paramount here.

Most of the structure was occupied by research laboratories. It was in this establishment that the concept of a MainBrain had been perfected, and the Gremlins were quarantined when they first arrived. Work was done here on the next generation of androids, truly organic beings with no artificial components and some hush-hush work on the mythical procedure of cloning.

One entire floor was designated for the advancement of pocket-docs and another for the purification and improvement of the Martian Youth Drug. A third dealt entirely with terraforming and its almost incalculable environmental impacts. Koop's Eco-Zoo contained the sole surviving members of the nigh extinct Martian dog-sponge and a genuine, card-carrying Communist.

Politically unbiased, owning allegiance and fidelity to no nation or world, Koop was truly neutral territory. Even the Free Police had been graciously admitted for emergency medical repairs, until that fateful day when they tried to take over the hospital; a traitorous act that prompted a unilateral military retaliation and the utter annihilation of their Io moon base.

Since then, even if escaped prisoners from the Rasputin Asylum for the Criminally Insane and Socially Ambivalent stop for assistance, they say "please" and "thank you," pay for the service received, and leave as quickly as possible. Often leaving a fifteen percent gratuity.

In the spacious reception area of the space hospital, an elderly man in a brown worsted jumpsuit with matching fedora hat used a cane to slowly hobble to the front desk. His face was careworn, deeply etched with lines, his bulbous nose red from decades of too much alcohol and his teeth far too perfect to be a product of nature.

All in white, the nurse greeted him with a brief but dazzling smile.

"How may I help you, sir?" she asked.

Harry smacked his gums and blinked. "My name is Horace B. Horace. I'm here to see my niece," he said, his ancient voice cracking.

"And is her name the same?"

Oops. What was the name Rikka had chosen again. Oh, yes.

"Gilman," he cackled. "Laura Anne Gilman."

Expert hands began riffling through the physical array of patient cards.

"The middle name is Anne," the oldster repeated. "With an 'E,' but it's silent, just like the 'E' in Rotary Club."

A weak smile forced its way into existence on the nurse, but just then a hairy behemoth in a hand-tailored Pierre Cardin, Jr., jumpsuit darkened the reception desk.

"Attend me," rumbled the huge Gremlin. "I am here to immediately speak with your superior."

"If you will wait just a minute, sir," started the nurse.

"No, I will not!" countered Michelangelo. "My name is Raymond Descartes of Tick-Doc Manufacturing. I have been given to understand that one of our portable medical units has reportedly malfunctioned and I demand to see the physician in charge of this facility at once!"

As if by magic, another nurse appeared behind the desk.

"Is there a problem?" she asked in a belligerent tone daring anybody to challenge her.

"No," said the trainee nurse.

"Yes," said Michelangelo rudely.

"Hi," said Harry, offering a paper bag. "Want a cookie?"

The offer was declined and the two nurses stepped away from the desk to hold a fast conference to ascertain the situation.

"Besides," finished the duty nurse to the trainee, "you should know better than to ever put a Descartes before a Horace."

With a prim snort, she glared at the alien and returned to her own, far less noisy office.

"I'm sorry, but there is no Gilman in residence at the present time," reported the nurse. "Nor has there been any space foot injuries admitted within a fortnight.

"And as for you, sir," she continued, icicles dripping off the last word. "There have been no reported incidents of any malfunctioning, or even a dysfunctioning doc of any caliber. Good-bye."

Stunned, Harry and Mike exchanged knowing glances. For some unknown reason, Koop Memorial was obviously hiding Rikka's presence. This was not according to plan.

"And by the way," inquired the nurse, crossing her arms and scowling. "If we have no record of an accident or admittance, then how do you two know of these events?"

Sweat broke out under his heavy cosmetics and Harry revved his brain to overload for some fancy lying.

"ARGHH!" throated Michelangelo, standing erect and spreading his arms as if to challenge the universe.

What the . . .?

"I'm about to *spartoone*!" cried the alien, doubling over and clutching his stomach. "Gods above and below! The pain! Argh . . ."

"Code Blue," said the nurse to the thin air. Seconds later teams of nurses and physicians poured into the reception area. Michelangelo was thrashing about on the floor, moaning and groaning and generally behaving in a most unseemly manner.

Puzzled, the physicians stared at each other.

"What do we do?"

"I have no idea. I'm a GYN, not an Exobiologist! Didn't think there was any money in it!"

Flipping into the air, Mike hit the floor with a crash that rattled bedpans under patients two floors away and made the ceiling-mounted light fixtures swing. Snarling and gnashing his teeth, the alien began rolling about on the floor *kisvikng* and screaming.

"What is he doing?!"

"I think it's called *kisvikng*."

"E-yuck!"

Four orderlies leaped upon the writhing giant and tried to pin him motionless. Mike rolled away from the moaning bodies and barreled down an intersection.

"The pain!" he howled, disappearing into the distance.

"Code Red!" said a physician into her collar mike upping the situation from Annoying to Drastic. "We have a . . . ah . . . oh, hell. We have a Gremlin about to harpoon, or spartum, I'm not sure what he screamed. I want a division chief of every, repeat EVERY department, at Emergency Room. Stat!"

Soon a crowd of concerned doctors poured from the elevators and doors to gather about the writhing alien. Harry fought the impulse to applaud his friend.

"Take his temperature and blood pressure," ordered a physician.

"How?" asked a nurse, ducking under a fist the size of Montana.

"Tranq him," commanded another.

"With what?" demanded an orderly. "Does Narcolip effect Gremlins?"

"Does he have a pocket-doc?" asked an intern. "That should be set for his species."

Hands reached downward, but Mike moved faster. *CRUNCH!*

"Damn, he just rolled over it!" wailed a nurse.

"But it was a nice try, kid," consoled a doctor.

Suddenly, the ravings of the alien being took on a lower, more incessant tone.

"What is he saying?"

A brave nurse bent closer. "He's asking for something."

"Water? A blanket?"

An intern stepped back. "He's not going to *kisvikng* again, is he?" asked the man in disgust.

"A cupcake!" reported the nurse, finally deciphering the alien mutterings. "We need a cupcake and a pencil!"

Foaming and twitching, Mike moaned a correction.

"A really sharp pencil!"

With everybody's attention elsewhere, Harry slid open an inspection port atop the reception desk computer, dropped in a handful of metallic things, closed the port, and ambled off to assist in the madness.

Inside the computer, the animated chips scurried about finding the boards and circuitry cubes they had been assigned. Then, warming their platinum legs, they sank into position and soldered the connections shut.

On the control board of the QSNT shuttle, a series of tones and squeals announced that they had established contact with the computer network of the hospital.

"Ready?" asked Jhonny, Velcroing shut his skintight camouflage jumpsuit. A bag of identical material was strapped to his chest.

AS I'LL EVER BE, scrolled Deitrich. HERE GOES.

"Luck."

YOU ALSO.

Standing alone in the office of his mansion, Uther Deitrich finished buttoning his uniform jacket closed and briefly inspected himself in the mirror. Tall, clean-shaven, blond, blue eyes, and heavily muscled enough to be a professional weight lifter or the "after" man from the Wilkes Toasted Yogurt Instant Health commercials.

Summoning his resolve, the MainBrain strode into the living room and threw open the front door. Before him was a tunnel of light stretching off into the distance.

The cybernetic Brain walked down the tunnel until reaching a plain plastic door at the other end. This was the mental representation of the superconductor access to the MainBrain of the hospital. All he had to do was keep the other Brain busy for about thirty minutes. Clever conversation, lewd jokes, anything was okay. Deitrich had never before confronted one of his own kind. Hopefully the experience would also be new for the other Brain and mutual examination would consume the time. But the pilot was prepared to eagerly listen to the most boring or inane stories, engage in witty banter or even simulated physical combat. It was the first time the news team had ever needed him on an assignment and Deitrich would be damned if he would let his friends down!

Bracing himself, the pilot knocked loudly. The MainBrain of a hospital should by its own definition be the most boring person in existence. He knocked again. But no matter how weird or pedantic the conversation became he would keep its attention concentrated on him. It would be a battle of wits. A mental chess game played on the infinite field of the human mind augmented by the Virtual Reality of the support computers.

The door opened.

Stepping inside, Deitrich found himself in the presence of a pair of stunningly beautiful Oriental women. Slim and beautiful, they were each dressed in flowing kimonos of gossamer silk, respectively decorated with a dragon and a peacock. The women stood very unnaturally close to each other, their opposing hips jutted sideways and Deitrich had the distinct impression that when they had bodies, they were joined at that point.

Siamese twin MainBrains. Ye God, this was going to be tougher than he had ever imagined.

"Hello," he said, removing his hat.

"We know," said the dragon.

". . . why you are here," said the peacock.

And the dragon lady threw her arms about Deitrich, kissing him passionately on the mouth, while the peacock grabbed hold of his pilot's uniform and tore the cloth from his hard body.

Female gasps of delight. "It has been . . ."

". . . so very long."

"Oh, God!"

". . . so very long!"

* * *

Watching through the cockpit windows, the android spied the security cameras start to take on a random movement in their sweeps. Attaboy, Deitrich! He must be in serious brain-to-brain combat. Kick some butt, guy!

Scrambling out the airlock, Jhonny dashed across the landing bay and hit the wall alongside a door marked "private." Steel fingers plus a number nine probe picked the lock easily and he silently closed the portal behind him.

Glancing at the blueprints displayed on his wrist secretary, the android moved fast and silent down a corridor, skipped down a flight of stairs, and picked the lock on a closet. At the rear of the cubicle was a grillwork easily removed. Wiggling to get inside the shaft beyond, Jhonny shimmied sideways along the conduit counting the intersections.

At the proper point, or so he hoped, Jhonny eased off the lattice and replaced the screen as he stood in the dim hallway. The security cameras up in the corner of the ceiling were still behaving strangely. Good ol' Deitrich. Doing his best for the team. What a man! Give 'em one for me, guy!

Consulting with his camcorder, the android eased through a maze of infrared laser sensors and stood triumphant on the other side. Now facing him was a slab of veined metal. A vault door whose hinges were larger than he.

Opening a service panel in his right forearm, Jhonny hardwired himself to the keypad on the door. He meshed with circuits through the slot for magnetic ID cards easily enough, but the small wall-mounted computer completely refused to recognize his authority. Plus, none of the standard override command codes worked with the lock. Anger welling within him, Jhonny J. Smith threw all of his prodigious will against the dumb brute machine. In a cybernetic fight of mind over machine, an android should have a definite edge because he was both.

The irresistible force of his brain and the immovable object of computer software clashed in a violent swirl of electromagnetic bombardment. The stubborn wall-mounted keypad actually grew warm under the forces Jhonny unleashed in the deadly serious cyber-battle. Deep within the incredible maze of circuitry, molecular doors were forced open and electrons rushed through, as always taking the easiest path. Some doors opened merely at his bold asking. At others, Jhonny had to knock politely first. Stronger barriers flatly refused him entry until they were unlocked. But the android constantly found their magnetic key hidden under a gallium/arsenic doormat. Once more the flood of electrons washed down another electrochemical tunnel with ever increasing speed; turn after turn, circuit by circuit, program to program, language after language, access, confirm, query, acknowledge, ARM, reverse, affirm, IPD, hold, access, reverse, dump, assimilate, dump, access, access, access, success!

With a rumble of thunder, the massive bolts slid free, the EM lock flashed a combination of digits, letters, musical notes, and obscure medical slang. Noiselessly, the twenty-megagram door swung aside.

Disconnecting himself, the panting android eased inside and pursued the vault. File cabinets lined one wall, safe deposit boxes the other. The far wall was blank.

"Bullshit," he said aloud, grinning widely.

Sensitive fingers found the access depressions in the wall and after a few minutes of experimental pressing, the camera-op was rewarded with a loud click as a section of the wall rose out of view exposing a safe.

A safe inside a vault. Yep. That had to be it.

Cracking the combination lock only took a minute, and while he rifled through the papers, his camcorder dutifully recorded everything. Matching the encoded transmission numbers, Jhonny found what what he was looking for in short order. Judiciously, he made copies, then slid the disk into his boot, made another copy of the material that he left inside the camcorder, and then got the hell out as fast as possible.

The recall signal was still buzzing on his wrist secretary when the rest of the team arrived: Rikka hauling a floating IV drip bottle and limping along on her heavily bandaged foot, Harry ripping off his disguise the second he hopped into the airlock, and Michelangelo munching on a cupcake with a pencil behind his ear. Never having physically left the shuttle, Deitrich returned with the snap of a switch cutting the illegal connection between the QSNT vessel and the hospital. However, although the medical status indicators showed the pilot was unharmed, actually in a remarkably relaxed condition, he refused to respond to a computer summons. Jhonny decided to let the poor guy rest. Lord only knows what the brave Brain had been through to maintain the attention of Johnson & Johnson, the Koop Memorial security MainBrains.

"What's happening?" demanded Harry, tearing off his nose and throwing it away. "Did you get the report? What was it?"

"Strap in," commanded Jhonny, priming the main engines.

"Where we going?" asked Rikka, her head bobbing about like a balloon on a string. The silly expression on her face told that the painkillers and regenerative ointments were hard at work.

"Ganymede!" cried the android and the shuttle blasted free of the hospital launch bay.

"Why?" rumbled Mike, wiping crumbs off his tattered jumpsuit. Spartooning just ruined clothes.

The camera-op tossed a bubble card over his shoulder. "Here!"

Harry made the catch with one hand.

As the android maneuvered the shuttle to Fatal position and made the acceleration to light speed, the team glanced over each other's shoulders to read the report scrolling on a display monitor.

"This is a medical report," stated Snyder, reading as fast as possible. "About the autopsy and biochemical analysis on the toxic effects of a secondary radiation field directly linked to . . . Jumping Jesus!"

Grimly, Jhonny nodded. "Close enough."

"The Apocalypse Drive," gasped Rikka, color returning to her cheeks and then abruptly leaving. Suddenly she was stone-cold sober and sincerely wished she wasn't.

"The what?" asked Michelangelo. The hospital report was woefully lacking in this obvious critical bit of information. Why would the United Planets Security Council think an autopsy report was classified information?

As Jhonny was piloting the shuttle, Deitrich was unavailable, and Rikka was trying not to fall over, Harry did the honors of explaining.

Ganymede was the fourteenth moon of Jupiter, nearly the dimension of Earth. Only minor terraforming would have been needed to give the world a breathable atmosphere. But this had not been done, because Ganymede was home for Laboratory 9. Better known as the BoomMoon.

Space Lab 9 is where the HNS laboratories experimented upon FTL drives whose principles of operation were too dangerous to use near inhabited worlds.

Mankind had an FTL drive, but one whose engines could sustain no more than a maximum of fifty-four hours of flight, not enough to even reach the nearest star of Alpha Centuri only two light-years away. At top speed, a mere month distant.

Over a dozen Fatal drives had been invented, but none was safe enough to use, such as Edwin's Magic Ion Drive, so-called because nobody was exactly sure why the silly thing didn't explode every time it was turned on. After exhaustive research, the scientist finally concluded that explosions occurred whenever the technicians wore blue, had the same last name, if it was too hot, too cold, too wet, a month with the letter "R" in it, or simply whenever the nutty engine damn well felt like exploding.

Or the Collier-Hayes Boron Drive, efficient, powerful, cheap, and capable of a prodigious thrust of eighty-five million foot-pounds, but it had an incredibly low specific impulse. It was used for maneuvering L5 colonies into position and little else.

However, the most infamous of them all was the Apocalypse Drive. Originally named the Trans-Dimension Shunt, that ambiguous moniker had long since been filed into trivia. It was known, now and forever, as the Apocalypse Drive. And with good reason.

When the scientist ran the prototype engine in a chained test, there were unexpected side effects. Under full power, the area of effect of the drive far outreached the confines of the model and extended beyond the safety barriers to engulf the control room of the attending scientists. Instantly, they all dropped dead.

With nobody at the controls, the engines ran wild, the lethal drive field of the model constantly expanding and killing every living thing it encountered, including the mold and mildew in the bathroom stalls. It was well on its way to depopulating Ganymede straight down to the bedrock when some bold jackdaffer climbed onboard a test drone and fired himself into space where he managed to get inside the *Sister Sue,* a hundred-million-ton HNS freighter that was delivering parts of a new tokamac to the base. The man hot-wired the engines to ignite and manhandled the navigation controls to violently crash the superfreighter on top of the lethal runaway.

But, incredibly, before the UP Security Council could move in and appropriate the killer engines, in an unprecedented move the HNS scientists decided the drive was too dangerous to let anybody get their hands on and deleted every file, burned every record, and destroyed the remaining prototypes.

"The Apocalypse Drive," rumbled Michelangelo, brushing crumbs off his fancy jumpsuit. "Yes, I had heard something vague about such an invention. Thought it was only a joke like 'fresh vacuum' or a 'snipe hunt.'"

"No, it was real enough," said Rikka in remembrance while playing with her navel. "I read about the story in journalism school."

"I helped cover the story," said Harry, pulling down her hospital gown.

"I was only a gleam in my computer's optical circuitry at the time," said Jhonny.

"Sound asleep in deep space," added Mike, reaching for his more comfortable tool vest and shorts.

U^RTY FHVB, scrolled Deitrich in a mild delirium.

The Apocalypse Drive, mused Snyder. If somebody had rediscovered the deadly propulsion engine, this could explain a lot. Say, the Free Police or some other criminal organization found an old file and were able to cobble together a working model. It would be the equivalent of the American Indians of the 1750s having a nuclear bomb. Or the Incas facing Cortés armed with antigravity laser cannons. They win! End of discussion.

The confrontation would be interesting to observe. But only from an extreme distance.

Maybe somebody was even mass producing the thing in a handgun model. A genuine honest to gosh death ray, unstoppable by the most advanced shield, forcefield, or even kilometers of planetary bedrock. The United Planets would pay millions to get ahold of that weapon and billions, trillions, to stop the Free Police from keeping it. Those loonies were quite dangerous enough without invincible superweapons.

The Apocalypse Drive in the hands of the Free Police.

Shiver.

"Ganymede, it is," agreed Snyder. "That's the only place where we can even hope to discover the true story."

Jhonny grinned. "My thoughts exactly."

Suddenly, the function lights on the control board flickered into an organized pattern announcing the return to consciousness of Lt. Major Uther Deitrich.

"Deitrich, buddy!" called Jhonny anxiously. "What happened, mon ami?"

The monitor crackled and fluttered incomprehensibly for a moment, then cleared abruptly.

I THINK I'M ENGAGED, scrolled the pilot.

CHAPTER ELEVEN

LOCATED DEEP IN a nameless mountain, carved from the living rock by slaves with chisels, was the main meeting room of the top secret headquarters of the Fraternal Order of Free Police. Spacious enough to hold a thousand ship captains as delegates, only half the chairs were filled, and more than a few were adorned with fresh funeral wreaths.

Standing at the head of the room, a grizzled man in laser-slashed spacearmor banged his gauntlet on the column of raw rock serving as a podium.

"Glad you could make it," he spat at them.

"Prack you, too!" chorused the assemblage of captains in ritual greeting.

"To business! Due to the recent loss of our main recruiting center, the ThunderBay Danger Club, and the added inducement of every pracking gunship in existence out there hunting for somebody, quite possibly us, I hereby formerly make the request that we all take an immediate vacation of undetermined length."

Grumblings sounded in the cavern.

"Where?" asked a burly woman, a robotic hand thoughtfully rubbing her acid-scarred chin.

"Here," replied the moderator, pounding the podium again. "Unless you have a taste for UP steel in your guts!"

"I'm no coward," shouted a bearded man, denying the known facts. "But I've seen the armada the worlds are building and I tell you it's pracking dangerous out there!"

After some minor discussion and a summary execution, the motion was passed unanimously. Immediately, they broke out the cards to while away some time.

"Deal," ordered a woman above the corpse-draped table.

Poker cards were dealt.

"I bet his left boot."

"Right glove."

"Helmet."

And the piecemeal game played on into the night.

White-robed trumpeters sounded a heavenly harmonized greeting, while pious monks swung open the giant stained-glass doors of the elaborate cathedral and heavily armed nuns watched the approaching visitors with trained eyes and nervous trigger fingers.

But just as the QINS team was about to step foot into the Martian Vatican, Susie Sunshine halted them with a curt hand motion.

"Hold it," commanded the buxom blonde, touching her collar where a surgically implanted BonePhone was vibrating a message along the mastoid bone to her inner ear. Nobody else could hear what was being said. This private mode of communication was what gave the reporter a seemingly endless array of information used to impress interview subjects, accounted for her twice escaping death and winning her elementary school spelling bee six years in a row.

"There's been an altercation at Koop Memorial Hospital," she reported aloud. "Something about a doc gone mad and a free-for-all with a Gremlin and a . . . harpoon?"

Jason Hardcopy spun about to face his diminutive associate. "What? You sure?"

"Yes!"

The rugged magnificence of his countenance flushed with anger, Jason raised a clenched fist to heaven and the stars beyond. "Them," he snarled. "It's gotta be them!"

A bleached nod. "Agreed."

With a leap, Hardcopy and Sunshine started down the stairs completely ignoring the safety regulation sign by taking the steps two at a time.

"Come on!" cried the reporters. "We're off to Koop!"

Staggering under a monstrous load of video recorders, 3-D lenses, tinted lights, power packs, and hastily borrowed religious artifacts, the QINS camera-op dropped a lot more than just his jaw at the outlandish command.

"B-but what about the audience with His Holiness the Pope?" stammered the fellow, almost beside himself with angst.

Hardcopy used a term definitely not endorsed by the Church, and Sunshine added a fillip that was physically impossible under the current laws of science.

Of course, the nuns immediately opened fire. But since the fleeing perpetrators were still on church property, they deliberately missed.

It was just a warning. This time.

"Boat," corrected Conway politely over his helmet radio.

Placing his stainless-steel equipment satchel on the rocky ground, Jhonny straightened in his spacesuit and glanced at the stocky metal figure standing next to the team.

His bulky armored spacesuit was a scathing orange, marking the man as a pilot. The reflection of their own lightweight blue spacesuits could faintly be seen in the tinted visor of his octagonal helmet.

"Beg pardon?" Harry asked, puzzled, into his throat mike.

"The craft that brought you here is classified as a spaceboat," Conway explained patiently. "Not a spaceship."

Rikka glanced about them. Off to one side, filling the horizon, was the giant planet Jupiter, its multicolored bands illuminating the barren valley in a soft muted rainbow. Behind was the sleek white-tiled space shuttle that had just deposited them on the moon Ganymede.

Inside the helmet, Collins tilted her head. "You mean the news shuttle?"

An armored thumb jerked upward. "Yes. And the boat in a parking orbit above us."

She glanced skyward. "The *Lady O'Grady*? But that's an HNS registered freighter!" the woman said. "It's got a crew of one hundred and must weigh a million tons! The only thing bigger in space is a goddamn L5 colony!"

Conway's helmet nodded. "Correct. A boat."

In the privacy of her own helmet, Collins lowered one eyebrow while raising the other. "Okay . . . and what exactly do you consider a ship around here?"

"Anything interstellar."

That gave her pause. Hmm, interplanetary boat, interstellar ship. As much as Rikka hated to admit it, the phraseology made sense. On Earth, a boat was a small unpowered vessel and ships were large, powered craft designed for long voyages.

"Okay, I buy that," the reporter relented.

"Salutations," said the man, extending his gloved hand, something he had not done when they first met at the landing strip. "It's a pleasure to greet you. I am Pilot Charles Conway and you just passed the Ganymede immigration test by displaying that rarest of abilities called common sense. Welcome to Fargo."

Their gloved hands shook.

"I thought it was pronounced Far-Go," Harry said.

"Only on high holy days."

They could hear the smile in his voice.

"Do many fail to pass the test?" asked Michelangelo, his voice sounding huge and powerful even over the radio.

"Sadly, yes."

"And what happens to them, sir?"

"They usually end up in Administration."

Gallantly, Conway gestured and they started to walk along the gravel trail that meandered along between bulbous fuel tanks and a small Quonset hut. Straight ahead was the twelve overlapping polished steel domes that made up the infamous UP Experimental Laboratory 9, nicknamed by the inhabiting mad scientists "Fargo Base." The rest of the solar system called it the BoomMoon.

As they started up a low hill, something on a distant mountaintop caught Jhonny's attention. "What are you doing with Bedlow laser cannons?"

Conway's helmet twisted about. "This is not a military base," the pilot stated firmly as if that was important. "We just tuned an old battery of obsolete Bedlows for a special job. To launch a lightsail ship."

"Interesting," said Jhonny, doing a wide-angle pan as an establishing shot and zooming in for a nice close-up of the towering weapon. "Did it work?"

Conway sighed. "Nope. No matter how we defused the beam, if we put in enough power to push the sail, the equipment pod would overheat to lethal temperatures." An armored shrug. "But then, what the whistle. I always thought it was a nutty idea anyway, leaving your engine at home."

Cresting the ridge, the path joined a road of hard-fused stone and walking became much easier. Rikka knew that Ganymede was almost the same size as Earth, but had not consciously realized that meant serious gravity. Not like the weak one-sixth available on Luna. Sadly, the reporter guessed there would be no flying bubble baths here. Sigh. Her brief interlude with the doc at her apartment seemed . . . she sniffed . . . smelled like a million years ago.

"Whistle?" Rikka asked, after a moment.

"A lot of things explode around here," Conway explained as he waved hello to the spacesuited driver in a passing wheeled lorry. The rear cargo bay was loaded with canisters whose stenciled markings bore the numbered code for weapons-grade plutonium. Harry made a note of the inventory numbers. He had a strong feeling that BoomMoon was not an affectionate affectation, but an accurate description.

Conway went on, "So, if you suddenly hear a sharp whistle . . ."

"There's a hole in your armor and pressure is dropping fast," she shuddered. "Ugly."

"Only nastier way to die I know of is to willfully eat the Wednesday meat loaf at the cafeteria."

"Not fit for human consumption, eh?" Jhonny asked with a private smile.

"Buddy, I wouldn't feed it to a politician."

Impressed at the leniency toward the natural enemy of astronauts everywhere, the camera-op started to whistle. But cut himself off in midnote. New places, new taboos. The android only hoped that singing in the shower was still okay.

"So, why are you here?" asked Conway. "Doing a story on why we're still alive? The history of high explosives? Sex in hyperspace?" He paused. "You're not here to help promote that stupid ion thing again?"

"You mean Edwin's Magic Ion Drive?" Rikka made a face, then realized that he could not see her. "Sorry, but my parents are not first cousins, nor was I repeatedly dropped on my head as a small child."

"Thank the Lord."

Chuckling, they stared walking along the fused path. In the distance, a team of people in tiger-striped Security spacesuits were running toward the Bedlow laser assembly.

"Curious," muttered the pilot.

"And what do you do, Mr. Conway?" asked Jhonny, letting his pet camcorder inside his helmet get photos of the guards and Bedlow.

"Retired jackdaffer, now HNS test pilot."

"Hmm, I didn't think the majority of the test vehicles would require live pilots," commented Harry, stepping around the crumbling edge of the fused path. Bits of glittering metal embedded in the surface told tales of yet another explosive blast.

"Most don't," Conway replied honestly. "But somebody has to be onboard for the final test. Remember the Apocalypse Drive."

The team pointedly said nothing. There were no computer records to trace here on Ganymede, no physical files to purloin. The sole source of information was the staff and what could be judiciously pried out of them. And even more important, specifically what they would not talk about.

Stopping for a moment, Charles pointed an orange finger at a rocky gray plain in the west. "When Jupiter is out of the sky, you can still see the glow from Crater One." He turned. "We're going to build the new launch field over there. Just beyond that really thick granite ridge."

"A wise move," noted Rikka, making sure her secretary was recording every word spoken.

"Our insurance company agrees."

Michelangelo gave a start. Insurance at Fargo Base? Ah, a joke. Most amusing. He was starting to like this human.

Approaching the seamless expanse of Florentine Plastic that constituted the main dome, Jhonny expertly noted that the airlock door was equipped with a keypad, hand sensor plate, female-type hardwire insert hole, manual wheel, and explosive bolts. This place seemed to expect disasters. But then, that's why the base was infamous, rather than just famous.

"Hold it," said the big alien, stopping him in the process of palming the sensor plate. "It was you, wasn't it? You're Charles 'Crash' Conway!"

"Guilty as charged, mate."

Jhonny swung the big camera around fast and adjusted the tint focus so he could see inside the faceplate of the helmet. "The hero of Ganymede! Why, you must have saved a hundred lives!" he prompted.

"Four hundred fifty," corrected Snyder. Who then bit his tongue. Damn, supposed to get info from them or else this would never work.

"All in a day's work, comrade," said the pilot. "Besides, it was a moral imperative that I stop the engine."

"Why?"

Rikka answered, "Because he helped design the drive."

"Ah. But then you know how to—"

"No!" interrupted the pilot hotly. "Everybody here underwent psychosurgery to remove all knowledge of the bedamned thing."

Suddenly, he turned on them. "Is that why you're here? To do a story on the A Drive?"

Hastily, they assured him it was not. Reluctantly, the pilot relaxed and seemed to accept their fervent denials.

Placing his gauntlet against the glowing plastic plate set into the metal side of the dome, Conway waited. As tiny sensors read the coded plate in his palm, the lights above the airlock door blinked from red, to yellow, to green. With a soft hiss, the segmented portal parted down the middle and they trundled in. The outer doors closed, and the inner doors of the actual airlock opened for admittance. There were a few minutes of silence as the group cycled their way through the military-style additional four doors until finally reaching the inside of the domed complex.

In the access foyer, surrounded by a jumbled rainbow of colored spacesuits, the six stripped off their outer garb, finally getting a look at each other. Charles resembled a spacetug; squat and powerful. His round face had more freckles than a moon and was topped by a stiff bristle array of crew-cut red hair. He seemed to radiate physical force.

Hanging their suits in numbered recharge brackets, Michelangelo fondled the flexible armor plating of Conway's worksuit. A civilian model of the military Samson powerarmor, the outfit was still many times more resilient than their own spacesuits. "If it can be told," started the alien. "Who makes these?"

"Samsung," replied Jhonny. "They are an old entertainment

company that holds the basic patent and do most of the assembly work themselves."

"And who does the rest?"

"A subcompany run by the owner's children," supplied Conway. The jackdaffer held a smile, knowing where this was going.

The furry technician chewed that over for a moment. "So what you're saying is that Samsung builds some of the Samson, and some of the Samson is made by Samsung and Son?"

"Yep!" smiled the android.

The big alien pinched his forehead to ease the pain. Humans. They did things like this to him on purpose. He just knew they did.

"Come on," said Conway amiably. "I'll show you to quarters, and then the base commander, Major Guido RunningHawk. He's regular Navy, and a old chemical rocket jockey, but a good guy anyway. Afterward we'll hit the cafeteria for dinner. S'kay?"

Time was of the essence, but the team played along as if they hadn't a care in the worlds.

Rikka chuckled. "Natch. As long as we avoid the meat loaf."

"You learn fast, Ms. Collins."

She dimpled. "Thank you, Mr. Conway."

"Crash," he corrected.

"Rikka."

Stoically, the reporter waited a moment for the dreaded Rikki-tikki-tavi joke but it was not forthcoming. Well, well, maybe this handsome fellow had never read any Kipling. She might have to find the time and help him . . . Kipple some night. Hmm.

As they proceeded along an angular corridor, its plastic floor scarred from a thousand boots, Jhonny casually observed that the buttressed walls were Kingston foam-insulated steel alloy. Ominously, there were numerous discolored areas where punctures had been patched.

Taking an elevator down two levels into the planetoid bedrock, their quarters proved to be functional, but Spartan. Everything folded from the insulated stone walls and there were automatic timers on both water faucets. Exactly as expected. However, the flowers in a vase were a lovely touch. But where the bloody hell had they gotten fresh flowers?

"If you gentlefolk will excuse me for a second," requested Rikka, heading for the refresher stall.

Once safe behind closed doors, Collins activated her collar mike and established a link with their shuttle.

"Well? How we doing?" she asked in an urgent whisper.

AT THIS POINT I HAVE INSUFFICIENT DATA FOR A PROPER ANALYSIS, scrolled Deitrich. ASK MORE LEADING QUESTIONS AND USE THE LETTER "A" WHENEVER POSSIBLE, TO JOG THEIR REACTIONS.

"Natch."

After noisily washing her hands, the reporter joined the waiting entourage of males in the outside corridor.

Returning to the main dome, Conway introduced her to the answer of the flower question. Near the entrance of the subsurface transit capsules, safe behind a flexible lattice of Armorlite glass, there was a tiered stonework waterfall. The ivy-covered rocks were based in a rocky pool brimming with tropical flowers. It was absolutely beautiful and totally useless, serving only the purely esthetic function of being something delicate and lovely amid the deadly high explosives and killing electronics of the experimental labs.

It was a nice humanizing touch. And the team's respect for the propulsion scientists rose a level.

Conway greeted a dozen people and introduced the team to a select handful as they strolled along the curved access corridor going from this dome to the next. Everywhere there were neatly welded patches and partially closed blast doors; the serrated, rubbery edges having a nasty used appearance to them. Constant reminders that this was a working laboratory, and not an enclave of theoretical dreamers.

Reaching a central access area, with side corridors branching off in every direction, Conway walked directly to a plain door whose nameplate bore the designation of the base commander and underneath was a sensor plate surrounded by a thick circle bisected by an equally thick diagonal line. The international NO symbol. The message was loud and clear. Don't bother the boss. The team gave the appropriate laugh as Conway knocked twice and they entered.

Inside, the room was huge; gently curving walls were lined with humming computer DPU banks, and in the center was a broken circle of control stations. Resembling small desks, each console boasted a plush swivel chair, a hooded monitor, computer keyboard, laser printer, cyber-link, and enough buttons, levers, dials, switches, meters, and digital readouts to record a 3-D rock music video. Even Mike was impressed.

But rather than the relaxed atmosphere of a laboratory office that she had expected, the command complex was jammed full of people scurrying every which way, shouting, whispering, and looking anxious. Many were talking on Hush phones, or typing madly on computer keyboards. Something important must be going on. And towering amid the bustling activity stood a tall, slim man whose uniform was so spotlessly clean he could only have been a desk jockey. Must be Major RunningHawk.

"Double-check those readings, lady!" snapped Guido, slamming the hood down on a console. "Conway, where the whistle have you been? Fuentes, sound recall to all external personnel!"

A harried man glanced up from his control board. "Sir, should I alert the tokamac crew?"

Glaring, Major RunningHawk turned brown in the face. "You mean it hasn't been done yet? Liptrot, you're an idiot! No wonder you're in Administration. Hell yes!"

"Hey, chief!" merrily called out Conway. "What's happening?"

Instantly, the whole room went totally quiet and slowly turned to face the people in the doorway. Unable to stop himself, Jhonny took a photograph of the group. Stepping behind Rikka, Harry kicked the android in the shin.

Who the . . . reporters! Geez, he had forgotten! A smile forced itself into existence on the Major's face.

"Ah, the visiting reporters," beamed Guido. "How very nice." But suddenly the man looked very sad. "Unfortunately, while I hate to be rude or untoward, we have an administrative problem that requires the immediate attendance of Pilot Conway. Charles, please see them to the door and join us?"

Slyly, Mike checked a sensor device in his multipocketed tool vest. Yep, the live percentage of bullshit in the atmosphere had just hit maximum.

Frowning in confusion, the pilot spread his arms. "Ah, sorry, folks. Business before PR. Catch you at dinner."

A squad of grim clerks appeared to gently, but forcibly, push the team into the hallway.

And the reporters smiled.

CHAPTER TWELVE

"WHAT IS IT, sir?" asked Conway, seriously concerned. One glance around the Ganymede control room and all thoughts of Rikka and dinner were gone from his mind.

"In a minute!" snapped Major RunningHawk over a shoulder.

"Wave form analysis complete!" cried a technician from his console, the monitor before him showed a moray pattern of wild undulating lines.

RunningHawk strode toward the man. "Talk to me, Syd."

"There's good news, bad news."

"Oh, shut up and talk!" growled the Major contradictorily.

"It's definitely the Apocalypse Drive," said the tech, running nervous fingers through his thin mustache. "And the vessel is headed straight for Earth."

The room went silent.

"What?" throated the base commander, his hair attempting to stand straight up in the air. The frigging military hadn't given him that little nugget of information! Earth!

Placing fists to temples, the officer visibly calmed. "Okay. Be calm. Data. More data. Is it still on a random course or heading directly for our homeworld?"

"Direct."

"Geez, you sure?"

"Confirmed with the Royal Martian SETI scanners in the Ort Cloud and SitComTac of the UPSC."

Bloody hell.

"What the prack is going on!" demanded Conway at the top of his lungs.

Frowning, then sighing, RunningHawk waved the pilot close. "Brace yourself, Chuck. We've got a problem."

"Okay, now what?" asked Jhonny, grinning broadly. Ah, the good old bum's rush! They had hoped for a reaction like this, but so soon? They must be really close to the core of the story.

"Roam the base and ask questions," said Harry, his nostrils dilating with the smell of a ripe mystery.

Removing her ear from the office door Collins agreed. "Whatever is happening here is on the point of breaking. We'd better move fast, or we'll end up interviewing cockroaches in the brig. Meet you at the garden when Deitrich sends the recall signal. Go."

And the four team members separated, eagerly searching for talkative victims. This should be a snap. People loved to chat about themselves, and scientists even more so than normal folk. They had so much more to say. None of it was usually interesting, but there was always tons of it. Along with quotes, footnotes, and often graphs and charts as well.

"Excuse me there, Professor, QSNT here. I was wondering if there was anything you really disliked . . . sorry, I mean really liked here at Fargo?"

"How is the food?"

"Does the constant danger drive you crazy?"

"What is your greatest triumph so far?"

"Fine. Just give me a summary from A to Z. Okay?"

"What is the biggest explosion you've had here?"

"Does the military ever interfere with your work?"

"Have there ever been any injured at the base?"

"Anything exciting ever happen here? Ha-ha."

"How did Ganymede get to be called the BoomMoon?"

BEEPBEEPBEEPBEEPBEEP!

After being escorted to Spartan steel accommodations by a Security officer, the team downloaded their recorded conversations from their wrist secretaries into a transmodem and fed the mess to Deitrich.

GIVE ME A MINUTE, scrolled the pilot. I HAVEN'T DONE A STATISTICAL LIE ANALYSIS IN QUITE A WHILE.

After putting fresh batteries in his camcorder, Jhonny checked his video disks for clarity while Harry lit a cigar, Mike cycled a small watermelon as a snack from the food dispenser, and Rikka dashed for the shower. A minute was all she needed. A minute was all she got.

DONE, announced the MainBrain.

"He's finished!" cried Snyder.

Rikka dashed out of the refresher in clean clothes, hand dryer still blowing her hair into a wild corona.

"Don't wait for me," she shouted above the strident air currents. "Talk!"

FOR THE SAKE OF BREVITY, I'LL DISPENSE WITH THE SLIDING PERCENT-AGE SCALE OF PROBABILITIES AND SECONDARY SUBCONSCIOUS REFER-ENCES, began the pilot. ALTHOUGH SOME OF THEM ARE REALLY FASCINATING.

"Thanks," puffed Harry. "Just shoot us the straight poop, guy."

NATCH, CHIEF, scrolled the wrist monitor. FIRST OFF, CONWAY KNOWS NOTHING OF WHAT REALLY HAPPENED.

Collins brightened at that information, then became deadly serious. "That's great news, but what the prack really did happen that day?"

IT WASN'T A BARE ENGINE THEY WERE TESTING THAT DAY, BUT A FULL-SCALE WORKING MODEL OF THE PROBE AND DRIVE.

"B-but that means there was a pilot onboard!"

YES. HE DIED AS SOON AS HE IGNITED THE PRIMARY COILS.

"Any chance of a name?"

NICKNAME STARTED WITH AN "M," THAT'S THE BEST I CAN DO.

Lost in rumination, Snyder blew smoke rings at the ventilator where they were sucked into the wall. A secret death. Well, that was okay for a beginning.

Tossing away the watermelon rind, Michelangelo made a paw motion toward his IBM portable and Jhonny nodded. Deitrich could chat now.

"Deitrich, how is it that you can do this?" asked the alien, tonguing his whiskers clean.

IT'S ACTUALLY QUITE SIMPLE IF YOU HAVE A MAINBRAIN WORKING IN CONJUNCTION WITH A GOOD COMPUTER TO CORRELATE THE QUESTION RESPONSES INTO AN INTELLIGENT PROFILE AND GRAPH WHAT THE FOLKS

ARE NOT SAYING. FORTUNATELY, I AM THE ONLY ROVING MAINBRAIN
OUTSIDE THE MILITARY.

"And why is that?"

GARDNER WILKES DONATES A LOT OF MONEY TO KOOP MEMORIAL.

"But . . ."

A *LOT* OF MONEY.

Thoughtfully, Mike began combing his face. Interesting.

THERE'S MORE TO THE REPORT, scrolled the MainBrain.

"You know who found or stole the plans for the Apocalypse
Drive?" asked Harry, leaning forward in his chair.

YES. There was a pause. NOBODY.

Puzzled looks filled the room.

"Explain, please," said Rikka, placing aside the dryer.

"Our probe?" demanded Conway, regaining control of his voice.
"Our *destroyed* probe! And how is that hellish little miracle occur-
ring?"

"When you smashed the containment building, it simply set the
probe free," said RunningHawk. "The HNS had a chance to destroy it while the probe headed toward deep space, but decided not
to. The autopilot was set to cruise a hundred different solar systems
looking for Earth-type planets and then come back. Why waste this
valuable chance? We might never get another one off the ground."

"You unleashed a known killer loose on the galaxy?" Conway
glared at the tall man.

"What the hell, who could care? There's nobody else out there,"
shrugged the Major. Then he glanced at the scanning monitors.

"Except for the Gremlins," the man added softly. But the probe
was launched before the alien bears had arrived to shatter the human ideal of an empty galaxy.

"As the chief test pilot," stormed Conway furiously, "why the
whistling hell wasn't I informed?"

"Because the HNS doesn't like you," came the calm reply.
"Your actions cost them a hundred million dollars Swiss last year
and Crash Conway is a hero so they can't take it out of your salary."

The pilot croggled. "I saved four hundred lives!"

"Correct," smiled RunningHawk tolerantly. "So, if you want to
date my virgin sister, borrow fifty bucks, or get a week off, just ask.

You got 'em. But I will not inform you of secret company matters until I am authorized to do so. You got that, amigo?"

In response, the pilot mumbled something under his breath.

"We're not dead yet!" barked RunningHawk. "We can stop it."

"How?" asked a technician in forced calm.

"Pirate the navigational computer." Commander RunningHawk turned toward the Communications people. "Use the Zed-prefix countercommand sequence. Change its course into the sun, abort the mission, scramble the memory, blow the engines, anything you can!"

Slumping into an empty chair, a technician drummed fingers on a tabletop. "None of those worked last time, why should they work now?"

"And what do you think I have been doing for the last fifteen minutes, ya old goat?" snapped the Chief of Communications, her slim hands trying to be in several places on the control board at the same time.

Diplomatically, Guido refused to reply. Good technicians were hard to get these days. Especially ones you married. Striding to his desk, the commander activated his personal keyboard and typed in a short command sequence. Suddenly, a new sound was added to the background clamor of the red alert Klaxon. Conway had to struggle to remember what it was. Battle stations?

"We'll wage electronic warfare from here," announced RunningHawk, taking his chair. "Conway, you saved our butts once. Wanna do it for Earth?"

"How? Got another megaton cruiser you want destroyed?"

"Your problem. I hereby promote you to acting Chief of Security. Now go and do something clever."

Like have Manufacturing start mass-producing gravestones, thought the test pilot wryly.

"Van Gelder, what's the tightest focus you can get on our maser?" asked the new Chief of Security, nervously cracking his knuckles.

"Four meters," said the sweaty man, then slowly his face scrunched. "Unless I take a hammer and smash the safeties, then I can get her down to maybe four inches! That'll punch a hole in anything this side of hell!"

Conway nodded. "Hammers are in Supply. Get."

Scrambling from his chair, the man got.

Frantically working on her wrist secretary, an engineer asked, "Any chance I can get a portable four-gigawatt magnetic ring with a Hanson Q-rig? I'll also need a Samson powersuit, laser welder, ninety-two-gauge coaxial superconductor cables, and some antiradiation coveralls."

Every head in the room turned.

"Whatever for?" asked RunningHawk, puzzled.

Conway snapped his fingers. "The power plant!"

The engineer nodded. "Given enough time I can modify a Bussard ramjet into a hydrogen lance from the tokamac. They only have a limited range and consume fuel like a prehistoric Atlas-Centaur, but it will toast our turnabout to slag in a microsecond."

"If you can hit that tiny a target."

She shrugged eloquently.

"I'll alert the t-mac operators," added RunningHawk.

Conway sent his mind through the floor plans of the complex furiously. "Analytical Laboratory 5," he told her. "There's a salvaged wreck of Edwin's Magic Ion Drive. Should have what you want. The rest will be delivered. Sergeant McShawn, show her the way!"

Wordless, the woman nodded, turned, and the two departed.

"Dr. Andrews, send an X-class radio message to Earth with all of the pertinent details, and every bit of information we have on the drive."

The woman didn't waste time confirming the order. She just started typing fast.

Glancing about the room, Conway found the next man he wanted. "Hey, Lars, how many remote-control drones do we have ready to fly?"

"Nine," said the tech, busy at his damage control board. "I'm preparing a flight plan for a rendezvous and ram with our incoming bird."

Thank God, somebody else was thinking fast.

"Also, have the *Lady O'Grady* strip down to a skeleton crew and prep for immediate launch."

RunningHawk touched his aching head. The UP Budget Committee would have shit kittens over another liner crash. Then he smiled. Of course, that was a point in its favor. Vacuum the politicians!

Conway racked his brain. Was that it for weapons? There might be a few handguns or laser pistols somewhere. But nothing useful for the present emergency. Damn-damn-damn! Biting a lip, Conway glanced at his wrist secretary. "How long?"

"Till it gets here?" concluded a WatchDog scanner operator. "At the present deceleration ETA with Uranus five hours. It'll pass us in six, the asteroid belt in seven, and reach Earth at ten."

Conway started doing calculations on his secretary. "So, our window of attack will be from 15:55 to 16:05." Giving them ten minutes to try to destroy the rogue.

Or else every living creature on Earth died.

"Holy crap!" cried Harry, dropping his lit cigar on his leg. There was a brief sizz of plastic, but the anchor failed to notice. The biggest news story of the decade? Hell, this might be the *last* news story. Period!

"Deitrich, are you sure?" demanded Rikka, feeling ill. "Are you absolutely pracking positive?"

NINETY-TWO PERCENT CERTAINTY. YES. CONWAY'S ACTION ONLY SET THE KILLER DRONE FREE TO RANDOMLY WANDER THE GALAXY.

"But why didn't HNS blast the drone before it left the solar system?" demanded Jhonny.

UNKNOWN.

"Probably to save money," growled Snyder, rubbing at a mysterious pain in his leg.

"Deitrich, get us a Z link to Media," snapped Collins. "Compress the data into the smallest, tightest blip you can and beep 'em twice! We have to alert the station. Hell, alert everybody!"

There was a pause.

DONE.

Another pause.

AND THE MILITARY INTERCEPTED.

"Unholy crap!" cursed Snyder, kicking an inoffensive bit of furniture out of his way.

I USE A TRANSPOSITIONAL BOOK CODE MADE BY PARSON, SO IT WILL TAKE THEM AN ESTIMATED HOUR TO DECIPHER. HOWEVER, THEY KNOW THE SOURCE AND TARGET OF THE TRANSMISSION AND THAT SAYS A LOT RIGHT THERE.

Snyder grabbed his coat and turned. The team was already

standing. "Let's boogie. Military Intelligence from three worlds are going to hit this place in about five minutes."

Jhonny agreed. "Yeah, this info is like a lead safe full of Kafka."

They all stared at him.

"*Very* heavy," explained the android.

The humans groaned while Mike accessed the name "Kafka" on his IBM.

"Leave the bags," directed Harry. "It may fool Security into thinking we're still on the moon for a couple of minutes."

Rikka stepped into the bathroom and turned the shower back on, Michelangelo used pillows to make fake bodies under the covers, Harry fed the CD player ten disks, and Jhonny left a 17:00 wake-up call for the whole team. Quietly, the news team left the room, Mike broke the doorlock to hinder entrance of nosey Security folk, and they headed swiftly for the main airlock.

"Our next move is obvious," said Rikka, stepping into the legs of her spacesuit and sliding on the arms.

"Proof," agreed Harry, closing his chest. "We gotta support this theory with some solid documentation."

"Seeing is believing," quoted Jhonny, pointing at his camcorder perched on his shoulder. His helmet went on to seal with a hiss and the conversation continued via radio link.

"Hassan?" asked Rikka.

"Hassan," agreed Harry.

A giant in white armor, Michelangelo paused in the act of donning his four-fingered gauntlets. "Hold," said the alien in harsh admonishment. "Am I to understand that we are going to leave the moon without proper authorization from the Ganymede Flight Controller or even Media?" He sounded worried. Almost frightened.

"Yeah. Sure. So?"

"But we can't do this. It's . . . it's immoral!"

Angrily, Rikka turned on the alien, but Harry gave her a hand signal. The tech had said immoral, not illegal.

"Son," said Collins in her best oratory, "if you're going to become a member of the news fraternity, then you have got to learn a few ground rules. We are the archenemy of the uncaring big business and corrupt government. Plus, the people have a right to know. And if we break a few minor rules to aid the greater good, where's the harm? We're not destroying anything, or hurting anybody. The shuttle is our own property. We're just removing it from Ganymede dock without proper authorization so the station will be in the clear in case there's trouble."

The big alien's resolve appeared to be weakening. "So, we are sort of protecting the station?"

Softly in the distance, an alarm began to sound.

"Exactly! Why, my fellow sentient . . ."

Harry started humming the theme of the United Planets and Jhonny pulled a small white-'n'-gold flag out of his sleeve.

"Yes, freedom of the press! Our most basic mandate of civilization positively demands that . . ."

The alien waved her silent. "Agreed. Let's go."

Smiling, Jhonny cavalierly tossed the flag away and they cycled open the airlock. "Told you it would come in useful someday," the android whispered to Rikka.

She patted him on the shoulder and closed the shuttle door. Through the tiny porthole, the reporter saw a group of people in tiger-striped Security spacesuits running toward them. But then abruptly stop and hastily retreat as Deitrich started the main engines with an unnecessary blast of flame from the belly jets.

Satisfied that the team was safe for the present, Rikka strapped herself into the cockpit seat. Next stop, the Independent Asteroids. A hunk of rock called Tannenbaum. And a visit to the biggest pornographer in the entire solar system. Abduhl Benny Hassan. A good friend or an archenemy, depending upon the circumstances of the visit.

And sometimes, he was both.

CHAPTER THIRTEEN

IN ANY SOLAR system the planets revolve about the central body at different speeds, depending upon their size, mass, proximity, and in some rare unearthly cases their political affiliation. Unusual was the time when all the worlds of any given system would be in perfect alignment like ducks in a row.

Very rare indeed.

In the Sol system of humanity, this was not such a time. But for the next few days a triad of planets were in direct confrontation, definitely the most distant of cousins: the fertile, blue/white Earth, so close and warm to the mother sun, the colossal planet Uranus with its hundred plus rings and Whitman's Sampler of assorted moons, and, at the extreme edge of the human solar system, the frozen ammonia world of Pluto. Small, dark, and virtually sunless, the barren planet had been voted at the Interplanetary Travel Agents convention of 2204 as the most boring place in known space. Which was really saying something when you considered such desolate locations as Outer Siberia, the Dead Mud Sea of Mars, and downtown Cincinnati.

Viewed from the arctic surface of Pluto, the mighty class-G star known as Sol was merely a slightly brighter than average point of light in the glory of the Milky Way Galaxy. Morning was only a scientific technicality. Seasons were generated by glacier pressure caused by gravity and subterranean tectonic plates. Professional football but a fleeting dream. Yet, although sans atmosphere, fast food restaurants, and with a mean temperature of bitterly cold, Pluto was not alone.

Locked in an roaming elliptical orbit about the sterile ice world was the tiny Charon moon, orbiting so far away from its mother world that for centuries it was thought to exist solely as a glitch in the mathematical calculations, or a fly speck on the telescope lens. Which was how over fourteen mysterious planets had been discovered before somebody finally put screens in the windows of the Mt. Wilson Observatory.

Charon was a barren hunk of primordial stone with no known resources, fuels, or minerals; very similar to New Jersey. The moon was an irregular sphere of congealed planetary excess of no conceivable use. Except, perhaps, to serve as a physical platform for men and machines looking to go elsewhere. For past the moon lay only the Ort Cloud, a nebulous ring of lost meteors and wandering comets whose incredibly complex trajectories were puzzling even to each other. Next came the great abyss of space. And beyond that, the stars themselves.

The unreachable stars.

But suddenly, an impossible dawn tinted the icy horizon of Charon. Rapidly increasing in brilliance, the strange greenish light flooded the barren landscape with heatless illumination. Yet as the encroaching glow swept across the crystalline landscape, the jagged mountains of superhard methane snow and the frozen oceans of ammonia did not reflect any sort of emerald sheen.

Steadily accelerating in speed, the aura of translucent green swept across a plateau, several mining outposts, and a valley.

As it departed, the rocks, permafrost, and ice seemed unaffected. The deserted smelting plant hummed along as always. But in the valley, a fleeing Land Rover slowed and came to a halt as it wandered off the snowy road and bumped into a ice boulder. There was no apparent reaction from the four spacesuited figures inside the heated cabin.

An ever-expanding sphere, the area of illumination moved on, fully engulfing the moon before reaching outward into space toward the mother planet.

Set in geosynchronous orbit above the north continent of Pluto, floating serenely in the starry sky, was the huge white cylinder of Relay Station 4; the silvery glass sheets of its solar energy collectors spread like the great wings of an exhibitionist butterfly.

On the bridge of the orbiter, a young man in a crisp orange UP Navy uniform worked a complex control panel with sure hands.

"Shoetown Transport, you are cleared for final approach," drawled Lt. Stewart, adjusting the gain on his radio.

"Roger that, Four," replied the grim man on the wall monitor. "Sorry we're late, but we ran into some trouble with a frigate of the Free Police."

A shrug. Could an hour make any real difference? "Kill 'em?"

"No. We let them go. Are your people ready for an immediate evac?"

Stewart nodded. Yeah, right. Probably just smacked them on the wrist and gave them a ticket for space piracy. Ha!

"Evac is confirmed, Ivan. But, ah . . . any chance you could tell us why we're being hustled out of here?"

"See you in five, Four."

"Three, two, one," finished the Lieutenant lamely in his standard good-bye joke.

The radio speaker cut off sans the usual laugh.

Frowning, the Lieutenant released the transmit switch.

Busy running a last-minute diagnostic on the MainFrame computer that would temporarily take over their duties, Commander Peggy Terrel harrumphed in disapproval. If Stewart had not been her current sex partner, the officer wouldn't have tolerated such nonsense on a duty shift. And especially during this impromtu emergency. Ah well, such was love.

Suddenly, an odd green glow broached the horizon, flooding the bridge vision with its lambent color.

Lowering her digital clipboard, Commander Terrel ceased her inspection of the console and arched a questioning eyebrow at the intrusion. What the prack?

"Beautiful," breathed the Lieutenant. "Of course I'm new here, sir, but I didn't know that Pluto had any sort of an aurora borealis."

"It doesn't," snapped the commander, scowling. Damn, but this certainly was a day for unusual occurrences. First the Brazilian crew operating the SETI scanners in the Ort Cloud failed to make their regular weekly report. Back home, the Lunar Rovers had somehow managed to beat the Chicago Cubbies and win the Worlds Series. Then UP Security demanded an immediate unexplained evacuation of all personnel off Pluto and the Charon moon. Next, the colonists at Titan declared war. And now this. Weird.

Just then the proximity alert sounded a warning keen. But before either of the naval officers could react, the awesome bulk of the transport ship violently filled the main monitor.

And was gone.

The two officers exchanged puzzled glances.

"Wide angle view!" ordered Terrel, stepping close to the sole window and craning her neck about.

In a flickering flash, the scene of the monitor shifted. Now visible, the Martian troop transport was veering away from the station and starting to tumble aft over keel as it continued on into deep space.

Trying to do two things at once, the Lieutenant activated his communications console. "Shoetown Transport, do you copy? Shoetown, do you copy? Ivan, what is your problem? Over!"

Only static sounded over the speaker.

A sudden suspicion filled Terrel's mind. "Lt. Stewart, give me reverse trajectory of the transport and that odd cloud."

Buttons were pushed and commands hastily typed.

In reverse motion the shuttle reappeared on the screen and the ship and gaseous formation retreated to converge below the space station and then separate again.

"Commander, look!"

Turning to face the tactical monitor, Terrel could see a distant path of greenish illumination expanding from the planet below and moving steadily toward the station. Tactical scrolled along, the monitor giving chemical composition, size, speed, and heading.

Only it didn't. The tactical monitor was clean. As if the cloud did not exist, or couldn't be analyzed.

"Raise shields and fields!" she barked. "Maximum distance."

The sweating man pounded on the control boards. "I already did!"

"And?"

"And the damn thing moved through the 488 forcefield as if it were a screen door!"

Prack, damn, and hell! Sprinting across the small bridge, the woman grabbed the command microphone from its rest in the arm of her chair.

"Red alert," her amplified voice echoed over the howling sirens. "Emergency procedure number two. Repeat, number two. Prepare for radiation protocol!"

And a soft pearlescence field engulfed Relay Station 4.

Instantly, the loading dock was awash with green, the crew members collapsing atop crates of supplies, and technicians slumping into the working innards of machinery with horrible results. In the main corridor, a frightened Security guard shouted into his collar radio and triggered his Peacemaker at the encroaching glow. But the multibarreled stun pistol had no noticeable effect on the radiation field.

Trapped inside the elevator, a doctor yanked a surgical laser from her bag and fired point-blank at the cloud with full power. The shimmering beam passed harmlessly through the fluorescent field, melting a neat hole in the wall beyond. Promptly, a small wind whipped over the still body of the physician as the atmosphere howled out into space. But the virulent storm did nothing to deter the creeping light.

Steadily, the glow moved onward. Airtight doors and adamantine walls of refractory armor did nothing to slow its inexorable advance: life support, living quarters, the tokamac reactor, the personnel in each was stilled in turn. And then the bridge was saturated; Lt. Stewart and Commander Terrel only having enough time to bleat an emergency warning to Verrilli Base before they went off the air.

Already ninety percent of the icy world of Pluto was immersed in the field as the lovely green swiftly moved in from every direction to close upon the insulated domes of Verrilli Base.

"Station Four, do you copy!" cried a physicist clumsily operating the communications console. "I repeat . . . aw, prack!" Throwing the microphone to the floor, he grabbed another. "Alert! All personnel board your shuttles and leave! Now! Immediately! The Ganymede drone is here! Repeat, the drone is here!"

As the weird glow moved smoothly through the four-meter hull of the base to fill the control room, the elderly scientist collapsed limply onto the console.

Down in the warm cafeteria, screaming scientists scrambled for the door, blocking the exit solid with their own bodies. Primordial fear overwhelmed sentience and the scholars howled and clawed for freedom like insane animals.

An emerald tidal wave, the luminescent field entered the room and quiet soon prevailed.

Down in the bowels of the base, a janitor yanked open the lead-lined portal to the irradiation chamber flooding the laboratory with hard radiation, preferring to chance cancer to this silent alien death. But the invisible torrent of alpha, beta, and gamma particles seemed to in no way effect the gentle glow and soon the man dropped like every other living creature.

Still warm and humming with power, the sensors of Verrilli Base ceased to register any living personnel.

Unstoppable, the cloud phased through ice, metal walls, and military forcefields of the base as if they did not exist. The nearby Brazilian Mining outpost was engulfed. An automated road maker. And finally the North Pole where a French construction team was wearing state-of-the-art Hercules powerarmor. Helmet radios turned off so they could concentrate on their delicate work, abruptly the builders ceased their assembling of a tokamac for a new observatory.

Ever on, the emerald wave swept across the remaining surface of the white planet, the dire translucent field extended kilometers deep into the frigid mantle. In only minutes, Pluto was totally engulfed, a dark mote in the center of a exothermic halo.

But soon, the lovely glow moved away from the silent frozen world, and stolidly proceeded deeper into the solar system.

Then it winked out.

CHAPTER FOURTEEN

RIDING THE TOP of a thick column of flame, the QSNT shuttle hit Fatal One before it left the gravitational field of Ganymede, Fatal Two as it streaked past Jupiter, and Fatal Three as Deitrich kicked in the overdrive, the after-thrusters, and jettisoned the luggage.

In the cockpit, the dashboard meters indicating the stability of the FTL engine components were visibly dropping toward zero.

Frantically working the controls, Rikka, Harry, and Jhonny terminated unnecessary ship functions to give a fractional boost to the electrical system feeding the main engines.

Damn, prack, and hell, stormed Collins mentally. It was just bad timing that Jupiter was on the wrong side of the solar system from the section of the asteroid belt they wanted. Hassan had what the team needed to record the ultimate story, but only if they could get to him before the military won and successfully hid the existence of the dire events. Or worse, the tiny probe evaded the huge armada and Earth was depopulated straight down to the game show hosts and the only slightly less evolved primordial slime at the bottom of the ocean!

With a sudden blurring effect, the stars changed from red to white and the shuttle slowed to a relative speed of only four thousand kilometers an hour. But even before the craft drifted to a halt, Michelangelo had spanner in paw and was removing the protective bolts that held the access hatch to the engine tightly shut. Callously, he ripped the depleted FTL element out of the motor and tossed it over a shoulder, as his other paw slammed in the auxiliary element.

"Go!" he cried, quickly winching the bolts into place.

And the shuttle streaked away again.

"Mike, how's our FTL status?" asked Harry over the PA.

"We're down to the emergency replacement element," replied the alien with a satisfied grin as he stepped away from the whining motors. Five seconds flat. Not bad for a beginner.

"What?!"

"There wasn't time to requisition another set from BoomMoon supplies prior to our departure."

Rikka spoke. "Will we make it to Tannenbaum?"

"Using the reserves, yes," said the tech, glancing at the grilled speaker on the white wall separating him from them.

Jhonny kicked in. "You'd better be sure, mon ami. Frankly, I don't relish drifting helplessly in deep space. Without the mains, we're a year away from home with a week's supply of air."

"Will we make it?" demanded Snyder. "Or should I call for a replacement team from Media?"

WE WILL REACH TANNENBAUM IF I HAVE TO GET OUT AND PUSH, scrolled Deitrich. I WANT A FRONT ROW SEAT FOR THE END OF CIVILIZATION.

"Agreed," stated Michelangelo as he removed the fuse for the safety cutoff. His job was to get the team to their goal. So get them there he would.

At any price. Honor demanded no less.

Hours passed in nervous anticipation. Up in the cockpit, Rikka was down to the cuticles of her fingers, Harry was developing a twitch, and Jhonny had worn the label off the memory disk he rhythmically loaded and unloaded in his camcorder. On the dashboard, the meters read zero, yet the shuttle was still Fatal Three; the exciters ripping every possible atom of althropic material from the FTL elements in the engine.

Down in Engineering, Mike had stripped to his glasses and boots because of the heat. Meanwhile Deitrich struggled to regulate life support. The outer casing of the motors had grown red-hot and wisps of bitter smoke from frying insulation wafted into view around the edges of the inspection hatch.

MIKE, scrolled Deitrich on the technician's wrist portable. I HATE TO SAY THIS, BUT I DON'T THINK WE'RE GOING—

Abruptly, the engines cut off. Stomachs flipped from the unbuffered transition. The keel creaked loudly. Somewhere glass shattered. But the stout vessel stayed intact and the status lights soon went from red, to yellow, to green again.

Stumbling to the porthole, the technician could see that the shuttle was now floating above a stream of tumbling boulders in the vast river of the asteroid belt.

. . . TO HAVE ANY WORRIES, continued the Brain unabashed.

"Thanks," sighed the alien, wiping his face with a towel. End of the human world or not, nothing smelled worse than damp fur.

In the cockpit, Rikka uncrossed her eyes and ignited the chemical engines. With renewed speed, the shuddering ship shot forward into an endless flow of irregularly shaped rocks.

Mountains and pebbles moved past the shuttle on all sides: the rocky flotsam was the sole remains of some dramatic prehistoric cataclysm. Definitely prime-time material in its day, but pure Sunday supplement filler nowadays.

Then in the distance, staining the natural purity of the avalanche to nowhere, there appeared a shiny flash of technology.

As Jhonny dialed for enhancement, Harry locked in the navigational beacon. Now showing on a submonitor was a clear dome of Armorlite sitting on top of a huge asteroid whose rocky surface twinkled with running lights and directional arrows.

Tannenbaum. The cursed jewel of the asteroid belt.

Traffic was sparse and the shuttle moved in quickly. Inside the adamantine bubble of military plastic was a perfectly ordinary city with streets and homes, factories and warehouse, malls and office buildings. The peak of the tallest spacescraper actually touched the pinnacle of the dome, beyond which shone the immortal stars.

Parking the shuttle in a landing bay whose louvered entrance offered armor of mythical proportions, the team disembarked at a run, unnecessarily flashing their press credentials to get past the sleeping Customs agents. There was law and order on the asteroid, but unless you directly disrupted the colonists, the tourists, or shouted out the surprise ending of a movie, you were free to do as you pleased. Although there were handy gallows established near every major theater for the swift retribution of loudmouths who spoiled the plot for everybody else.

The imposing bulk of Michelangelo assisted greatly in their swift exodus from the crowded terminal. Pushing and shoving a path to the sidewalk, the team managed to grab a Hovercraft at the curb.

Rikka took the wheel, Harry paid the robotic meter the rental fee for the car, Jhonny apologized to the crowd showing his QSNT identity card, and Mike carried in the equipment bags. Although why they had so many for such a short assignment he had no idea.

In a billowing breath of warm air, the hovercar lifted from the pavement and started skimming along the smooth roadway. Taking an off ramp to a lower level, Rikka floored the rheostat and the electrostatic engines whined with unchained fury. Soon, the city was behind them and a lush forest lined the left side of the road, while to the right, a steel safety barrier underlined the brick wall dividing the roadway from the thick dome wall and stars beyond.

"Who is this Hassan that we seek?" asked the big alien, his hair blown wild by the whipping wind of the car. On some strange impulse, he placed both paws outside the window and lagged his tongue in the wind. Whee!

"Mike, do you have criminals on your world?" asked Jhonny.

Politely, the technician turned from the window and offered an elbow to the android so the camera-op could see that it was fully covered with the pelt of an adult.

"Well, Abduhl Benny Hassan is our number one criminal."

"Why?" asked the alien.

"Mostly because the police can never find him, capture him, or successfully prosecute," explained Harry, fumbling about in the bag on his lap.

"He is a killer? Sells drugs?" asked Mike curiously.

"Pornographer," said Rikka, curving her mouth about as if the words themselves possessed a bad flavor.

"Mostly," corrected Jhonny ominously. "And he's about as dangerous as having Bruno in your bathtub."

The alien shuddered. What a horrid visual. But after consulting his IBM, Michelangelo was even more confused. "Illegal sexual positions? You have regulations on sex?"

"Human conduct is very complicated," offered Snyder hesitantly.

Patiently, the alien waited for enlightenment.

"Deitrich will explain it to you later," said Collins, maneuvering past a lumbering McBurger truck full of miniature cows, their symbiotic pickles and lettuce already attached.

THE BIRDS AND THE BEES? OKAY, scrolled the MainBrain. FIRST, YOU NEEDED A MOTEL, A TRAMPOLINE, A CUCUMBER . . .

Curling her lips in scorn and exceeding the speed limit, Rikka felt invigorated by the crisp country air, rich and sweet with the scent of laurel, the short evergreen trees that the asteroid was named after. Tannenbaum was only two kilometers long, but the inhabitants had packed a whole world inside the colossal dome. Actually it was not surprising. When building a world from the ground up, and you even had to supply the ground, only a simpleton would make it anything but totally pleasant. Although it was generally conceded that the hedonistic folks over at the Tower of Babel Bubble had taken this genial philosophy of delight just a tad too far.

"Everybody prep a weapon," said Harry, lifting a Smith & Wesson 2mm needler into view. The trim black pistol shone like polished sin.

"Weapons!" roared Michelangelo. "B-b-b-"

"Of course, we'll be wearing weapons," explained Rikka, adroitly sliding on a shoulder holster. "Hassan knows we're reporters, so it shows our respect for the man."

"And gives his guards something to take off us," added Jhonny, checking the action on an AVM Neutrino pistol. Hmm, a little stiff. Must be dusty again. The android placed an eye on the barrel and worked the trigger to see how things were down there.

Snapping the flap on his holster, Snyder agreed. "If we walked in clean, they'd be so suspicious they would vivisect us searching for guns."

Reluctantly, the technician admitted the wisdom of the action. Gangsters on any world were like unused batteries, their own power made them corrode from within.

"But I have no weapon," stated the alien. "Perhaps a club? Or knife?"

IN YOUR EQUIPMENT BAG.

Eh? Opening the valise on the floor between his legs, Mike accordioned apart the trays and there lay an elongated bundle of synthocloth. Lifting the wrapping, he drew apart the material and found a huge, short-barreled pistol whose maw could easily accommodate his snout.

"What is it?" asked the alien, keeping his hands far from the guardless trigger.

AN M79 GRENADE LAUNCHER, CIRCA 1995, scrolled Deitrich. I REQUISITIONED IT FROM MEDIA SECURITY ARCHIVES FOR THE SHUTTLE'S ONBOARD ARSENAL. THE MECHANISM IS A SINGLE-ACTION BREECH-LOADER THAT LAUNCHES A 40MM CANISTER OF LIGHT ARMOR-PIERCING HIGH EXPLOSIVE.

Mike stared at the thing as if it had sprouted live snakes.

NASTY LITTLE THING, ISN'T IT?

A dumb nod. What was this horrid mechanism designed for? To put critically ill planets out of their misery?

DON'T WORRY, IT'S UNLOADED. SHELLS ARE IN THE BAG.

"Thanks," growled the alien uncertainly. Was that a plus, or a minus?

SORRY ABOUT THE ANTIQUE. BUT IT'S THE ONLY WEAPON I COULD FIND LARGE ENOUGH TO SERVE YOU AS A HANDGUN. I TRIED TO GET A SHOULDER HOLSTER BUT WARDROBE DIDN'T HAVE ENOUGH LEATHER TO DO A PROPER JOB. THEY RARELY HAVE A NEED FOR A 95 EXTRA-EXTRA-EXTRA-LARGE.

"Ever fire a weapon in combat?" asked Harry, checking the magazine in his needler. The collection of steel slivers glistened oily in the light of the asteroid's artificial sun.

Summoning his resolve, Mike told the truth. "Actually, I am a devoted pacifist/vegetarian. I have never physically harmed a living soul and would rather die than do so."

Stunned silence.

"However I do lie outrageously," grinned the leviathan in unabashed glee.

Reaching an intersection, Rikka turned onto a private concrete road that led into a sprawling parking lot alongside a large industrial park. Surrounded by a stout wire-link fence of no appreciable military value was the executive complex. Neat hedges edged rows of low redbrick buildings laid out in orderly strips. Warehouses? Manufacturing plants? To the west was a carpeted landing grid for Hovercraft. On the east was a small parking lot for automobiles, but only a handful of expensive ground cars there.

At the front gate was a brick kiosk with a pair of uniformed guards apparently chosen for their surly attitudes and love of boot polish. The dour two stopped the hovercar and probed everybody and everything with an illegal WatchDog scanner.

"Weapons, please," politely demanded the woman with the scar, while the scowling man with the eye patch proffered a wicker hamper.

Dutifully, the news team handed over the collection of death dealers. The exchange went smoothly until Mike doffed his M79 monster. Something seemed to catch the guard's attention, and fumbling about with it for a minute, she then passed the weapon to her associate who took the weapon and reverently laid the huge pistol in plain view on the shelf above the desk in their kiosk.

"Pass," waved the woman pleasantly, the man incredibly offered a salute.

As the team drove slowly away, Rikka had to ask what the prack was that about?

"Apparently," rumbled the alien, "a hundred-credit note was inserted in the barrel of the gun."

The human and android exchanged smiles.

"I have a semi-cousin," explained the technician. "She runs around on all fours, mates out of season, eats chocolate for breakfast. You know the type."

"Hell, I am that type," smirked Rikka softly.

Facing the window, Harry agreed, but not too loudly.

Passing the entrance for trucks, then the rampway for delivery vans, Collins slowed just enough to roll over a speed bump and landed the rented coupe in a reserved spot near the front walk.

Gathering recorders and cameras, the team left the vehicle not bothering to activate the lock. At their departure, a duo of android attendants lurched forward to clean and wax the hovercar. Jhonny viewed them sadly, but stayed with the group.

Covering several hexacres in the center of the complex was a fifteen-story office building of classic design, a gigantic rectangle of mirrored glass. A pavilion of trimmed hedges lined the cubist edifice.

Pushing through a revolving door, the reporters entered an air-conditioned lobby dominated by a tiered water fountain and a stunningly beautiful receptionist at the information desk. Like the water fountain, the woman was purely for decoration. The android clerk beside her did any important work.

A floating holographic directory listed the 250 companies that had offices in the building. Not listed was the organization that owned the companies, along with the office building and the entire asteroid that held the complex.

The lobby proved to be jammed full of people scurrying about. A jostling crowd had formed at the central elevator bank, the mass of suits and briefcases inching their way forward. Detouring around the crush, Harry led the gang toward a private elevator set in an alcove decorated with mosaic tiles. The burnished metal doors parted at his approach and closed behind them.

Touching nothing, the reporters impatiently waited as another tight beam security scanner checked for unauthorized contraband. On the wall, there was a standard bank of buttons with numbers, but having been here before as guests, the team knew that pressing any of them would result in the floor unhinging and a fast trip to the furnace in the basement.

A soft ding announced they would live and the elevator began its upward climb. Classic movie sound tracks were today's musical entree for the journey and in spite of the tense situation the news team was humming along with an old Fred Astaire tune as they reached the only floor the lift went to.

Practically speaking, this level did not exist. Situated between the eighth and ninth stories, this special elevator was the only way in or out. No access tunnels or air ducts stopped here. The stairs artfully wound on by. It did not appear on the registered floor plans or blueprints. And any window washer or janitor unfortunate enough to accidentally discover the nonfloor would painfully suffer early retirement due to rapid concrete poisoning.

Striding along a stark white corridor, the QSNT people kept their hands in plain sight and tried not to stare at the blank walls on either side. There were no obvious guards, but the rooms beyond were filled with a small army of heavily beweaponed enforcers chosen for their marksmanship and fanatical loyalty to the boss.

At the end of the hallway was a spaceship-type airlock set into the painted Armorlite wall. Cycling through, the team stepped out the other side.

...g the room was a plain square bunker of unprocessed concrete, a squat military pillbox as incongruous and serious as the man it contained: Abduhl Benny Hassan, godfather supreme, crime lord of slime, smut peddler, video pirate, pornographer, and owner of at least four illegal cable hookups. There were no known bounds to his villainy or premium channels.

"Enter, my friends," announced a pinhead speaker next to the armored door. "But please leave your wet dog outside."

"Dog!" challenged Michelangelo, rattling the rafters.

"Ah! The Gremlin with money speaks. Well then, please admit this most interesting personage."

Wary of getting crushed, the reporters stepped past the already closing door. Hopefully the action was going to be prophetic. Hassan was dangerous with a capital G, as in grave.

The interior of the spacious pillbox was softened with real wood paneling and a pastel blue carpet. A gleaming white drop ceiling hid the overhead steel support beams and a hologram of Lunar City at daybreak dominated the far wall.

Sheik Don Abduhl Benny Hassan was sipping a drink and sitting behind a curved wooden desk lined with video monitors, each scrolling a different financial report or showing colorful sale graphs.

Even reclining, Abduhl was an impressive man. Well over six feet tall, his stylish Slash shirt displayed an incredibly muscular chest. His blond hair was cut in an old style called crew cut and both of his eyes were blue, although the right was clearly artificial.

Lying openly on a polished wooden rack behind him was the largest weapon any of the team had ever seen. The brass plate underneath boasted the designation GIBRALTAR ASSAULT CANNON. With as many barrels as a steam organ, a body harness of straps and cushioned supports helped to distribute the eighty-five pounds of weight. The composite superweapon was theoretically capable of delivering more assorted destruction than a platoon of drunk Marines. UP Security all but loved the weapons biblically and possession was punishable by having to try to run away from one firing on full auto. Presently, the score stood: Gibraltar—437, criminals—1.

At the team's approach, Abduhl rotated his chair away from a monitor displaying a zoo of some kind. Although the animals seemed to be wearing lingerie.

"As this is an unexpected visit, I assume you have a favor to ask?" he said without preamble. A smile was there, but it meant nothing. The sheik often killed his enemies while in the middle of telling a joke. It helped relieve the tension, and drove the ghosts to spend the rest of eternity trying to find somebody who knew the punch line.

Chairs cycled up from the floor and the reporters took seats when the action on the monitor caught everybody's attention.

"What is that rhino doing?" demanded Rikka, blushing and going pale at the same moment.

Then the unexpected happened, with the expected results.

"Oh . . . !"

". . . My!"

". . . GOD!"

". . . s, above and below!"

And the team turned away trying not to barf on the carpet.

"Animal snuff films," said Hassan, unperturbed. "The very latest thing in nouveau decadence. Very popular on Venus and in Los Angeles."

"That," panted Harry, wiping his mouth with the back of a hand, "that is absolutely the sickest thing I have ever witnessed!"

Politely, the crime lord turned off the monitor. It was a repeat, anyway. "Nonsense! Wait till you see the one with the ostrich!"

"Pass!" cried Jhonny, backing away, hands over eyes.

Chuckling, Hassan worked the keyboard of his primary computer for a moment, information flowing across the shaded screen.

"Interested in making a movie?" the gangster asked the hirsute Goliath.

Michelangelo glowered down at the tiny human.

"Only with you as my costar," he rumbled dangerously.

The team gasped for breath.

Faceless guards in ninja black stepped into view from out of the well-lit corners.

The Gibraltar automatically clicked on by itself.

And throwing back his head, Hassan roared with laughter.

"That," he stopped to breathe. "That is a wonderful idea! I could make a million dollars on such a movie. The death of Hassan. Ha!"

Then his attitude and demeanor changed. "I also am not interested, but it is a splendid notion."

However, Abduhl made a note on his wrist secretary to check into the possibility of a computer simulation film.

"So, why are you here?" he asked, resting elbows on the desk and templing his fingers.

"Sir, we need access to your telescope," said Harry, with a dry mouth. The minutes were flashing away on his secretary.

The gentleman pornographer hemmed and hawed. "Well, I am in the middle of a time-lapse series on the Crab Nebula. But I could probably work you in next week."

"Sir, we need it now," amended Rikka.

Jhonny added, "As in five minutes ago."

"Is it that important?"

"Yes!"

In silent contemplation, Hassan surveyed the reporters. The impatience of the news team was almost a tangible thing, along with their fear. That was good. QSNT had done him many a good turn and he likewise. Was the slate even? He thought so. Then this would place them under an obligation to him. That would be payment enough. Having the press on your side often came in handy more than the lunar refueling station in Toronto.

"What exactly are we trying to do?" asked Hassan inquisitively.

Frothing with impatience, the team told him the bare facts as briefly as possible.

"Sorry. Can't do it," he apologized sadly. "Would anybody like some tea?"

"What the prack do you mean we can't?" angrily shouted Collins, standing.

The guards stepped closer and Rikka quickly sat back down and repeated her request for information with a sickly smile and a much more reasonable tone of voice.

"The probe you wish to observe is coming in Fatal. To maintain proper focus means a constant motion of the scope in infinitesimal increments. My computer is not designed for that."

"Sahib, should I go steal another computer?" offered one of the masked guardians.

Abduhl smiled at the killer. Such a kind and thoughtful son. "Thank you, but no, Phillip. Just go break the legs of that woman who cheated me on the last delivery of Strip Chess games."

A bow. "Yes, my father."

"And get some Danish on the way back!" He smiled at the news team. "I know how you reporters love a fresh Danish," he chided them in a friendly manner.

I CAN DO IT, scrolled Deitrich on the desk monitor.

"Ah, my bodiless friend," cried Hassan in delight. "I am so glad you could join us. And how is your celibate life in a jar?"

CELIBATE? HAHAHAHAHAHAHAHAHAHAHAHAHAHAHAHAHAHAHAHAHA-HAHAHAHAHAHAHAHAHHAHAHAHAHAHAHAHAHAHAHAHAHAHAHAHAHA-HAHAHAHAHAHAHAHAHAHAHAHHAHAHAHAHAHAHA . . .

As the scrolling continued, Hassan was shocked and pleased at the reaction. The Brain had sex? Fascinating!

"Tell me about it," asked the crime lord eagerly. "Was she another Brain? Was it good?"

"Is sex ever bad?" asked Jhonny, askance.

"Yes, quite frequently," admitted Hassan matter-of-factly.

The roll stopped in mid-ha. MEANING NO DISRESPECT, BUT A GENTLEMAN NEVER KISSES AND TELLS.

"Ah," hissed the man in delight. "You only kissed like children. How sweet."

KISS? YES, ONCE. AT THE BEGINNING.

Gnashing her teeth, Rikka started making guttural noises. Moving fast to cut her off, Harry leaned forward in his chair. "Of course, purely out of courtesy and respect, we will give you duplicates of all recordings made to dispose of as you wish."

Suddenly, the monetary implications became quite clear to the crime lord. If civilization did not end, he could make a fortune! This could be even better than his own death! Or better yet, he could put them together as a double feature!

And then, there was always the possibility of a spin-off series and a line of stuffed toys.

"Come," he said, rising and walking away.

The news team and guards followed close behind. Another private elevator took them to the top floor of the spacescraper. The room was a half globe, similar to the protective dome outside. The floor was covered with cork to muffle the disrupting vibrations of footsteps, the walls were adorned with astronomical charts and diagrams of the solar system heavily notated with corrections. A row of computer consoles encircled an exposed array of meshed gears that directly connected to the supporting steelloy beams, each thick as an aircar. And completely filling the middle of the room was a seamless column of black ferruled metal over eighty feet in circumference with a tiny little periscope attached at the bottom. A catwalk artfully encased the scope, allowing easy access to dozens of observation ports and maintenance points of the monster telescope.

A devoted technophile, Jhonny knew the statistics by heart. The main reflecting mirror was a disk of glass 475 inches in diameter, backed by a cold-fused, molecularly perfect sheet of silver/iridium alloy worth over a million on the legit market. Which Hassan had gotten for $3.95, no tax, a rebate, and a discount coupon on the next one.

As the group went forward, the team glanced out the windows, where the asteroid city spread below them with the wonder and majesty of an amusement park seen from the top of the Ferris wheel. In the distance, stately asteroids moved on regulated courses, colorful beacons winking and blinking the silent language of warning.

As they approached a prominent console, a billowing cloud of white fog erupted from the telescope and a bitter chill swept across the cavernous room.

"Do not be alarmed," explained Hassan, taking a seat. "It is only periodic cleaning with frozen carbon dioxide."

"Why?" asked Collins, fighting a shiver.

The pornographer stared at her askance. "Why? Because anything else would pit the glass!"

Rikka was fascinated. He stated that possibility as if it were the worst thing that could happen.

"Amazing," sighed Snyder, his breath visible for only an instant as the life support efficiently regulated the room temperature. "How did you get started in this hobby?"

A smarmy smile. "As a young boy, my next-door neighbor was a voluptuous redhead, and Allah be praised, every night she would not completely close the curtains just before—"

The interest in their faces quickly fled and Hassan soon stopped his monologue. In good humor, he accepted the mild rebuff. Some people just didn't like anecdotal humor. He was sure Mark Twain had constantly encountered similar prejudice himself. It was TriD that did it. Ruined everybody's patience. Filthy thing. Which was why Abduhl only sold porno to show on the nasty viewers.

Placing his camcorder on an open area among the controls, Jhonny took the seat of the prime director. Nimble hands threw switches and rotated dials with professional abandonment. The operating lights changed pattern and indicators flickered in strobing response.

LINK IS ESTABLISHED, Deitrich scrolled in his familiar font on the console monitor. I WILL BEGIN RELINING NOW.

The colossal tube seemed to quiver. Then nothing happened.

GOT IT. FOUND THE PROBE.

"How?" demanded Rikka, sharing a look with Harry and Mike. "The scope didn't move."

YES IT DID. AN INCH HERE MEANS A MILLION KILOMETERS THERE.

Incredulously, the reporter sniffed at the gargantuan device. WatchDog scanners gave a much better picture and a lot easier. Unfortunately, they were active, not passive scanners, telling the armada that it was being watched, which could mean fifty years on Neptune for having top secret data. A news reporter's immunity could only work if they could hide behind the battalion of lawyers at their parent station. Out in the field, it was be discreet or stand-quietly-and-place-your-hands-above-your-head. As the saying goes, freedom of speech stopped at the atmosphere.

"It's going to be difficult to get a good sighting with all those lights on," said the android, tentatively adjusting the controls of the mammoth scope.

Hassan raised a wrist. "Achmed?"

"Yes, sahib?" responded a voice from his secretary.

"Turn off the city, please."

And the asteroid outside the windows went black.

"It's good to be the boss," the crime lord smirked in the stygian darkness.

Slowly increasing illumination, safety bars glowed into existence around all doorways, windows, and consoles. The ghostly glowing lines gave the observatory a spooky atmosphere and seemed to enhance the feelings of tension.

"This is only a visible light telescope," stated Michelangelo, literally looking over the console. "So what we will be seeing are events that already happened. Uranus is some four hours away at light speed."

"That is so," nodded Hassan, obviously pleased that somebody understood the simple laws of optical telemetry.

Harry grunted. Which is why they had had to hurry, or else the team would have missed the war.

Hands in pockets, Rikka arched her neck to stare at the slit in the high curved ceiling. Then the fate of mankind had already been settled. Had the united fleet stopped the runaway drone? Or was it now streaking toward the asteroid belt and then Earth. Uncontrollably, she started to shake and then got command of herself. It was only a story. Just another story. Nothing personal.

Yeah, right.

READY TO RECORD? scrolled Deitrich.

The camera-op had his face pressed tight against the cushioned rim of a hooded monitor. "Tones and bars, pal. The picture is crystal clear . . . and here it comes!" There was a pause. "Hmm, it seems larger than the blueprints indicated."

Rikka waved that aside. "Probably just some last-minute modifications by the Ganymede scientists."

"Or it's still dragging around a chunk of the test building or chains," postulated Harry, taking out a silver case. He placed a fresh cigar in his mouth and Hassan removed the stogie, returning the broken halves to the anchor and shaking his head vehemently no. Smoke bothered the telescope? Sheesh.

"No," said Jhonny in an urgent tone. "The probe is bigger." The android raised his head from the cushioned viewer. "A lot bigger."

CHAPTER FIFTEEN

IT WAS KNOWN only as The Ship.

Sleeker than a surgical needle, the military craft was painted a dead flat, reflectionless black. She possessed no external running lights or operational lights. Even the glow bars in the airlock had been removed.

A complex series of baffles muffled the nuclear flame of her sublight engines, the material of the baffles themselves absorbing the heat and radiation.

There was no iron or steel used anywhere in its composition. Indeed, very little metal of any kind had been incorporated into the unique vessel. Even the teeth of the crew had ceramic fillings instead of gold or silver.

Radar proved it wasn't there, masers indicated the same. Z-band sensors and WatchDog scanners registered not even an anomaly. It had no heat signature; on infrared or ultraviolet it showed as nothing. Even the usually reliable proximity indicators had trouble locating the vessel when they were immediately alongside. Indeed, twice The Ship had been listed as AWOL when the stealthship was safely ensconced in her home port.

On the tiny bridge, a grim man sat hunched over in a command chair, the arm panels covered with miniature controls. Before him, the crew was in a semicircle of instrument panels. Nearby, attached to the wooden handle of the weapons locker with a plastic leash, was a Gila lizard munching contentedly in a bowl full of food.

"Mark," called out the Tactical officer. "Two light minutes till rendezvous with target."

"Drop the mines," commanded the Captain. "Launch the missiles, release the torpedoes, evasive maneuvers."

162

The crew obeyed.

Moving off on an angle, the empty area of space aligned itself bow toward the rapidly oncoming drone. On the main monitor of the bridge, the sphere of lambent green was readily visible at only magnification five. Damn thing must be three thousand klicks in diameter!

"Missiles will impact at five," announced the Tactical officer, ". . . four . . . three . . . two . . . we have a malfunction."

"What?!" roared the Captain, rising from his chair.

"The missiles went random just prior to impact."

Ruefully, the man crunched his face in concentration. "At what distance?"

"Roughly three thousand klicks."

A fist slammed onto a knee. It was the Apocalypse Drive! That damn field must be scrambling the electronic guidance systems of the missiles!

"Weapons officer! Prep a volley of dead missiles. Auto navigation and gyroscopes only. No electronic lock."

The plump man nodded. "Aye, sir. Ten minutes!"

"Do it in five." No audible warning followed.

A gulp. "Aye, aye, Skipper!"

Softly, the Medical officer said a short prayer in Gaelic.

"We have contact," said the Gunnery officer in a thick Russian accent. "There is a shape on the Z-band scanners."

"Wait for it," growled the Captain.

Near the Communications officer the WatchDog scanner went blip.

"Wait . . ."

At the console of the Navigation officer, the sublight radar pinged with a bogey at ten thousand.

"Fire!"

And empty space erupted with pyrotechnic fury. Bedlow lasers stabbed into the distant darkness. Antiship torpedoes disappeared on searing cones of flame. A salvo of Fatal missiles blurred out of sight at six times the speed of light. The neutrino cannon vomited invisible torrents of death, enough to fry the circuitry of any possible machine. Then a brilliant point of light flashed into existence as the atomic mines detonated.

A precious moment passed as The Ship waited impatiently for the swirling plasma of destruction to dissipate.

"It's undamaged!" cried the Sensor officer.

"Confirmed," added Tactical.

"Ramming speed!" ordered the Captain, cinching his safety belt.

Resolutely, Navigation flipped a switch and The Ship took off in hot pursuit after the rogue probe.

Toying with the wedding ring on his hand, the Captain watched as his crew prepared for close-order combat. The Ganymede drone was now bracketed by hostile forces from before and behind. All the fleet had to do was slow the bugger down and The Ship would plow into it. He and his crew had no qualms in sacrificing their lives in this battle. They had faced infinitely worse battling the Free Police. This would be a clean death in the service of humanity.

So much for his retirement next month.

"Alert!" called Navigation. "Target is slowing!"

Madre mia! "Evasive maneuvers!"

And a sudden wash of green light sweep over the stealth craft and every crew member slumped at their posts, including the lizard.

"Nothing so far," announced Jhonny. "Just some light flashes."

"Probably a salvo of ultra-long-distance Fatal missiles," guessed Rikka.

"UP has probably been pounding the drone with those since it cleared Pluto," noted Hassan sagely. "Or, at least, I would have."

Collins glanced at the starry sky toward the ninth planet. "Lord, I hope the scientists had enough time to evac."

"Or maybe it was a daring attack by The Ship," offered Snyder, chewing discontentedly on a cigar flavor stick.

Annoyed, Hassan scowled at the man. "Sir, you don't actually believe in that prattle about an undetectable warship?"

The anchor shrugged eloquently.

Mike accessed the word "prattle."

Side by side, Admiral Davis and a translucent Admiral Hamilton stood on the bridge of *Prime,* the mobile command center for the Unified Solar Defense Armada. Filling the triptych of monitors that spanned the bow wall spread a panorama of warships from half a dozen worlds, enough amassed firepower to extinguish the very sun itself.

Should anybody be stupid enough to wish that event.

"The Ship has been neutralized, sir," announced an ensign, busy hands everywhere on her console.

A Colonel turned to face the woman. "And how do you know?" he demanded hotly.

"Activation signal from the Dead Man beacon."

Admiral Davis removed the pipe from his mouth and tapped the hot ashes into a hand so badly scarred it couldn't feel the heat. Normally it was a neat trick for impressing the troops. Today he did it without thinking. So far, this war was a debacle. They had lost over eighty-five ultra-long-range Fatal missiles in abortive attempts to blow the drone apart, the poor bastards at Pluto never escaped in time, and now The Ship failed. It was coming very close to open warfare—something impossible to hide from the civilian population. And how many innocent deaths would occur in the resulting panic and riots? But there was one chance remaining.

"Your turn, Kat," drawled the southerner, reloading his pipe with fresh shag.

On the Uranus moon of Titania, Admiral Hamilton looked at the laser hologram of her male counterpart.

"See you in hell, Mad Dog."

"Give 'em hell, Kat."

With a shimmer, the Earth Admiral disappeared and Kathryn Hamilton was alone in her own mobile command center. She knew that the tacticians had wished each Admiral to watch the other, looking for weak points in the attacks and to assist whenever possible. But in truth each of the Admirals simply couldn't stand having somebody watch over their shoulder as they worked.

The control room was bustling with officers and crew, all wearing spacesuits and helmets. It was a standard precaution against explosive decompression and, in the case of Titania, toxic methane poisoning. It registered almost as bad as Los Angeles smog on the environmental scale.

Uranus, with its hundred razor-thin rings, filled the aft sky, and the Titan fleet was haloed by the rapidly encroaching green glow from space.

Kat nodded. Good. It wasn't going to try to swing around them.

The mindless machine was coming straight in like a monorail express train.

"Magnification one hundred?" asked the Admiral, hands clasped behind her back.

An ensign swiveled about in his chair at the tactical console. "But, sir, we can see it good enough to target."

"One hundred," she repeated in a no-nonsense tone.

Quickly the screen enlarged for maximum. Now clearly discernible in the middle of the huge drive field was a black silhouette. A technician placed the vector graphic of the drone archived from Ganymede also on the screen for comparison. Gasps and curses arose at the image.

The two did not match.

The original probe was a bare bones array of struts, engines, and reactor. This invader was five times as large, with a smooth humped hull indicating armor. Lots of armor.

In cold fury, the Titan troops wondered how many of the missiles had gotten through only to impact uselessly on the outside of the thick hull.

"Missiles officer, reset for penetration!" snapped Hamilton.

"Already on it, A!" called the Colonel, typing on a keyboard with both hands. Titan had always relied upon individual initiative, instead of the silly sheep-go-to-war notion of Earth.

"Informing Prime," announced the Communications Lieutenant.

"Aye," said Kat in authorization. Damnation, their attacks and defenses had been established for an unarmed drone whose sole protection was that damnable drive field. Furiously, she snapped orders to reorganize the fleet and lunar defenses. But in a remarkably short time, there was a beep as the drone was tracked on the radar.

"Outer perimeter, fire at will," said Admiral Hamilton with deceptive calm.

Buttons were pressed. At extreme range, the scintillating beams of a hundred Bedlow lasers lanced into space, illuminating an immaterial globe about the machine.

It had a forceshield.

"Gods above and below," whispered a Gremlin technician. Suddenly, her enlistment in the military didn't seem like such a wise career move.

Hamilton turned about. "Weapons officer, launch all missiles! DTR, converge the mines! And pull those ships back! I want a minimum distance of four thousand klicks!" The naval officer was unwilling to lose any more human lives than was absolutely necessary. But they would stop that drone!

Swiftly, the Titan warships retreated to allow the drone easy access through to the moon of Titania and its infinitely more powerful land-based weaponry.

Constantly bombarded by the stabbing fury of the human lasers, the radiating drone rapidly passed by the moon, the green glow of the deadly Apocalypse Drive overpowered the reflected sunlight from Uranus.

A flurry of sublight rockets streaked up from a battery emplacement atop a rocky butte. The drone easily dodged the lumbering attack. Then more missiles lifted into space. Dozens. Hundreds! But upon entering the drive field, the missiles became unguided rockets and zigzagged willy-nilly. However, there were precisely too many of them. The sublight missiles collided constantly and streamers of flame blossomed to fill the horizon below Uranus as half-molten debris shotgunned every which way.

A random chunk slammed into the probe scoring the armor hull. Quickly, the drone maneuvered to the west.

. . . and an entire mountain range glowed with an incandescent light! Then sixteen blinding white stilettos lanced out tracking toward the enemy. Awesome in their raw destructive power, the searing beams of fusing hydrogen swept ever closer toward the deadly intruder—when the green glow suddenly expanded to twice its original dimensions and the hellish drive field engulfed the entire base.

The lances winked out. Armored spacesuits toppled over at their stations. Hellcat Hamilton shouted a final warning to her troops and Titania went off the air.

"Negative!" announced Jhonny.

"What?" snapped Rikka.

The technician at the glowing WatchDog scanner console had a worried expression on his plastic face. "That isn't our probe."

"Eh?"

"Qua?"

"Huh?"

"Bullshit!" Harry looked over the android's shoulder at the rotating green bands on the monitor. "Run a diagnostic."

"See for yourself," offered the camera-op, gesturing. "The system is fine and the pattern of the Apocalypse Drive is close, but not exact. I accessed the Media files of their previous earlier attempts. It is not our probe. Check the wave frequency modulations yourself."

Squiggly lines snaked across a submonitor window on the main screen in the infamous pattern. There was some variation. Not much. But enough.

"Aliens?" asked Rikka, her voice taking on an excited quality.

"Yes?" replied Mike, glancing toward her. "Oh, sorry. Old habit."

"From aliens," corrected Mike. "Nothing carbon-based is alive on that ship."

Wringing his hands, Hassan demanded to know why.

"Turnabout," whispered Snyder, heart pounding in his chest. "That bedamned probe went to some inhabited system and killed who knows how many of the locals before they stopped it. The Apocalypse Drive may have wiped out an entire planet!"

Collins went pale. "So now they are sending the probe back to its creators as retribution." Retribution. What a lofty and noble-sounding word until you are on the receiving end.

"Why to Earth?" queried Hassan from behind a sheaf of computer printouts.

"Those coordinates the onboard computer had," snorted Jhonny, worrying his chin. "According to the probe ship, that is where it came from originally!"

"So what can we do?" demanded Michelangelo.

"Us?" snorted the news reporter. "We can do our job and record everything for posterity and hope the military is as good as they boast."

A tense moment passed.

"No. Really," the alien insisted. "What can we do?"

"Pray," said Hassan, closing his eyes. "Early and often."

* * *

15:54 . . . 15:55 . . .

"The probe has left Uranus!" announced a Ganymede tech.

Then the Titan fleet at Titania was destroyed. Conway ground his teeth. The course the probe was taking was too damn far outside the effective range of their feeble masers. They had the power, but not an effective focus. And the operational range of the hydrogen lances was too short for such a distance. Damn-damn-damn!

"Launch the experimental drones!" he commanded.

Major RunningHawk pointed a finger as an added incentive for quick movement.

Rising from every launch bay on the moon came a crude attack squadron of remote-controlled drones, each powered by a different experimental engine. Straight and true, the makeshift armada hurled themselves directly at the invader at absolute maximum speed. It was a hastily cobbled technological avalanche moving at just under the unbelievable velocity of Fatal Ten.

Across the intervening millions of kilometers the drones flashed in their dimension-bending race for death. Then from the aft of the alien probe came a stuttering beam of energy. Every visual scanner blanked from the onslaught of blinding light that erupted from the staggering multiple explosions.

Prayers now battled with curses for supremacy in the control room. Gone were any questions as to the machine's intentions.

This was no warning.

It was war.

Onboard the USDA *Prime,* Admiral Davis lit his pipe and puffed a cloud of thoughts about himself. Armed and armored. He was glad the Ark was safely on its way out of the system.

Rapidly forming around the flagship of the armada was a wall of ships, linked together with tractor and pressure beams into an unbreakable space web directly in the path of the alien killer.

According to Tactical, nothing should be able to get through.

But then, Tactical had designed the defenses of Titania.

"Target at six thousand klicks," called an ensign.

"Outer four rings, independent fire," said the Admiral.

Glowing daggers of pure force stabbed out of the web. The drone jerked violently to starboard, and a scintillating laser beam, as big as a house, passed on the left. The deadly dance had begun.

Searing energy pulses came at the drone in a tightening cone of near misses, almost faster than it could compensate for. Wildly, the probe went crashing through an endless series of crazy maneuvers, things that no missile or crewed ship could do; twisting, turning, spinning, spiraling, looping backward, jumping, dancing, darting up and down, back and forth. It was a roller-coaster ride through a cocktail shaker bouncing down a flight of stairs. Yet, every random shunt eventually brought the drone closer and closer to the web.

A hundred times the USDA missiles got acquisition, only to have the probe dodge free again. The Martian carriers released swarms of Tarantula interceptors, but whether the cyborg fighters dived in from the sides, charged in head on, or spiraled up from the bottom, the drone outdistanced them and their weapons with contemptuous ease.

Taking an insane chance, the military threw firepower across space, expending gigawatts of energy in a brutal display of pyrotechnic fury. In that wave, a pulse impacted directly on the drone. Its forceshield ran through the visible spectrum in a second and dropped. Unstoppable, the beam carried onward only to splash harmlessly against another, tougher shield underneath the first.

"It has a shield within a shield?" croggled an ensign.

"That's impossible!" denounced an elderly Major. "You can not propagate a forcefield through another forcefield! Gotterstein's Third Law of Forcefield Dynamics!"

"Prack Gotterstein and the asteroid he came in on!" spat Davis around his pipe. "All ships, at my mark, cease fire! Then a four-second pause and then blanket fire pattern Ticonderoga! Communications officer, relay and confirm!"

Precisely on the mark, the random firing ceased and the drone zoomed in, sweeping through the center of the web to eliminate this boisterous competition once and for good.

Which was exactly what Davis wanted.

"How can this be?" cried Hassan, tearing at his hair and beard. "One lone ship dealing disaster to the entire human armada?"

"A lone ship rebuilt by a very pissed-off alien culture," reminded Snyder. "Who knows how much effort and money they put into the conversion. Millions? Billions?"

"Trillions!" added Rikka.

"Googols!" finished Jhonny.

Quickly Mike accessed that word also. Ah, unknown aliens spent enough money to make their eyes bulge out. Yes, that was a lot.

The drone neared, and then entered Point Zero.

Instantly, the entire armada discharged every weapon they possessed in a single staggering barrage: lasers, disrupters, missiles, rockets, torpedoes, shells, bombs, mines, drones, neutrino beams, hydrogen lances, the titanic outpouring of energy so illuminated space that it was visible to the naked eye on the daylight side of Earth.

Pausing in their daily routine, the civilians wondered which side of the war was winning.

Then the Einstein Gatlings cut loose with their special brand of destruction and a shotgun blast of thermonuclear bullets peppered all of nearby space. But still the trapped drone fought on, nimbly dodging the titanic thrust of raw cosmic power. Again and again, the probe was targeted. A hundred times the multitiered power ray came close to the drone, but always the silvery machine spiraled away from the stabbing fury of the deadly composite gigawatt beam.

Then, as the reserve troops on the Titan ships seized control of their decimated base, from Titania moon came a spiraling rod of turbulent energy. Across the trillion miles of space the quasi-solid energy pulse sliced in from the sidelines, the flaring thrust of counterforce bisecting the offensive bombardment to create a staggering explosion of cosmic proportions!

In *Prime*, the bridge monitors went blank from sensory overload.

"Cease fire!" cried Davis at last. It took a few moments, but the awful expenditure was slowly staged down and the monitors cleared to display hot black space.

"Full scans from the L5s!"

"Attack horizon is clear!"

"We zaped it!" cried an ensign and the bridge crew began to cheer.

"Silence!" roared Davis. "Tactical confirm with SitComTac and Lunar Base Gagarin!"

A tense minute passed.

"Negative," cried an aghast ensign, turning pale. "Target is twenty thousand klicks behind us!"

Dashing his pipe to the deck, Admiral Davis violently cursed as he stomped the family heirloom to bits. The alien machine had somehow jumped around the web and the whole damn asteroid belt! Had it only been playing with them this whole time? Ye God, how fast could the bloody thing go? Did it even have a speed limit?

"Flight Commander, disengage all lines! Reverse headings! Independent firing from dreadnoughts and up! Volley fire from battleships and down! Corsairs and frigates try for a ram!"

But the naval officer knew the situation was hopeless. The drone was already far ahead of them and Davis was aware this last try was a feeble gesture at best. The military had done their best—and failed.

Earth was doomed.

CHAPTER SIXTEEN

IN THE CHILLY darkness of the asteroid observatory, the news team and Hassan watched with waxy expressions as the killer drone dwindled off into the distance toward Earth. It was an unusual experience to be able to write your own epitaph, and know that nobody would ever hear it. Bummer.

But suddenly the Ganymede probe exploded into a brilliant fireball of lambent nuclear vapors!

There was a blink.

And then they could see the drone again. Whole and intact.

Stupefied, the team and gangster could only stare in dumb wonderment. What the hell was going on here?

THAT WAS A COMPUTER SIMULATION, scrolled Deitrich.

"Thanks for the heart attack," groaned Harry, clutching his chest in mock agony. Then the anchor straightened. "But hey! If you show us this—"

THEN I CAN SHOW THE DRONE WHAT IT WANTS TO SEE. YES.

"The destruction of Earth!" cried Rikka. "Is there anything we can do to help?"

LOTS. IT'LL BE TOUGH ENOUGH BALANCING THE TRANSMISSION TO FOOL THE DRONE. I WILL NEED AS BIG A DATA BASE OF INFO AS POSSIBLE.

Data base? "News clips of disasters do?" asked Jhonny.

YES. ANYTHING LIKE THAT.

"And we could cannibalize the shuttle's movie collection," offered Michelangelo, fumbling for a transmodem in his tool vest.

With a shudder Hassan rejoined the conversation. "You are seriously going to send a phony picture of the Earth being destroyed to the probe? How? The craft has more shields and protective fields than the whole armada!"

AND THAT IS ITS WEAKNESS.

Jhonny and Michelangelo nodded in understanding, busy with their computers.

Rikka decided to explain, "With so many shields, Z-band transmissions can't go in or out."

From the expression on his dour face, the crime lord plainly did not comprehend.

"How does it see?" explained Jhonny, speaking loudly in his excitement. "Fatal ships normally utilize a Z-band sensor, or a WatchDog, when traveling faster than light. But that many shields would scramble the transmission."

"And radar only travels at light speed," added Snyder. "Useless to FTL travel."

"Light," said Rikka, standing straight. "It's using plain old visible light to see where it's going."

The crime lord was having difficulty believing this. "They built a superprobe and it can only look where it is going?"

"Certainly. Simple is almost always the best procedure," noted Jhonny pragmatically. "But if light can get in, then a maser can get in also."

Mike had a flashback to their long-ago conversation about the Geneva L5. Yes, it could be done! Where brute force did fail, guile may prevail! Hmm, that rhymed. "And we can give the drone the show of a lifetime!"

This was becoming simply too much for Abduhl. Uncaring of the consequences, he strode to a star map on the wall, pressed Betelgeuse three times and the chart swung out on a hidden hinge. Behind the map, in a refrigerated recess, was a two-hundred-year-old bottle of Napoleon brandy. Cracking the seal with a thumbnail, Hassan upended the bottle and took a long draft.

Then made a horrible face and spit the spirits back into the chilled container. Allah's revenge! No wonder this was forbidden. But a pleasure? Feh! And if this was a very popular beverage of booze, then he could not even imagine what a pork sandwich would taste like!

Unaware of the religious drama being conducted near them, the team went on with its preparations for video combat.

"We can send a Z-band transmission to our Earth affiliate," said Mike, expertly working his wrist portable with one talon.

"And they can beam it toward the drone on a maser!" finished Jhonny, mimicking the action.

Harry dropped his flavor stick to the floor, crushing it underfoot, grinning widely. Reporters had always been purveyors of information. And during wartime, often masters of propaganda. This was surely a worse case scenario, but still, there was a chance.

And the only chance Earth had.

"Should we go back to the shuttle?" asked Rikka, taking a step toward the elevator.

NOT NECESSARY. YOU ALREADY HAVE A HOT LINK ESTABLISHED WITH ME. YOU FOUR CAN DO THE SCUT WORK FROM THE CONSOLES OF THE TELESCOPE.

"But the distance . . ." complained Hassan.

WHAT'S TWO KILOMETERS COMPARED TO THE FIFTY MILLION KILOMETERS WE'LL BE BROADCASTING OVER?

True enough.

Grabbing seats, the reporters accessed the appropriate files and memory banks from the shuttle and threw themselves into assembling the absolutely most important special report of their professional lives.

They started with news footage of Earth as seen from space, then dollied in and started a wild shotgun series of classic disasters: panic in the streets from the crash of Wall Street, the riots in Chicago when the Cubs finally won a World Series, Dallas when President Kennedy was shot, the tearing down of the Berlin Wall, protests against the Vietnam War, the victory celebration of the Six-Day War, plus World War I, II, and III, state lottery madness, food riots, mass escapes from prison, and numerous Beatles concerts. Anything with wild cheering crowds by adroit editing became wild screaming crowds. The reporters had no idea how the drive field killed, but it was always a sure bet that humanity would meet its end as noisily as possible.

"Cue!"

"Mark!"

"Set!"

"Jhonny," asked the alien technician, adjusting different dials with both paws at the same time. "Couldn't you do this faster and better by establishing a link with your positronic brain?"

Balancing colors and tinting old black-and-white videotapes, the cameraman shook his head. "Nope. That would require a positronic computer the size of a refrigerator! Originally I was built to be an underwater farmer. Most of my brain space is occupied with subprograms that let me walk upright. My limbs have no muscle memory," he explained.

Reluctantly the alien accepted that. Made sense.

But the busy android wasn't finished. "And my brain isn't what I have that's the size of a refrigerator," he smirked, hitching the lower half of his jumpsuit.

"Liar," puffed Harry, splicing like a madman. "It's no bigger than a flashlight."

Adjusting volume and level controls, Jhonny squinted at the anchor. "You been peeking in the showers again?"

Michelangelo and Hassan snorted volcanic laughs.

"Gentlemen, the war?" growled Rikka, her head tight against the cushioned rim of a hood visor as she blended cuts and crossfades with equal aplomb.

Soon the basic scut work was done and deemed insufficient. So now the team raided the more difficult archives. News footage of poison gas attacks from World War I had the gas neatly deleted out, leaving only dying bodies. Then they added hundreds of assorted shots of planes crashing, highway collisions, trains derailing, ships sinking, cities on fire, spaceships exploding in takeoff, buildings falling over, bridges collapsing, forest fires, earthquakes, tidal waves, hurricanes, tornadoes, volcanoes, nuclear explosions, the reelection of Dan Quayle. Anything and everything that seemed even faintly reasonable they trimmed, adjusted, and clipped onto the growing footage of the montage of doom.

"Cue!"

"Mark!"

"Set!"

Harry wiped sweat from his eyes with a sleeve. "God, I wish Parson was here."

"Deitrich, are you sure that you can harmonize the sound track?" asked Rikka, splicing and dicing as if her fingers had a life of their own.

SASHA MAY BE THE BEST THERE IS, BUT I'M THE BEST WE'VE GOT.

"Sorry," mumbled the woman. Geeze, some Brains were so sensitive.

SHADDUP AND WORK. I HAVE THE AFFILIATE READY TO GO.

Finished with his wanton rummaging, Snyder now fed Deitrich his own contributions from movieland: the mass hysteria scenes from *Cleopatra*, *Antony and Cleopatra*, *Caesar and Cleopatra*, and *Cleopatra Goes to Hawaii*. Endless screaming crowd shots from a plethora of goofy monster flicks. The opening from *Children of the Damned* where everybody falls over unconscious. A similar scene from *Day of the Triffids*. A lovely pair of apparently pointless riots from *Soylent Green*. Brutal hand-to-hand combat melees from the end of *Enter the Dragon* and a seemingly endless series of nuclear explosions from the trailer of *Dr. Strangelove* that he then crossfaded to the depopulated planet scenes from *The Last Beach*. Somber, dreary, gut-wrenching stuff, it was more appropriately nightmare visions than light entertainment.

Tearfully, Hassan completed his own work and keyed in all the pertinent shots from his entire collection of vintage and antique snuff films.

"Time?" asked Rikka, panting.

TEN SECONDS TO SPARE.

Relaxing at their consoles, everybody breathed a sigh of relief.

HERE WE GO.

Hands tightened and everybody held their breath.

"Well," barked Harry after a moment. "Is it working? Deitrich? Hey, Deitrich!"

Rikka waved him silent. "He's too busy to answer."

"But how do we know if it's working!" cried Hassan, chewing on the ragged end of his once-long beard.

"Use the Z-band sensors!" snapped Harry. "Who cares if the military arrests us later?"

"Good point," conceded Jhonny as he linked up the monitor to the new shuttle. He found the drone almost immediately.

On the monitor screen, the green glow was just passing the orbit of Mars and charging in straight toward Earth.

Gradually, the drone began to slow, as if unsure what to make of this bizarre time slip. It was receiving a picture of the target world way ahead of schedule. Inquisitively, the drone extended its drive field and the planet promptly turned green. Then suddenly the machine was bombarded by endless ground-level views of the indigenous population dying most dramatically. Hesitantly at first, the drone slowed to a complete stop. There was something wrong here, but it wasn't quite sure what that could be.

The machine would wait a bit before dropping its twelve shields for a full Z-band scan.

Then, disaster.

"Shit!" cried Jhonny, his hands all over the console.

"What?" demanded Rikka.

"We lost the audio! Blew a pracking transmitter! Hassan's equipment is old crap and couldn't take the load!"

Abduhl started to hotly contest that statement, then shrugged in silence. There was no defense against the truth. Except for money, guns, and lawyers, of course.

"Well, switch to another!" shouted Collins, almost dancing with barely restrained hysterics.

Futilely, Jhonny pounded on the console. "He doesn't have another!"

"I don't have another," said the gangster a moment too late.

Whiskers quivering, Mike swiveled about hard in his chair, making the steel support rod creak ominously. "So what do we do?"

Impulsively, Collins flexed her fingers in the air, as if to pull an answer or miracle out of nothingness. For once, her bag of tricks was empty. There was no gimmick, no sham that came to mind to pull their fat from the fire this time.

Then suddenly, Harry screamed, disrupting their worry convention. And the anchor continued screaming in as many different voices and languages as the talented man knew.

Taking their cue, the rest of the team joined in, and after a moment, so did Hassan. Soon a frantic squad of guards arrived and the gangster added their puzzled vocals to the painful throatings.

With the noise relayed through their wrist secretaries, Deitrich caught up the slack and modified the lag time. Sadly however, the vocal outpourings were a valiant effort. But it wasn't enough. Not by half. They needed more voices. A lot more.

And the MainBrain knew exactly where to find them.

"Horny Toad," sang out MacKenzie cheerfully on his telephone.

SHUT UP! scrolled Deitrich on the phone monitor. LISTEN AND MOVE FAST, MAC. THE ONLY CONCEIVABLE REASON WILKES LETS YOU

OWN THE TOAD IS THAT YOU HAVE SOMETHING ON HIM. USE IT! CALL THE
BOSS AND ORDER HIM TO HAVE THE WHOLE STATION START SCREAMING.
SCREAM FOR THEIR LIVES! AND NOT TO STOP UNTIL I SAY SO. AND UN-
LESS THEY DO, IN ABOUT TWENTY SECONDS WE'RE GOING TO HAVE THE
BIGGEST GODDAMN SLAUGHTER IN THE HISTORY OF MANKIND!

"But why?" asked MacKenzie.

THAT'S ONE!

Bartenders are trained listeners and can usually tell when a person is lying. It is a prerequisite in their business. And to the best of
the Scotsman's knowledge the pilot was dead serious.

Disconnecting the telephone monitor, the bartender typed in a
number Alonzo knew by heart but had honestly thought he would
never dial.

"Wilkes? MacKenzie here. We got a problem."

"Now here this!" boomed the voice of Gardner Wilkes over the
PA system of Media. "All personnel are to stop whatever they are
doing and start screaming. At the top of their lungs and in as many
different voices and languages you know." He gave them a precious
moment to absorb that. "And anybody who doesn't give me their
best effort will be fired with prejudice, lose their severance pay, un-
employment benefits, be blackballed from the entire news business,
and make a dire enemy of me and my 750 million dollars!"

Throughout the station, people stared at each other in puzzlement, shock, and then fear. A cub reporter with nothing to lose
started caterwauling and that set off the rest. Soon, the cries of anguish and death spread from room to room, level to level, even
Bruno gnashing his teeth and chewing noisily on the glass of his
home. In ragged chorus everybody but the dead moose in the saloon bathroom joined in on the sonic cavalcade.

Minutes passed, as the alien killer contentedly watched the de-
mise of the human race. As the nuclear fireballs sprouted mush-
room clouds of radioactive death across the wartorn world, the
drone lowered its multiple shields and started a class-one probe of
the planet with its sensors and scanners.

Immediately, it sensed something was wrong. Earth still registered as brimming with life!

* * *

. . . one second later, nine hundred Fatal missiles armed with thermonuclear warheads converged on the unprotected drone from every possible direction.

The USDA could also take a cue when necessary.

In a staggering series of silent explosions, a fusillade of atomic fireballs blossomed in a volume of space not capable of containing the raw elemental fury of that many nuclei tortured beyond endurance. In perfect spheres, the ruptured atoms released their quotas of lethal quantum energy.

Unable to counter inertia fast enough to escape the power of their own annihilation, the overlapping areas of fission reactions condensed into the fiercer nuclear fusion and even more explosive force was added to the violent tempest. The insane boiling mixture reached, equaled, and then surpassed the ultra-hot temperature/pressures at the core of a white dwarf sun.

And in the next instant, the rapidly melting antimatter generator of the vaporizing drone cut loose. The sheer, mind-shattering superblast threatened to rival the primordial divine boom that had created the macrocosmic universe.

New elements were formed and disintegrated in the nanosecond of their creation, such was the cosmic malestrom of the multiple megaton blasts. Neutrons, protons, and electrons were torn asunder into their base parts of quarks, mesons, tachyons, and a thousand other subatomic particles. The resulting lambent brew spread with the deadly speed of a miniature nova, the searing concentrated plasma nearly ripping apart the very fabric of the local time/space continuum.

The sun dimmed in comparison.

Without even atmosphere or gravity to assist in containing the riotous explosions, the superheated gases and mono-atomic vapors dissipated in every direction at sublight speed. The blinding light flashes and magnetic pulses radiated away even faster from the thinning ethereal mists until, seconds later, the rapidly expanding cloud of death stretched out scintillating daggers of pure death to claim its own creator. Soon there was absolutely nothing remaining in that black volume of cold space to mark that the event had ever happened.

Atop the spacescraper of Tannenbaum, the news reporters tried to shout in victory, but only hoarse squeaks emerged. So they danced with Hassan and the guards until eventually collapsing from total joyous exhaustion.

EPILOGUE

SMILING AT THE eight billion TriD viewers of the solar system, Harry Snyder turned a page and finished his news report. "So in summation, it was solely due to the fast and decisive action of the United Solar Defense Alliance that the probe was finally stopped, literally within striking distance of our beloved mother planet, Earth."

In the control room, a technician nudged Ambocksky. "Hey, Box, why did he list the name?"

Radiating total pleasure, Paul chuckled. "For our beloved idiot viewers who don't know which pracking world we came from."

"Ah, so."

On stage Snyder continued. "And although we mourn the brave soldiers and scientists who died fighting this unearthly threat, we should also give thanks that the dead number in but the thousands, instead of the billions." A page turn. "On a lighter note, the majority of the human race exposed during the destruction of the probe have developed a bad case of sunburn, but—considering the alternative—there have been no complaints and only a few hundred lawsuits."

Another page. "On a more serious matter, the United Planets Security Council has arrested all of the board members of the HNS Corporation and most of the executive personnel at Ganymede Laboratory for criminal negligence, reckless endangerment, public lying, and general stupidity. The court cases should start within the year and are scheduled to go into the next decade. We will cover these proceedings when, and if, anything interesting happens."

Page. "The sole notable exception to this role of dishonor is Pilot Charles Conway, who has been established as the acting head of the BoomMoon until further notice. Good luck, Crash!"

Page down. "And that's the rest of the story about this turnabout invasion from deep space. Will we ever meet the aliens? Can an honorable peace be negotiated with this justly hostile and superior culture? This reporter strongly hopes so."

A hundred-watt smile. "This is Harry Snyder, anchoring for the Satellite News Team. And now over to Lois Kent, for a general look at the worlds news. Lois?"

Cut to Kent, smiling and confident. "Thank you, Harry. Today, on the lighter side of the news, QINS reporters Jason Hardcopy and Susie Sunshine were arrested for attempting to break into the medical files of Koop Memorial Space Hospital. Apparently, their own camera-operator turned them in, aided by fellow journalists Lord Alexander Hyde-White from QBBC and Hanna O'Toole from QCNN. This reporter congratulates their joint honesty and integrity."

A new page. "We will have a rebroadcast of the Satellite News Team *exclusive* video report on the grand finale of the aborted alien invasion with *exclusive* footage of the destruction of the Ganymede probe right after this important commercial message!"

Cut to the geometric logo of Enigma Industries.

"Enigma Industries!" boomed an off-camera announcer as the animated logo began to dance. "Yes, *Enigma Industries!* What we make—"

Chorus: *"Is none of your damn business!"*

Down in The Horny Toad, Rikka turned off the TriD monitor and the team gave a round of applause. Harry took a silent bow. He loved to watch himself on the tube. Thank God for prerecording. The war with the drone had been his first live broadcast in over twenty years. Kinda fun actually.

"Thank you, my friends," said Jhonny in a good mimic of Snyder's voice. "Thank you."

Tonight, the bar was crowded with a line of QSNT employees trailing out into the lobby as the wheezing staff trundled in for large steaming mugs of strong tea laced with whiskey and honey. In a victory spirit, MacKenzie was charging the whole thing to

Wilkes's private account. Nobody was complaining. Or, at least, not very loudly. The space station hadn't been this quiet since Christmas two years ago when the Accounting computer glitched and added an extra zero to everybody's paycheck.

"If you hadn't been under the desk speaking for me," whispered Harry in a throaty croak, "it might have been my job."

The camera-op dismissed it with a wave. "No prob, chief," he chuckled. "Androids don't get sore throats."

"So who is talking for Lois?" wheezed Rikka, hugging her mug of healing elixir.

"Danny J.," said the camera-op with a sneer. "It'll be a nice change for him to work under somebody other than Maria."

Sweet tea sprayed across the table and the pedestal quickly delivered a pile of napkins and a small book on basic etiquette.

As they mopped and cleaned, Harry reviewed his broadcast in detail. On the whole, not bad. The military had truly appreciated their assistance in making the drone lower its shields. But since the team had broken half a zillion laws doing so, a deal had been quickly cut. QSNT gave USDA all of the credit for stopping the drone and in exchange the Satellite News Team didn't do hard time on Neptune.

What the hell. The reporters hadn't really wanted to receive worlds renown for saving mankind. Just professional credit for getting the story and scooping the other three networks. That's what counted on your résumé.

Meanwhile, Jhonny was content to finally get his first chance to do the news. Albeit secretly. A lot of good came from this adventure. Hassan had sworn off porno, although God only knew what devilment he would get into next. And currently, Deitrich was using his tremendous accumulation of vacation days to recuperate at Koop Memorial. Oddly, the MainBrain at the hospital seemed to be off-line all the time.

Hee-hee-hee. Ain't love grand?

Reclining in her chair, Rikka lowered her mug and licked the dissolving honey off her lips. "Jhonny," she whispered, "first chance you get, please send an E-Mail to the QINS legal department and inform them that we'll go to court and be character witnesses for Hardcopy and Sunshine."

His whiskers dangling limply off his face, Mike lifted a snout

from his brimming bowl of tea. Already his throat felt better and
his coat had a definite stiff appearance.

"Professional courtesy?" he meowed. And then hiccuped.

Feeling a bit woozy herself, Collins gave a wink. "Natch."

"Besides," exhaled Harry, refilling his mug from the bottle of
whiskey on the table. "This way, they'll owe us one big favor."

Evil smiles grew and the team cackled fiendishly. Then they
clutched their throats and moaned in pain.

Suddenly in the background, a violent commotion started among
the temporary replacement personnel getting refreshments at the
busy bar.

"No . . . !" screamed a man, struggling wildly in the grip of five
laughing people. They were hauling him off toward the rest room.

"Kiss the moose! Kiss the moose!" they chanted.

"But I don't wanna!"

"You play, you pay!" they laughed in wicked merriment.

Behind the people-jammed counter, MacKenzie spoke into his
wrist secretary and the ceiling-mounted PA boomed, "And mind
ya, no tongue!"

"Wah . . . !" cried the victim.

"Hey, what the hell happened?" called out Jhonny curiously as
the boisterous crowd passed by.

"Never," sobbed the victim. "*Ever,* draw to an inside straight!"

And at that moment, Michelangelo made a solemn vow to the
gods above, below, between, and to himself, to not even attempt a
round of poker until he was intimately familiar with absolutely all
of the pertinent rules. That damn card game was dangerous!

Almost as dangerous as being a news reporter.